ARANSAS
EVENING

ARANSAS
EVENING

A NOVEL BY
JEFF HAMPTON

THE SEQUEL TO ARANSAS MORNING

Jeff Hampton, Writer / JL Books and Creations
901 W. Avenue E
Garland, Texas 75040
www.jeffhamptonwriter.com

Publisher's Note: This is a work of fiction. Names, characters, places, and incidents are a product of the author's imagination. Locales and public names are sometimes used for atmospheric purposes. Any resemblance to actual people, living or dead, or to businesses, companies, events, institutions, or locales is completely coincidental.

Book Layout © 2014 BookDesignTemplates.com

Aransas Evening / Jeff Hampton -- 1st edition
ISBN 978-0-9966448-4-6

Cover Photo: Sunset at Port Aransas, Texas, January 20, 2013. By Jeff Hampton.

Dedicated to the people of Port Aransas—for their unbreakable spirit as they rebuild their lives on the Texas Gulf Coast.

Acknowledgments

This second trip to Port Aransas would not have happened without the cajoling of friends and family who read *Aransas Morning* and kept asking, "So what happens next?" Among them:

- LeAnn, who has been my Shelly and has shown me the way to live fearlessly and love unconditionally.
- The Weardens and Welborns, who welcomed me into their family and introduced me to life near the Texas Gulf Coast.
- The people of Wilshire Baptist Church, who have shown me the true nature of family beyond family, have encouraged my writing over the years, and have given me the courage to tell my stories whether real or fictional.
- Nancy, Chip, Gary, and Tom, my writers group who earned their way into the Demolition Crew with their generous and honest critique.
- Alison, who helps keep my grammar and punctuation on the straight and narrow while letting my characters and plot lines run free.
- My parents, Mack and Ann, who have been my biggest cheerleaders and best editors since day one.

—Jeff Hampton

Chapter 1

The summer sun pressed down hard on the Aransas shoreline, turning the loose, dry sand on the beach into a pale, gritty ash that burned the bottoms of even the toughest feet and sent the tourists retreating to the cool of their condos and restaurants. The only movement along that thin line where earth and sea meet was the dancing heat waves that seemed to bend and buckle the tankers and drilling platforms out on the horizon.

Even the coastal breeze—which caressed the tiny port town on most days—was in hiding somewhere, leaving the breakers to crawl onto the beach under their own weak power. Only later, when the devil sun sank out of sight to pester the inhabitants on the other side of the planet, would the pale moon take to the sky to pull a cool breeze across the top of the water and fluff up the breakers, sending them foaming onto the thirsty sand once more.

Even so, a rogue burst of wind came from somewhere far away off the northern coast of Mexico and rocked the trailer just enough to throw it off level. On the table, an apple shuddered into motion and rolled a few inches before plunging onto the floor, hitting the laminate with a dull thud and rolling the length of the trailer to where Sam was enjoying a noontime nap.

Sam was awakened, not by the hollow sound of the apple bumping against the wooden base of his bed but by the sickly, sweet smell of the over-ripe fruit just out of his sight. He sat up and rubbed his eyes. Something had changed but he wasn't quite sure what.

~ ~ ~ ~ ~

"I'm going out." Bo bellowed, not so much at Allie, but at the world.

"Where?" she asked, not looking up from her newspaper.

"I'm going back out on the water. I'm gonna buy a boat."

Allie sat up straight on the sofa and lowered the paper that separated her from the hulking man sitting back in the recliner, still wearing the stained coveralls of a shrimper. Bo's burly hand felt around for a moment, found the handle, and pushed it forward, popping himself up to where he was facing his daughter.

"What do you mean, buy a boat?" She searched his eyes for any hint of a joke, but instead she saw frustration and irritation. He was serious.

"I mean hand someone some money and they give me a boat." He was being literal—in his usual smartass way—and she didn't appreciate that at all.

"You know that's not what I'm asking. I'm asking: when and where and why and from whom?"

"I don't have any of that worked out yet, but I'm going to do it. I'm bored, sweetheart. It's not enough to stand ankle deep in the water and throw out a line. That's amateur fishing."

"But we all thought that you were doing well with it."

"I was for a while. But now the season has started up again, and when I see the boats going out . . . I haven't missed a season in fifty years."

Allie sighed. She felt responsible because she had insisted on moving from Freeport to Port Aransas to begin a new life with her father Bo. But then she grumbled because she wouldn't have moved if Bo hadn't come looking for Cassandra—her mother and the woman he abandoned years earlier and named his boat after—and if he hadn't sought the daughter he didn't know he had. And wasn't he the one who demanded they move all of her belongings down the coast on a boat that shouldn't have been out in that storm? She wanted to push all of that back on him, but when she looked into his weary eyes her heart softened, because if Bo hadn't been so bullheaded and impulsive, she would never have met her father.

"Oh Daddy, I know that has to be tough. I understand that, but I just can't have you going out there on your own and getting into trouble. You're not as steady and strong as you once were. You might . . ."

"Might what?"

"You might get hurt again. Or worse."

"You mean I might die? Well of course I might die. I might die sitting in this chair or laying in that bed in there. Or just crossing the street." He got up to walk into the kitchen. "I'm dying anyway . . ."

"What was that?"

"I said we're all dying."

But that's not what he said, and that's not what he meant. In the weeks since the *Cassie* had been resurrected and placed on dry land next door to Shelly's Dream Bean coffee shop, Bo had gotten up early most mornings and grabbed his tackle off her deck, stopped at the Dream Bean to fill up his cup, and then walked down to the pylons or the beach to put out his line and see what was biting. Most days he caught at least something, and sometimes there was almost more than he could carry back to the *Cassie* on his own. And then three weeks ago he found his arms and legs cramping and he had to stop several times on the way back. He thought it was just the size of the load until the next morning when he felt the same way—and all he was carrying was his pole. And then a few days later there came the tightness in his shoulders and shortness of breath.

Now, looking out the kitchen window toward the forest of boat masts rocking in the afternoon breeze, he knew the truth of it. He was dying. He wasn't afraid of that, but what did scare him was to have his last earthly sight be the cheap paneling on the den wall or the speckled texture of the bedroom ceiling. When he closed his eyes for the last time, he wanted to be looking out across the rolling surface of the Gulf, whether it be under a bright blue sky or a dark gray dome.

He was still staring out the window and thinking when Allie walked up behind him and put her arms around his thick middle.

"I just don't belong here, sitting and doing nothing," he said. "You might as well saw off my legs and stuff me in a box."

He turned around to face his daughter, whose troubled expression from a moment earlier had melted into empathy. She put her head on his shoulder and hugged him again.

"I know it's been difficult changing your ways, and you've been a good sport about it. But I don't think buying a boat is a good idea." She lifted her head and looked him in the eyes. "Maybe . . . you could go out with one of the guys."

Bo broke into a wheezy, coughing laugh. "That's not going to happen. Those men don't want an old fart like me around any more than I would want one of them on my crew."

Allie watched closely, trying to measure Bo's mood as he patted her on the head and then creaked down the hallway toward his room. She heard him bump and bang around and then watched him come back down the hall and turn toward the front door.

"Where are you going?"

"*Cassie* . . . the pier maybe . . . won't know for sure until I get down there."

"Well, don't go buying a boat," she said loudly as he stepped outside and pulled the door shut.

Bo walked the four blocks to the corner where the bow of the *Cassie* leaned out toward the street corner. There was none of the ominous pain that he'd felt in recent weeks, and if it hadn't been for the grinding and popping of cartilage that is common beneath the skin of an aging man, he might have defied Allie and walked another block to the pier to begin negotiating. Instead, he climbed onto the deck of the *Cassie* and pulled his old chair around so that he could see and hear all that was important to him—the masts and rigging of the shrimp boats, the front porch of the Dream Bean, and the Gulf of Mexico out beyond the shops and sheds.

Inside the Dream Bean, Shelly and Dave cleaned up after the light noonday crowd. Business had settled into a predictable, comfortable rhythm with a nice rush in the morning for coffee and Shelly's no-menu breakfast. Sam still worked the early shift in the kitchen with Dave if he didn't have an appointment at the Pier Association; as its president and only employee he could make his own schedule. Allie worked full-time at the Dream Bean, but with Bo spending more time at home recently she had started to check on him at noon.

Afraid that her father might actually pull a stunt and buy a boat, Allie called Shelly at the Dream Bean. "Have you seen Bo down there?"

"No, but I can look. Is everything all right?"

"He's just in a mood."

Shelly stuck her head out the front door of the coffee shop and looked down the porch and across the side to the *Cassie*. She pulled her head back inside and quietly closed the door.

"He's on the *Cassie*. Looks like he's in deep thought, or deep sleep."

"Great," said Allie. "I'm coming down there in a little while to help you set up for tomorrow, but I need to go down to the pier first and take care of something. If you see Bo walking that way, call him back to the Bean, will you?"

"Sure, but what's up?"

"Just trying to prevent him from making a dangerous mistake."

Allie pulled on her shoes and left in a hurry. She circled around through the backstreets and entered the pier area from the south, where she found a handful of shrimpers stowing their gear and talking about the morning's catch.

"Hey Miss Allie," said an old Cajun cleaning up the deck of his boat. "What brings you down here this afternoon without Pére Bo?"

"I've come looking for help."

"Oh, my little one, what has happened?" He stopped what he was doing and stepped onto the pier. Seeing Allie now, some other men gathered around them.

"What's happened?" they asked.

"Nothing yet, and that's where you can help me. Bo's grumbling about buying a boat and going back out, and I need you to tell him no."

A murmur of agreement—that nobody had a boat to sell—passed through the men, and the old Cajun told her they would spread the word that nobody was to accept any offers from Bo.

"Great . . . now I have another favor to ask," Allie said. "If Bo comes down to talk about boats, could someone invite him to go out on the water? That's really all he wants to do."

This time it was grumbling and head shaking that circled through the men.

"I don't know, Miss Allie, this Bo . . . no offense . . . but your pére . . . he's a . . . ." The old Cajun struggled with how to say it, so Allie filled the gap.

"He's a sonofabitch, yes, we all know that," she said, "but he's lonely and bored in dry dock the way he is. Put yourself in his boots for a moment."

There was head scratching and feet shuffling and staring at the ground until the old Cajun spoke again. "Come on now, she's right. There's not a man among us who wouldn't rather be dead than to never go out on the water again. We can all do this together. I'll be first."

There was more grumbling and a few reluctant nods, but Allie took the Cajun's word as a yes.

"Great! Now one last thing: You can't tell Bo we had this talk. This needs to come from you."

Allie hugged the old Cajun—his arms fell to his sides as if he'd been taken up in the tentacles of a giant squid—and then she slipped back down the pier and circled around to the Dream Bean and the *Cassie* where Bo was sitting in the sunshine. Standing still for a moment to see the rise and fall of his chest, she walked up the steps and into the Dream Bean.

"Got it taken care of?" Shelly asked.

Allie explained the whole thing to Shelly and Dave.

"That sounds reasonable, but you can't smother him with protection," Dave said. "He's gone his own way all these years, and you can't suddenly take away his control."

"I'm not," said Allie. "He wants to go back out on the water and I'll let him do that. Just making sure he doesn't go out there by himself. He might have been on his own up until now, but I can't undo my responsibility for him now."

"Responsibility? You make it sound like a burden," said Shelly, but she regretted those words immediately as she saw the damp redness in Allie's eyes. Allie was so headstrong and determined, and it was easy for others to forget that she was still grieving the loss of her mother in Hurricane Ike. Shelly thought about the death of her

9

own parents and knew that if she still had just one of them, she'd hang on tightly too.

Allie walked to the storage room to check supplies, leaving Shelly to look at Dave and whisper, "Oops."

~ ~ ~ ~ ~

Inside his trailer, Sam checked the clock as he pulled on his khakis, blue shirt, and loafers. It was as dressed up as he'd been since coming to the island three years earlier. He'd been all flash and dash during his corporate days in Dallas, but after the car wreck that killed the girl and ended his career and marriage, he'd run as far from that lifestyle as he could. Now in his fifties and head of the Port Aransas Pier Association, he couldn't imagine ever again wearing a starched shirt and silk necktie.

Sam looked at himself in the mirror and knew he was overdressed even for Port Aransas, but he'd gotten a call a few days earlier from a woman from Houston who wanted to look at retail space. He'd sat at the office for a month and, like Bo, had grown restless without much to do. He'd helped a few businesses with some minor marketing upgrades and he'd ordered some seasonal banners to hang from light poles around the pier area. But this was his first appointment with someone from out of town, so he made sure that everything was in place. He had maps, rental rates, and tourist demographics from the chamber of commerce, and in a show of hospitality he arranged with Shelly to have a fresh pot of coffee ready and some cookies just out of the oven.

He was sitting at his desk at three o'clock when the front door opened and in walked a woman who immediately commanded his attention. She was of average height and shape for a woman who appeared to be leaning toward fifty, but what caught his eye was her full shoulder-length hair that had been allowed to turn gray naturally, creating pleasing ropes of dark brown and gray.

Sam stood up at his desk and the woman met him with a warm smile and an outstretched hand.

"You must be Sam. I'm Rosemary."

"Pleased to meet you," he said, extending his own hand and inviting her to sit down. "Any problem finding the way?"

"No, your directions were perfect, all the way down to the ferry and on across. That's some ride." As if cued to punctuate her enthusiasm, the low wail of the ferry horn drifted through the thin walls of the office.

"Yes it is, and many who have floated across have not gone back, myself included," Sam said.

"Is that so? You'll have to share that story with me some day. But as I said on the phone, my interest is probably just seasonal."

And for the next few minutes she went into further detail about what she had explained on the phone—how she was divorced and her children were grown, and with some money in the bank and time on her hands, she was interested in opening a shop and gallery where she could sell original arts and crafts as well as pursue her hobby as a painter. As she spoke she opened a small flat portfolio case and lay it flat on the desk to reveal a wrinkled painting of the sun rising over the beach. She turned it toward Sam and he raised his eyebrows, which she saw and caused her to ask, "What?"

"You've captured all the elements and textures beautifully, but the colors . . . they aren't quite right."

"You speak like you've seen a few sunrises."

"A thousand probably, and when I look out over the water I see more than just shades of gray, green, and blue. There are pinks, oranges, reds, purples, lavenders. And that's not just on the water or in the sky, but in the puddles on the beach and the wet sand itself and even on the backs of the gulls."

"I see, well you'll have to show me sometime," she said, closing and zipping the portfolio. "But right now I'd like to look at whatever you can show me in the way of retail space."

"Sure," said Sam. He motioned to the door and they stepped outside. "I hope you don't think I was being critical. I didn't begin to see all the colors on the water until I'd been here a few months."

"No, not at all," she said. "I'm really just starting to paint and I need more time to experiment. I painted that scene from memory. Like you suggested, I need to spend more time just observing."

They walked together in the fading afternoon sunshine as the clouds began to gather and the breeze began to stir. Sam led Rosemary to several vacant storefronts where she cupped her hands to look inside the windows. He offered to call the landlords but she said that wouldn't be necessary. Sam noticed that she had her own method of evaluation. In every location she'd stand across the street to judge its curb appeal, as they say, and then she'd stand with her back to the front door to observe the view from that position as well.

Noticing the quizzical look on Sam's face, she explained. "The location can't just be good for the customers. If I'm going to spend time someplace, I want to like it too, and for me that begins with the view."

Their walking tour led them to the shell of what had been the Sea Siren.

"This is interesting. What was it?" she asked, looking inside at the empty, nicely decorated space. Sam started to tell her how the national coffee house had come and gone with a little shove from Shelly and friends, but his words were overrun by the sudden rush of traffic around the corner as cars coming off the ferry turned to go down the highway toward Corpus Christi or dispersed into town.

"Do they ever stop?" she asked.

"It's a busy corner, that's for sure," Sam said.

"Well this will never do. I might as well set up shop on the shoulder of Interstate 45. I don't like this at all."

When the light changed and traffic stopped, they crossed the street and walked back toward the quieter, older part of the downtown area. When they came to a small stand-alone building with a covered porch like that of the Dream Bean, Rosemary sat down in a plastic chair and turned her head slowly from left to right. Sam followed her stare to see what she was observing: another strip of brightly painted shops, a cluster of weathered tourist cabins, a little park with swings and palm trees, and the growing shadows from the buildings and palms as the sun descended behind them.

"Now this is nice," she said.

"Do you want me to call about it?"

"No, let's do that tomorrow. But I could sure go for a cup of coffee."

"Good, because I know just the place," he said.

They walked back toward the pier, and when they turned the corner toward the Dream Bean, Rosemary laughed out loud.

"What is that?" she asked, staring at the bow of the boat that appeared to be rising up out of the ground and onto the street.

"That's the *Cassie*, one of the most beloved boats in Port Aransas."

"But how did she get up here . . . and why?"

"That's a long story. We can talk about that next door at Shelly's."

Rosemary followed Sam's gesture and burst into

laughter again as she read "Dream Bean" on the sign above the awning. "This is just delightful . . . delightful," she said. "This is where I need to be."

Stepping inside, they found Allie working behind the counter and Bo sitting alone at a table by the window. Shelly and Dave sat with hands clasped at a table in the middle of the room—she talking a mile a minute about an idea for the business and he listening patiently. Dave wished Shelly could be more laid back like most island natives, but he had been charmed by the way her blunt energy often gave way to a soft vulnerability. He was grateful that Sam had introduced them when he first came to town with his own burdens. She had given him a new life that they had talked about sharing.

Sam nodded at the others. "This is Rosemary—I didn't get your last name—from Houston."

"It's Chase," she said. "Rosemary Viola Chase, but my friends just call me Rosie."

After everyone had introduced themselves, except Bo, who didn't budge from his seat and as usual was skeptical of the presence of anyone from out of town—especially a big city like Houston—Shelly invited Sam and Rosie to sit with them at their table. Allie came from the kitchen with a tray of mugs and a plate of cookies.

Sam began to explain the reason for Rosie's visit, but it soon became clear that this woman didn't need anyone to do her talking. She laid out the entire plan and ended it with, "So . . . what do you think?"

"I think . . . it sounds like something you ought to do," said Dave. "Did you and Sam find a space that suits your needs?"

"Well, we found one a few blocks over with a nice big porch like you have here. But what really has my head spinning is that crazy boat docked next door."

Bo's hands hit the table hard and he stood up loudly. "That crazy boat is the *Cassie*. She's mine and you can't have her—at least not until I'm dead," he said. He nodded to Allie and Shelly and walked out the door, letting it slam loudly behind him.

"I'm so sorry; I hope I didn't offend him," Rosie said. "I had no idea . . ."

"That's okay, he's just having a bad week," said Allie. She watched as Bo walked across the street and down toward the piers. She silently hoped that if there was anyone down there, they'd keep their promise and offer him a ride and not the title to their vessel.

Noticing that the Dream Bean was empty of any other customers, Rosie took a big gulp of coffee and put her mug down. "It looks like I'm keeping you from closing shop so I better get on to my room," she said.

Nobody argued the point and Sam walked her to the door. "Are you staying down on the highway?" he asked.

"No, I'm right over here at the Island Palms." She stuck out her hand again. "Thank you so much for your hospitality and the tour. I'll sleep on what we looked at and get back with you tomorrow around ten."

"See you then," Sam said. He opened the door and watched as she walked down the steps, across the street, and down the block.

Going back into the shop, he was met by the questioning eyes of the others, except for Shelly who never stayed silent for long.

"Do you think she'll pull the trigger and rent some space?"

"I don't know," said Sam. "She seems to like it here okay."

"It's a big change from Houston," said Allie.

"And more precisely, River Oaks," said Dave.

"What's that?" Allie asked.

"Just one of the richest neighborhoods in Texas," said Shelly.

"Tough transition, huh?"

"What do you think, Sam?" Dave asked. "You came from North Dallas, which isn't much different."

"I think I'm going home. See you in the morning."

"Goodnight Sam." they each said as he walked out the door.

Walking down the highway to his trailer, Sam thought about it all. His transition hadn't just been from North Dallas. He'd come up out of a much darker place.

Chapter 2

Rosie kept her promise and was waiting on the porch outside Sam's office when he arrived a little after ten o'clock.

"Sorry to keep you waiting. I often work early mornings at the Dream Bean," he said as he unlocked the door.

She laughed out loud as she had the night before. "Does everyone on the island just pitch in and help each other like that all the time?"

"I don't really know because I don't know too many people." He directed her to the chair across from his desk.

"Well, the ones of you I've met seem really close," she said.

"I suppose we are." Sam didn't say more. Seeing the look on Rosie's face, Sam knew she wanted to hear more, but it wasn't his place to tell, so he quickly went to the reason for their meeting. "Did you have time to think about the properties we looked at yesterday?"

Rosie cackled again. "So, we're gonna stick to business, huh? Very well, yes, I liked that stand-alone building with the porch like you have here and at the coffee shop. Now what I really liked was that boat, but since I can't wait for that old pirate to die . . ." She leaned back and laughed some more.

"He's a shrimper," Sam said seriously, "and there's not enough room there for what you want to do."

"Oh honey, I was just pulling your leg about that. If I wanted a boat I'd go buy a real big one and park it by the docks and let people just walk on board and shop. Anyway . . . let's go ahead and secure the property with the porch."

"Do you want to know the rent?"

"No, just ask them for their best price and call me with the details if you need to," and she pushed a check across the desk. "Meanwhile, here's a down payment— you can fill in their name—and I'll sign the lease when I get back. Now, I need to get back to Houston and decide what's staying and what's coming back with me."

She stood up and stuck out her hand for Sam to shake, which he did, and which she held onto for what seemed to him like the longest time.

"So good to meet you and do business with you, Sam, and I'm so looking forward to coming down here and being with you all and seeing what fun we can have. Tell your friends I'll be back soon . . . and tell that old pirate that his crazy old boat is safe!"

She laughed and turned and was quickly out the door, down the steps, and on across the street toward the

Island Palms Hotel. Sam looked closely at the check for the first time, which was fringed with drawings of bright white magnolia blossoms. And then, there below her name—Rosemary Viola Chase, which was written in a hand as flowery as the magnolias—was the sum of her down payment: five thousand dollars. He let go a little whistle with the thought that while five thousand might get her just a month at the Galleria in Houston, in Port Aransas, it would buy a full year if not more. Sam looked out the window, following the imaginary trail of the storm that had just blown into his office and back out into the town.

Down at the pier, Bo sat against a piling, hands in his pockets, and stared at the empty slips and then out at the channel and the Gulf beyond that. He'd seen nobody when he walked down there the night before, which relieved Allie when he came home too late for dinner and went to bed without any big announcements about wanting to buy a boat. And she was pleased again when she saw him walking away from the *Cassie* around seven thirty that morning with his fishing tackle. But she didn't know that he had never made it down to the beach to fish but instead had gone back to the piers.

Bo was still sitting there a little before noon when one by one the boats came in, churning into reverse and cutting their engines as they drifted back into their slips. And then there were shouts and the sounds of stowing and shutting down and putting away. He closed his eyes to listen. The years rolled back to an earlier time when the *Cassie* was new and he was captain of a small crew that fished the waters off the coast for shrimp, tarpon, grouper, and snapper.

It was a happy time, going out in the mornings with those men, working hard all day, and then hanging out at Shorty's bar to drink and tell stories until closing time. And it went that way for a few good years until they left him to start their own crews or to go to work in town, which Bo could never quite understand. There would be replacements but none would ever stay long—Bo never saw that he was the reason they would leave because they could never do anything right in his eyes.

That's what happened with Louie, who Bo regarded as a son but pushed him too hard until one day it was just too much.

"What the hell are you doing?" Bo shouted.

"I'm tying off the boom shrouds," said Louie.

"Well that's no good way to do it."

"That's the way I do it."

"Not on my boat you don't."

"Fine." Louie let the line fall loose to the deck and then stepped over the gunwale and onto the pier.

"Where do you think you're going?" Bo asked.

"I'm going to get my own boat so I can do it my own way."

Louie walked away and as he did, Bo shouted back, "You go do that then."

Bo shook his head. "Oh . . . Louie . . ."

"Huh? . . . what's wrong with you old man?"

Bo felt a kick against the sole of his boot and his eyes fluttered open. He looked around, disoriented, and then his head cleared and he realized he'd been dreaming.

"Are you okay?"

Bo looked up to see Louie standing over him. Bo raised up onto his knees and then grabbed hold of the piling and lifted himself up on his feet.

"Must've dozed off," Bo said, glancing sideways into Louie's eyes.

"It's a good day for it, although I reckon I might want a softer place," Louie said.

"You would."

Louie resisted the temptation to reply in a way that would lead to an argument. So he changed the subject.

"Listen, some of us were thinking that you might want to go out from time to time."

"What makes you think that?"

"Well, we thought you might be missing it a little . . ."

"Well you thought wrong. I'm doing what I want to be doing. Besides . . ."

"Besides what?"

"I don't take orders from no one, least of all some of you who don't know a lead block from a tail block."

"Nobody was asking you to crew with them," Louie said, working hard to hold his temper.

"Then what's the point of me going out?"

"We just thought you'd like to go out. You could sort of . . . I don't know . . . consult."

"Consult . . . ha."

"Never mind." Louie had heard enough and walked away. He was twenty yards down the pier when Bo shouted back at him. "What time are you going out tomorrow?"

Louie turned around. "You're the expert. You tell me." And then he turned around and continued on.

Bo stretched and scratched his bald head and then walked back to the *Cassie* with his fishing gear. He stowed it away and then rummaged around in the pilothouse and found his pocket knife, a compass, his best cap, some matches, and the stub of an old cigar that still had some life in it. He slapped the cap onto his head and shoved the other items into the deep pockets of his coveralls. He was ready.

Bo was up and out before sunrise the next morning—so early that Allie was still sound asleep when he left the house, and the Dream Bean was dark and locked tight when he arrived with his metal mug in hand. He shoved the empty mug down into the pocket of his baggy coveralls and walked down to the pier. He was sitting on the deck of Louie's boat, the *Rainbow*, when her captain arrived. Seeing Bo sitting on a crate sent a momentary surge of irritation through Louie's bones, but then he drew in a deep breath, exhaled, and climbed on board.

"You're late," Bo said gruffly.

"No, you're early." Louie brushed past Bo and walked into the pilothouse where he put down his lunchbox and got ready for the morning work—which included setting up a beat-up coffee pot. Stepping back outside, he saw the top of Bo's mug poking up out of his pocket.

"My men take care of themselves when it comes to food and drink," Louie said. "You might catch Shelly before we leave, but we push off at seven."

"No matter, don't need it." Bo stood up, pulled the mug out of his pocket, and stuffed it into a cubbyhole under the gunwale. "Where are the others?"

"There's just one today, Paco, and he'll be here directly. He's a good man. Knows his job. Doesn't say much." Louie spoke firmly, hoping that last little statement would find its way into Bo's thick skull.

Bo sat back down on the crate he'd been using as a chair. He stared down the pier, avoiding eye contact with Louie, who went to the stern to work on the rigging. A few minutes later, a short man with dark brown skin and jet-black hair hanging out from under a stained cap came walking quietly up the pier and climbed onto the *Rainbow*. He carried a grease-stained paper bag in his hand

"Good morning Señor," he said. "You ride today?"

"Yes."

"Bueno. I'm Paco." He held out his hand.

"Bo." He shook Paco's hand without standing up.

"Buenos dias," Louie said from the stern.

"Good morning, Mr. Louie." Paco held up his bag. "Burritos. Enough for Mr. Bo too."

"Good. Stow them and let's get started."

Bo stayed seated as Louie and Paco worked all around him to get the boat ready. The same thing was starting to happen on the decks of boats up and down the pier, and Bo closed his eyes and listened for a moment. But then he felt a brush against his shoulder and realized he was in Paco's way. He stood up, and feeling out of place, he stepped off the deck and onto the pier. Looking over at the boat in the next slip, his eyes were met by those of another crewman, and the man nodded. Bo nodded back. And then Louie called out to him, "cast off those lines."

Bo untied and tossed one line on board, and then a second. He hopped heavily onto the deck and caught hold of the rigging to steady himself before returning to sit on the crate. In the pilothouse, Louie throttled the engine. The water stirred around the pilings and the *Rainbow* shuddered out of its slip. Paco stood on the starboard side to check the clearance as the *Rainbow* turned out into the channel. Taking the cue, Bo stood and leaned out over the port side, then turned and nodded to Paco, who shouted "Vámonos."

Bo sat back down on the crate and turned his weathered face toward the rising sun, its warmth loosening his muscles and releasing the tightness from his chest. As the *Rainbow* puttered out into Turtle Cove and turned east into the channel, Bo's spirit began to rise. The *Rainbow* wasn't his boat, and he wasn't her captain, but he had helped turn her loose and set her free, and that little bit of work soothed his soul like a prayer.

Chapter 3

Allie wasn't thinking about Bo when she stepped through the front door of the Pier Association later that morning. She didn't give any thought to whether he was on a shrimp boat or standing thigh-deep in the surf with his fishing pole or sound asleep on the deck of the *Cassie*. She was thinking about the note in her hand and what she was going to do about it, if anything.

"Hey Allie, what brings you here? I thought Shelly gave you the morning off?" Sam asked as she came through the door.

"She did, but I was wondering if I could borrow your computer for a moment?"

"You don't have a computer? I thought everyone had a computer—I thought I was the last person on the planet to get one."

Allie laughed. "No, I think that must be me, and that's created a problem that I need to take care of."

And then she explained that with Bo out of the house early and no work to go to, she had decided to clean house and was going through a stack of papers when she came upon the note left at the Dream Bean by Justin.

The tall, redheaded college boy had dropped in with his rude friends in early May during the annual SandFest celebration that filled the tiny town with thousands of people. Allie's face flushed red with her next words: "I guess I got busy and forgot all about it and, well, he left me his email address."

"Aha." Sam stood up from his chair and motioned for Allie to come around and sit at the desk. He leaned over, moved the mouse, and made a few keystrokes. "You can send him a message from my email with your name in the subject line—like 'From Allie' or something like that."

Allie, grateful but embarrassed, thanked Sam and sat down at the computer. Her disconnection from technology had come accidentally during her move from Freeport. Her old laptop had been in a crate that washed off the deck of the *Cassie* during the storm. She looked at Sam's monitor a moment and then took the mouse in her palm and moved the cursor into position on the screen. She glanced up a moment.

"I'm going over to Shelly's for lunch. You can lock up and bring me the keys when you're finished," Sam said.

In a moment Allie was alone, and for the first time in almost a year she placed her fingers on a keyboard and began to type. The familiar feeling and sounds of writing returned quickly, but she also rediscovered the delete key because she didn't know what to say.

"Hey Justin, Allie here, from the Dream Bean coffee shop in

Port A. Bet you thought you'd never hear from me. Lost your note. LOL. How's school? Coming back? Would like to see you. Allie."

She read and reread, typed and deleted, and then with her eyes squinting in mock pain, she clicked send. "He'll never reply," she thought as she stood up from the desk, but then the computer made a soft ding sound and she was shocked to see that she had an immediate response.

"Hey, wondering about you too. Probably back down in a couple weeks. We'll see. Later!"

Allie looked up to make sure she was really alone, then she sat down again, thought a moment, and typed, *"See you soon!"* and clicked send. She waited a moment, and when there was no further reply, she deleted the outgoing and incoming emails, stuffed Justin's paper note into her back pocket, and left the office.

A few moments later, she walked into the Dream Bean to find Shelly, Dave, and Sam sitting at a table. She walked nonchalantly to the counter and poured herself a cup of coffee, and then sat down with them, took a sip, and searched their eyes to see if Sam had kept her little bit of personal business a secret.

Dave was the first to speak to her, but not about Justin. "I was just telling Sam and Shelly that Kent from the marina thought he saw Bo on the *Rainbow* going out."

"Oh really," Allie said. "I was hoping that would happen."

That got Shelly's attention. "Did you plan this?"

"I might have suggested it." Allie took another sip from her cup and then put it down on the table.

"Oh my. Nothing could go wrong with that, could it?" Shelly said.

"What?" Allie asked.

"I'm just saying . . . hey, if you want to stick around for a while, we've got a new load of beans to grind. Might help you kill the time until the boats come in and then . . ."

"And then what?"

Dave stepped in. "I think what Shelly is suggesting is that you can hang out here and then when Bo gets off the boat you can see how his morning went."

Shelly snorted. "No, I was thinking she could go down to the pier and see who was still alive and who wasn't."

"Nah, he'll be fine," Allie said. She took another sip and looked out the window. She wasn't so sure.

Allie's worries were confirmed in the early afternoon when the drone of engines floating over the rooftops told her that the boats were coming in. Pulling off her apron, she ran for the door. Sam had come in to help with the lunch crowd and she stopped to look at him, which he saw as a silent plea, and he followed her.

When they got to the pier, the boats were at different stages of puttering into their slips. The *Rainbow* was just bumping into the rubber tires, with Louie and Paco tying her off. Allie couldn't see Bo at all, but then something caught Sam's eye and he looked down the pier and saw him climbing off another boat. He nudged Allie, and when she saw her father walking back toward town in another direction, she shouted at Louie.

"You want to tell me what happened?" she asked, pointing toward her father who was almost out of sight.

"Listen, Allie, we gave it a try, but it just isn't going to work."

"What happened?"

"He . . . he just wouldn't . . . leave us be."

"Oh dear." Allie shook her head.

"He started barking orders and telling us what to do and how to do it and . . . I tried to remind him whose boat he was on, and well . . ."

Paco spoke up. "He went loco, shouting and cursing. He's a loco old man. Scary!"

"What do you mean?" Allie asked.

Louie reached down, picked up the end of a rope, and began coiling it around his hand and elbow. He looked at Sam, and then at Allie, and then returned to his rope.

"What do you mean? Please tell me."

Louie finished coiling the rope, pulled it off his arm and tied up the loose end. He tossed it onto the deck and then looked Allie in the eye.

"I was afraid for his safety—for all of our safety, really."

"He's mostly just bluster," Sam said. "He surely wouldn't harm someone."

Louie shook his head. "I don't know. The deck gets smaller out there on the open water. He got a look in his eye, a tone in his voice . . . we had to do something."

"He shook his knife at me," Paco said. "We had to fix it."

"Fix it. What do you mean?"

Paco pointed at the rope. Allie looked at it too.

"Really . . . you tied him up?"

"We tried, but he was loco," Paco said.

Allie exhaled loudly. . . . "What . . .?"

Louie answered: "We were going to restrain him, we warned him, but he . . . jumped off the boat."

"What the hell?!"

"He's a good swimmer," Paco said. "Like a fat dolphin."

Louie put out his hand to silence Paco. "The other boats were close by and he got picked up right away."

Allie's face turned red. Her nostrils flared. "How could you?!" She clinched her fist and pounded Louie hard in the shoulder and then turned and ran after her father.

Louie rubbed his stung arm as he, Sam, and Paco watched Allie run up the pier and off toward her home and her father.

"She's loco too," Paco said.

Sam spoke: "Maybe just a little, but she's got good reason. He's all she has."

"Well, you might as well tell her that Bo won't be

sailing with me again," Louie said. "I doubt anyone will take him after what happened out there."

Sam nodded and followed slowly after the daughter and father who had become family to him. It hurt to watch Bo get more cranky by the day—"locc" as Paco had called him—and even more to see what that was doing to Allie.

~ ~ ~ ~ ~

Allie burst through the front door of the house, calling Bo's name as she walked down the hall to his room, but nobody was there. She walked back to the *Cassie* and he wasn't there either, but she noticed that his rod and tackle were gone. Stopping briefly at the Dream Bean to tell Shelly she'd be out for a while, Allie walked down to the public beach and followed its curve southward a short ways until she saw her father standing thigh deep in the surf. She walked toward him quietly, and when she saw him glance her way and then turn back toward the water, she simply said, "Hey."

Bo didn't reply. He kept his eyes fixed on the fishing line that was stretched out about thirty yards to where a bright orange bobber was floating on the surface. He cranked the reel slowly with his right hand while holding the butt of the rod against his belly, popping it every so often to see if anything would tug on the end of the line.

"Anything biting?" Allie waited for an answer, but there was none. Understanding that her small talk was not going to lure her father into a conversation, let alone bring a confession about what had happened on the *Rainbow*, Allie sat down in the soft, warm sand next to where Bo had piled his tackle.

With Bo's back turned, Allie watched as he reeled the line in slowly, cast it out again, and reeled it back in. She hadn't noticed before how his right shoulder dipped down and his head leaned to the left, or how he stood with one leg thrust out in front of the other. She guessed that his posture came from years of standing at the wheel of his boat, bracing himself against the bucking of the waves, much like he was doing now in the churning surf. And beneath his dirty red cap, which sat askew on his bald head so the brim would shade his eyes from the sun, she saw for the first time that the cartilage shaping the back of this left ear was not cupped but instead was dented and wrinkled. She'd seen that before—at the pound in Freeport when she was thinking about adopting an abused mutt. She wondered if something had happened in her father's boyhood—perhaps a fight with another kid—to reshape his ear. Or maybe it was a souvenir from an accident at sea. She had been with him that night when the *Cassie* pitched in the storm and tossed him on his back. Perhaps he had busted up his ear on a similar night.

As she studied Bo from behind, Allie realized that as little as she knew about his physical characteristics, she knew even less about what had shaped his personality.

He had told her about how he had met her mother and what had driven him away, but she didn't know anything about his childhood and what might have produced his infamous bluster, his hard, crusty shell, his sometimes soft center.

Allie knew that as much as she wanted to know more about her father, he wasn't going to sit down beside her and start telling his story. She sighed and started to get up off the sand, when Bo cocked his head a little and cast a few words over his shoulder.

"Leavin' already?"

Allie stood up and brushed the grit off her jeans. "Yeah, gotta get back to Shelly's."

"Leave too soon you might miss something."

"You mean, like watching you stand there in the water? I think I've seen enough."

"Takes patience to fish these waters. They don't come walking through the door like they do at Shelly's."

"Yeah, and it takes patience, and courage, to let someone else captain the ship." Allie didn't wait for a response but began walking back up the beach. Just then she heard a loud splash and a "whoop" and she turned to see Bo backpedaling in the water, cranking his reel with the top of his rod pointing sharply toward the horizon.

"Get the net!" Bo shouted. Allie dashed back to the tackle and grabbed the net by the handle, and without hesitation she waded out into the water and stood at Bo's left side. Bo continued to crank and pull backwards until the water in front of their legs began to churn and splash. With both hands firmly on the rod, Bo leaned backward with all his weight, and Allie leaned forward and scooped the net into the boiling water and pulled it upward around the silvery flashes of fin and tail. Now the weight of the thrashing fish was in Allie's hands and not Bo's. He let the rod fall into the thin brine and he put his arms around Allie's waist and pulled her backward until man and girl and fish fell onto the firm wet sand. The fish flopped around on the sand between them as Bo lay there a moment catching his breath. Allie laughed out loud.

"She's a beauty, Daddy. You got her!"

"What do you mean? We both got her."

"Yes we did," Allie said.

That night, with Shelly, Dave, and Sam sitting with them around the table, they feasted on pan-fried black drum and laughed aloud as Allie and Bo recounted how they had landed their big catch. Nobody laughed louder that Bo, who embellished and bragged and wove in new pieces of story until he was battling a giant sailfish in the open water.

"She fought hard but we got her on the boat. Liked to have taken Louie's arm off!"

Allie looked into the eyes of the others and confirmed what she knew was happening. The day's story was for Bo every story he had ever told. He wasn't just weaving a yarn. His memories were becoming tangled.

In the days that followed Allie watched her father's actions and listened to his words carefully for any hint that indeed his memory was slipping. She worked backward through her most recent memories of time with him to see if she could recount any distinct moments where he seemed to be forgetful or to speak out of context. Nothing stood out, so she decided to not make too much of it. Talking across the counter at the Dream Bean one day, Sam concurred with the strategy.

"If you're overprotective, he's likely to push back or even turn away," Sam said.

"How do you know so much about it?" Allie asked.

"I went through the same thing with my mother. The best thing is to just let Bo be Bo. That will change over time—who he is—but he won't be much aware of it so there's no point in trying to fix him or correct him. Just keep loving him."

One thing that did get settled in Bo's mind was that he seemed to be content with fishing the beach again. Maybe it was the excitement of the catch with Allie—having a "crew" to work with and even to boss around—that inspired him, or maybe it was a full understanding that he had blown his chances to ever be invited back out on a boat; Allie didn't know for sure. It didn't really matter. Bo seemed to have found a comfortable place to be once more, and in her own way Allie found her own role in that place, walking down to the beach from time to time to check on him.

One afternoon, Allie was sitting in the sand, watching Bo fish, and the most basic of all questions she could ask came to her.

"Daddy, where'd you learn how to fish?"

"My uncle Bob."

"He fished for a living?"

"No, he sold insurance. He and my father both."

Allie dug at the sand with her toe. "Your father didn't teach you?"

"No, he never had time. He was always traveling."

Bo reeled in his line, checked the lure, and then sent it back out past the breakers into the calm warm water. He unspooled more line as he backed out onto the beach, then dug through his tackle and found a rod stand, planted it into the sand, and dropped in the rod. He sat down next to Allie.

"So where'd your father go?" she asked.

"So many questions today?" Bo leaned away a little to get a better look at his daughter.

"Just curious," she said. "You've told me about you and mother, but I really don't know anything about how you grew up. So . . . ?"

"So?" Bo scuffed at the sand with his wet boot.

"Your father traveled?"

"Oh . . . yes . . . my father and uncle had a small agency. My father was the oldest and he did all the traveling. He left Bob to run the office. He was single and lived with us, so he had time to fish."

"You never fished with your father?"

"A few times." Bo leaned forward to check his rod and reel.

"Where was this?"

"Port Arthur."

"How come you never told me this before?"

"You never asked. But nothing much to it anyway. Pretty much a normal raising. Mother ran the house, and my father and uncle covered the bills with the insurance business."

Allie sat quietly for a moment. She never asked because Bo was always so private. But more than that she had focused so much on just getting to know the father that was with her now that she hadn't thought much about what lay in his past. But now with his memory perhaps fading, she wanted to know more and remember more—perhaps for both of them.

"So who was the better fisherman, Uncle Bob or your father?"

Now it was Bo's turn to pause in silence for a moment. He tilted his head back and closed his eyes.

"What is it?" Allie asked.

Bo lowered his head again, with one eye open, his finger rubbing the sweat from the other. Or was it a tear? Allie wasn't sure. Bo rubbed his finger on his pants.

"My father was good a fisherman, better than Bob, but he was tough."

"How so?"

"Nobody could ever do anything right by his measure. He'd lose his patience and walk away. Said he was too busy to waste his time with someone not willing to do it right."

Allie thought about that a moment and then put her hand on her father's knee. "Sort of sounds like someone I know."

"Maybe. Grown-ups can handle that, but I was just a kid."

"It hurt, huh?"

Bo didn't answer, so Allie tacked the conversation in a new direction.

"Well, neither your father or your uncle had their own shrimp boat, and I bet they never pulled up some of the whoppers you've reeled in here on this beach."

Bo was quiet, then turned toward Allie as if he hadn't heard her. "What?"

"You know, the big fish, like what you and I pulled out of here last week."

Bo looked puzzled, and then his face brightened. "Oh, yes, she was a beauty. We need to get her on the grill."

"We did, that same night." Just as she said that Allie realized she had stumbled into Bo's forgetfulness, and she wished she had kept her mouth shut. Bo was not bothered as much as she was.

"Oh, yes, that's right, we did." And then he looked out at his line. "Well . . . I hope we have something in the freezer. Doesn't look like we'll be taking anything home tonight."

Allie stood up and reached a hand down to her father. He knew he was too heavy for her, so he scooted forward onto his knees and then clasped her hand and stood up as she pulled. He reeled in his line, and they gathered up the tackle and started walking back up into town.

"Don't let it bother you," Bo said as they turned the corner and came into view of the *Cassie* in her landlocked birth.

"What's that?"

"Me forgetting things. It's just the ways of an old man."

Chapter 4

As June rolled into July, Shelly and Dave began poking at the proposal that Dave had never actually made and that Shelly had accepted without ever hearing. She had said "yes," and they both knew that one small word represented a future together and more than that, a lifetime together. What hadn't been discussed aloud is whether they were talking about just living together or actually getting married. And if they were talking about getting married, would it be a simple civil ceremony or would there be a minister and music and all that usually came with that?

Dave had the full-blown church wedding with Debby, and while he didn't necessarily want to go through that again, he wanted Shelly to have the full experience if that was her dream. It would be smaller than his wedding in Dallas because their circle of friends in Port Aransas was small, and neither had family anywhere, at least not nearby. Like Shelly, Dave's parents had died some years earlier, although they had been older and so there wasn't the drama and tragedy that Shelly had experienced when her parents were killed on the highway. And his only brother had run off to the Pacific Northwest right out of college; they hadn't talked in several years.

This was on Dave's mind one late afternoon when he and Shelly were walking on the beach.

"So . . . where do you want to do the deed?"

"Huh!?"

"You know, make this thing between us official."

"Oh . . . that . . . I thought you were talking about something else."

"I'd never talk about that, I'd just do it," he said, pulling her close as if to demonstrate a move. She laughed and pushed him away.

Dave continued. "But seriously, we've not talked about 'the question' I raised and we need to be a little more direct about it." He took her by the hands and turned her so they were facing each other. "So . . . church? Courthouse? Dream Bean? Deck of the *Cassie*?"

"Definitely *not* the *Cassie*," Shelly said, and began walking again. "And not the Dream Bean either."

"Why not?"

"We'd end up waiting tables and washing dishes, and that's not what I have in mind for my wedding night."

Dave whistled through his teeth and tugged on Shelly's hand. Their eyes met and they both failed to hide their grins. "I'm glad we at least agree on that," he said. "Okay, so that leaves a church or the courthouse."

They stopped walking and sat down on the edge of a wood shower platform. The sun was beginning to go down behind them, softening the light. Shelly sat up straight and looked over her shoulder, and then turned forward again and looked out across the water. She pointed.

"Here."

"Huh?"

"We'll do it here!"

"Do what?" Dave said. He looked into her face and raised his eyebrows.

"The ceremony . . . the wedding. *Our* wedding," she said. "Look." She pointed out across the water, where as if on cue the puffy clouds and foaming breakers began to glow with touches of pink, orange, and rose.

"I like it," Dave said. "Whatever God paints on the sky—that will be our backdrop."

"And those will be our colors," Shelly added. She wrapped her arm around Dave's waist and leaned her head on his shoulder.

"Bo will give you away, of course," he said.

"Bo? Why not Sam?"

"Because Bo is as close as you have to a father, and because Sam will be my best man. And Allie . . . your maid of honor?" He was careful to pose a question and not dictate, but when Shelly didn't answer for a moment, he worried that he had said too much. "Sorry, I didn't mean to overstep . . ."

"No, it's not that," Shelly said. "It's just . . . I always thought my dad would give me away and my mother would be sitting on the front row."

Dave sighed. "Yeah, I know it's not the way you wanted it. We're both a little battered in that regard."

Shelly heard those words and understood what Dave was saying. He'd been married before and hadn't counted on going through it again after Debby's death. She was sensitive to that but she also felt awkward. She knew Dave loved her, and while she often wondered what other emotions were lingering in his head and in his heart, she was too afraid to ask. Instead, she stood up, brushed off the back of her jeans, and forced herself to take a more practical perspective.

"It's not going to help either one of us to focus on the past. All we have is this moment, so let's make the most of it." She held out her hand, signaling for Dave to stand up and join her on the walk back to the Dream Bean. "First thing we need to do is share our plans with the others."

"I'm guessing you want a June wedding," Dave said as they walked.

"June? No, let's make it early May."

"Why May?"

"Because everyone gets married in June, and we're not everyone. I'd really rather do it in April but that's SandFest."

"That could be fun . . . a big crowd of drunken crazies to watch us tie the knot."

Shelly pushed Dave aside and started running toward

the Dream Bean. When they both arrived on the porch, they stopped and enjoyed a lingering kiss and then went their separate ways.

The next morning when Bo burst into the Dream Bean with Allie right behind him, Shelly asked, "Hey, Bo, don't go anywhere in May, okay?"

Bo stopped and looked at her, and then at Allie. "What month is it now?"

"It's July, of course," Allie said.

Bo tapped his foot. "May is a long ways off. Don't know if I can keep it open. Might have some business in Mexico."

"Yeah, sure," Allie said. "So what's up in May, Shelly?"

Shelly stopped arranging things and came around the counter. "Me and Dave . . . we've decided to go into business together."

"Yes, and we need you to witness the transaction," Dave added as he came from the storeroom.

Allie's eyes lit up. "Really . . . you're actually gonna do it?!" She lunged at both of them and pulled them together in a big hug. "That's wonderful. I'm so happy for you. Of course we'll be here, won't we Daddy?"

Bo stood silently, not understanding. Allie turned and looked at him. "They're getting married . . . in May . . . and they want us to be there."

"Not just be there," said Shelly. She turned loose of Allie and stepped up beside Bo, bent his right arm across his middle and then placed her hand under his elbow. "I'm gonna need some help getting down the aisle, or in our case, the beach."

Bo scratched his head with his free hand and then looked down at the pose he and Shelly were making and he understood. He brought his hand down and patted Shelly's.

"Oh look at you." Shelly said. She reached up to stop one little trickle of moisture that had begun its journey down his leathery cheek. "And we've got jobs for you and Sam too." She motioned for Allie to come stand by her side.

"Definitely!" Allie said.

When Sam came in a little while later, he found the Dream Bean buzzing as the news about the engagement and wedding was spreading among the regulars who came in for their morning coffee. For his part, Sam was pleased for Dave and Shelly and honored to stand beside Dave. He was nervous too, as it had been years since he had been anywhere near a wedding. They had come in waves those first few years out of college as friend after friend got married and stepped out into the world as couples to make their marks. And then his head dropped as he thought about how many of those marriages had been shipwrecked by complacency or immaturity or any number of storms that can sink a relationship. And of course he and Brenda had been part of that wreckage— that was what ultimately drove him to the coast and placed him in the company of these strangers who now were his family. Sam raised his head and looked across the room where Shelly and Dave were standing, shoulder to shoulder, grinning and laughing with one of their neighbors. The sight of their new love brightened Sam, and he prayed silently that they would have a safe voyage together.

Chapter 5

Sam sat in his office on a Friday morning, staring blankly at the calendar, trying to brainstorm a way to drum up some end-of-the-season tourism. Labor Day Weekend was coming and that marked the end of the high season. The winter Texans would start coming from Wisconsin and Michigan, but they didn't spend as freely as the summertime crowds. He was turning that around in his head when he heard the grind of tires on the oyster shell parking lot outside. He looked out the window. "Oh Lord."

It was Rosie, driving up in her red Cadillac and dragging an orange U-Haul trailer. He watched her pull off her goggle-like sunglasses and toss them on the dashboard, and then the car door swung open and she climbed out, leaning on the horn as her feet touched the ground.

"Oh Lord," he said again, and for an instant he contemplated an escape. But realizing he had no back door, he decided he could at least make a pre-emptive move and go out on the porch before she came inside and parked herself at his desk.

Stepping out into the bright of day, he squinted and said, "Hello Ms. Chase."

She cackled upon seeing him. "Now Sam, I thought I told you to call me Rosie. This formal talk just isn't going to work with me."

Sam started down the steps. "Saw you coming and knew you'd want your keys."

He jingled them a little, as if she were a cat and he was trying to get her attention.

"Well yes, that's very kind indeed," she said. "I do want to start unloading soon, and I was hoping I could get some help with that."

Sam looked at the trailer, and then the back of the car, which was stuffed. "There's a couple of young men at the grocery who might be able to help you tomorrow."

"Yes, that would be just fine. Most of what I need till then is in the car," she said.

Sam held out the keys again and stood his ground just below the steps until Rosie finally reached for them. "Well then, I guess I better get started," she said.

"Yes ma'am," Sam said. He waited and watched her get back in the car and roll away. Certain that she was gone and not coming back, at least not for the rest of the day, he walked back into the office, called the market, and asked for Marty. Sam arranged for Marty and a new kid named Stu to stop by Rosie's shop the next morning and help her empty the trailer. He told them that Rosie would certainly pay them, but if not, he would take care of them out of the Pier Association funds.

The next day around mid-morning, Sam walked to the shop and found the trailer parked in front, its doors wide open. Looking in, he found it was empty, and then he heard voices and followed the sound into the shop. Sam weaved his way past stacks of crates and boxes until he came to Rosie and the two boys, who were sitting on crates, drinking Cokes and laughing. Rosie looked up and saw Sam standing with his hands on his waist.

"Marty was just telling me about how you ran Sea Siren out of town. That was some doing," she said.

Sam shrugged. "Just protecting our local interests."

"Well it was more than that. It was brilliant. Like I've said, you folks look out for each other, and that's a big reason I want to be here."

"We do what we can," Sam said. "I noticed the trailer is empty. I guess that means you boys can run on if you need to. I'm sure Ms. Chase can do the arranging herself."

"I suppose so," Marty said. He turned to Rosie. "Same time next week?"

She stood up to shake their hands. "That will be just fine."

The boys walked toward the front door, and Rosie turned to see the question on Sam's face.

"I have a truck coming next week, so I've arranged for the boys to come back and help with that."

Sam looked around the room, which was already

crowded with boxes full of stuff. "You have more?"

"Yes, some large oak and mahogany pieces, and then some shelves and cases for all this other mess." She explained that in addition to opening a gallery, she had a large collection of antique furniture and knickknacks to sell. "I'm downsizing in a big way and I have a lifetime of gathering to give away."

"Give away?"

"You can ask a million dollars and get just that, but if it holds memories, then no price will really matter and you might as well give it away."

Sam peeked into the top of an open box and saw china teacups and saucers, each piece emblazed with a large monogrammed C.

"I see what you mean," he said softly.

"I thought you would," and then she cackled, "but a million dollars would be pretty nice."

Sam tried to suppress a smile and a laugh, but he couldn't. He shook his head again. "Well, if you can squeeze a million dollars out of the tourists here, then we'll order a plaque and name you business person of the year."

"No, not me," she said. "I'd vote for that cute little Dream Bean coffee shop. That seems to be the popular place. And Sherry . . ."

"That's Shelly," Sam corrected.

"She's made of tough coastal stuff for sure. A man would be lucky to get serious with her."

"And a man is," Sam said.

Rosie perked up and Sam caught her look.

"She's marrying Dave, her partner at the Dream Bean, in May. They just announced it last week."

"Well that's delightful. I hope they'll be happy together."

"They'll do fine," Sam said, and then he realized he was telling too much and turned the conversation back into less interesting waters. "Unless you need something else right now, I'll let you unpack."

Sam pointed toward the front door, gave Rosie a little wave, and wound his way back past the boxes.

Rosie took a sip from her Coke and watched Sam make his way out. She smacked her lips and then let out a soft chuckle.

And Sam . . . he looked back over his shoulder just as he walked out the door. He noticed when Rosie first stood up that she was wearing black jeans instead of the print dress he had first seen her in. And he noticed that the jeans fit her nicely, and that she was in fine shape for a woman of her age. And then Sam squashed that thought as he walked back to the office.

Over the next week Rosie kept to herself, spending long days at the shop going through the boxes and taking inventory of thirty years of a marriage that started out heady and passionate and ended distant and empty. She'd managed to distance herself from the past while everything was in storage, but now with it staring up at her from the gaping jaws of dozens of cardboard boxes, it was a little overwhelming even for a woman with her sunny disposition.

She was sitting at an antique oak table, chin resting on her palm, when from across the room she heard, "Everything okay?" She looked up to find Allie standing in the aisle.

"Oh, I'm just thinking I should have hired an estate company to sell all of this. I don't know the first thing about how to price these things."

"I might be able to help," Allie said.

"How so?"

"I sold a lot of stuff like this when Momma died. I had a big garage sale and got a good lesson on what folks are willing to pay. And it isn't nearly as much as you think." As Allie talked, she dipped her hand into a box and eased out a little bundle of tissue paper, unwrapped it, and held up a delicate hand-painted teacup. "But then my stuff wasn't nearly this nice. Is this French?"

"Why yes, it is," Rosie beamed. "I picked that up on one of our trips to Paris—at a fun little flea market on the Left Bank. You have a good eye."

"I took some art and interior design classes at the junior college before Momma died and I had to start working."

"You want to tell me about it?" Rosie motioned to an empty chair across from hers, and a hot plate and tea kettle sitting on the edge of the table. "I've just made some tea. You can sip from that French teacup."

Allie sat at the table while Rosie poured hot water over teabags that she laid just so in the bottom of Allie's cup and another one just like it. As they waited for the hot liquid to turn from pale yellow to deep brown, Allie told her story: how she grew up in Freeport with just her mother, and how her mother was swept away by Hurricane Ike, and how she was working at Walmart one day when Bo walked in and collapsed at the sight of her. "And that's when I learned that Bo was my father and that's when I came to Port Aransas."

"No!" Rosie shrieked. "That's just the most amazing story I've ever heard. You should write that into one of those Southern novels that are so popular. You could call it *Port Aransas Morning* or something cute like that."

"Nah," Allie said, then took a sip of tea. "Like your teacups and knickknacks, it's probably of interest just to me." Allie took another long sip of tea and then looked at Rosie. "So . . . I've told you how I came to Port Aransas. Now it's your turn."

Rosie chuckled. "I'm afraid my story is not nearly as interesting. It's really just the story of a River Oaks housewife who spent too much time going to parties and let her dreams slip away."

Allie tilted her head down as if looking at Rosie over the top of a book. "Spill, girlfriend."

So Rosie explained how she and her husband Thomas met at Texas A&M University where he studied petroleum engineering and she, like Allie, studied interior design. With a job right out of school at Texaco for him and the anticipation of her getting work with a local decorator, they moved to a little house in the Bellaire area of Houston. They had a great time together in the early years. Thomas advanced quickly and they eventually settled into a spacious red-brick house among the shady live oaks and pecans of River Oaks. But Thomas' job took him overseas for longer and longer stints, and she filled the void with social clubs and fundraisers. And then when he called one day and told her that his job was moving to Europe permanently, divorce seemed the logical move.

"I got a couple of great kids out of it, but they have families of their own now and live up north. They don't have much time for me, and I suppose that's okay since I didn't give them much attention when they were little. We had nannies and all of that. They managed to grow up to be responsible adults in spite of me."

Allie reached over and patted Rosie's hand. "Don't be so hard on yourself. I'm sure you did fine. So . . . how'd you end up here?"

Rosie's face brightened. "Just dumb luck, really. I was packing up the house and I found a shoebox full of brochures for places we never found time to visit. I saw the pictures of this cute little town and decided to come take a look."

Allie took a final sip of tea and pushed back her chair.

"Well, we're all glad that you picked us out of the box and decided to give Port Aransas a try. I think you're going to like it here."

Rosie walked Allie to the door and out on the porch, where Allie turned around and looked up at the blank canvas awning. "Got a name yet?"

"I've been thinking about that. 'Forgotten Dreams' would be appropriate, but that doesn't have much street appeal, does it?"

"No, it doesn't," Allie said. "Besides, Shelly has the 'Dream' thing tied up. You could just call it 'Rosie's' for now. I'm sure the perfect name will come after you've spent a little time here. That's sort of the way it works in Port A."

By the time the truck arrived from Houston that weekend, Rosie had marked the floors with blue tape. Marty and Stu had only to carry in the shelves and furniture and place them according to Rosie's precise instructions. Over the next few days she and Allie arranged all the knickknacks and Allie priced them. With Sam running out of time to organize a Labor Day celebration, he decided that the opening of the new shop and gallery would be part of a day-long festival. Restaurants set up food stands, other shops rolled out sidewalk racks, and local artists set up booths featuring seashell wind chimes, driftwood carvings, and the like.

With a crowd gathered at ten in the morning, Sam welcomed Rosie to Port Aransas and the Pier

Association. She blushed and cackled in her signature way, and then when the crowd counted down from three, Rosie pulled a cord and a sheet fell from across the awning to reveal the name of Port Aransas' newest shop and gallery: Second Chances.

Chapter 6

While Rosie settled into the shop, others came down to visit, help her out, and even check her out. Allie had been won over by Rosie's brash yet honest charm, and she spent some of her free time at the shop helping out. Shelly had her own business to run, but she'd send Dave down occasionally with a cup of coffee and a cookie.

Bo rumbled in one day looking for Allie. Rosie thought he was just putting on an act and she gamely tried to play along.

"So what is this . . . one of those indoor flea markets?" Bo asked after walking in a few feet, nose in the air like he was sniffing things out.

"Well good morning to you Mr. Savoy, and no it's not a flea market. It's a proper antique shop and gallery."

Bo picked up a figurine in his large leathery hand and looked it over.

"That's a Hummel. You collect those?" Rosie laughed at the incongruity of such a thing.

"That'll be the day," he growled.

"Oh, perhaps you're a Precious Moments man." She cackled, knowing those pale, big-eyed figures were an even further distance from Bo's personality.

Bo scowled. "A what? Hell no, lady."

"Then is there something else I can help you with?"

He set the figurine down hard, rattling the other curious on the shelf. "I was looking for Allie. I hear she's been spending time down here."

"She's been a doll helping me get set up, but she's not been in today. Don't you live with her? Seems you'd see her all the time, or maybe you've been out on that boat of yours? What's that name again . . . *Caroline*?"

"It's *Cassie*, and I've not been out on her because we're out of season. Everyone knows that."

"Oh, I didn't know you had seasons like farmers. That's just so interesting."

"Well we do but it's a helluva lot tougher than farming. I never heard of any farmer drowning in his field, but it can happen out there on the Gulf sure enough. There ain't no comparison at all."

"I wasn't implying that it's the same . . ."

"You'd best stick to what you know, and that's fleas."

Bo wheeled around and pushed out through the door.

"Oh my," Rosie sighed as the door slammed behind him.

The exchange was on Rosie's mind later in the day when Sam stopped by. "I just thought he was putting on a show. I didn't mean to provoke him," she said.

"Well first thing you need to know is that Bo doesn't put on shows. He's rough and crusty, and sometimes he's rude, and that's real. But underneath that he's a kind man who would fall on a grenade for you. And he's not as strong as he thinks he is."

"He seems pretty sturdy to me."

"We've learned recently that his memory is failing, so we try not to say anything that might confuse him."

"I'm so sorry."

"No worries. Just don't take his barbs personally, and talk straight with him."

What Sam and Rosie didn't know was that the conversation with Rosie stirred up a storm in Bo's confused head. That night, as he settled into bed, Bo began arranging in his mind everything he would need to go out on the *Cassie* for the shrimping season.

Louie went down to the pier at five the next morning, still rubbing the crust from the corners of his eyes. He backtracked when he thought he had walked too far, then he rubbed his face again and confirmed what he was seeing, or rather not seeing: the slip where he had docked the *Rainbow* for a dozen years was empty. At first he suspected theft, but the more he thought about it the more he realized that shrimp boats just never get stolen. Still, the boat was missing and the news of it drifted up to the streets and shops, where it became the center of conversation. It was a curiosity at the Dream Bean, and several people wondered aloud what Bo might have to say about it.

"He'd hunt down the perp with a rusty screwdriver

and a grappling hook," said one of the sailors.

"That's why he used to sleep on the *Cassie*," said another. "He always said someone was going to run away with a boat some day, but I never believed him. I guess he was right."

"He was crazy, and mean, and a pain in the ass sometimes, but he was hardly ever wrong when it came to boats."

Allie, hearing all the chatter from behind the counter, stomped her foot. "I appreciate what you're saying, but you're talking like he's dead and that's a little creepy."

"We're sorry," said the one who started the conversation. "So where is Bo anyway?"

"Fishing I'm sure," said Allie. "Last night he said he'd be going out early."

She didn't think more of it until midafternoon when Bo hadn't walked back to the *Cassie* with his catch. With business at the Dream Bean slowing down and Shelly ready to close for the day, Allie turned in her apron and walked down to the beach. With the tourists gone for the fall and a storm beginning to churn a couple of miles off the shoreline, it didn't take her long to scan the beach and see that she was alone save for a couple of people taking an afternoon stroll. Turning to go back around to the piers, she saw a flash of lightning way out on the water and that's when it all came into focus: Louie's boat was missing, and Bo was nowhere to be found. "No!" she screamed and began running.

Allie turned the corner to the pier and saw a police car and Louie and a group of men gathered around talking.

"They've found her," Louie said. "The *Rainbow* is drifting but she's okay."

"It's Bo," Allie shouted as she ran up and stopped to catch her breath. "Bo took her out."

"What are you talking about?" the police captain asked.

She explained how Bo had told her before going to bed that he was leaving early for the catch, but he also had said something to Rosie about the shrimping season.

"He's been . . . confused . . . lately. I think he walked down to the pier this morning and thought he was getting on the *Cassie*."

"The Coast Guard sent a chopper out and they didn't see anyone on board," said the captain. "That might just be because he's inside, but we won't know for sure until they get a boat to her."

Out on the water, the *Rainbow* rose and fell in the growing storm. Indeed, Bo was on board, and he was in the pilothouse, at the wheel, barking orders at a crew that wasn't there. And when nobody did what he told them to do, he climbed out on the deck to do it himself. The cold spray washed his face and soaked through his clothing until his skin tingled with the chill of autumn. A shiver raced up his spine and his senses awakened to the full awareness that he was alone. He pulled and grasped his way back to the pilothouse and inside where he closed the door. Looking around, he had it in his mind that he should write a note in case things didn't turn out well, but he couldn't find the pencil and pad he kept in his toolbox because the toolbox wasn't on the floor in the corner where he usually stowed it.

"Dammit, always wanting to clean things up . . . why don't they just leave me alone," he growled. He scrounged around in the cubbyholes built into the cabin walls until he found a brown paper bag and a grease pencil. He dragged his way back to the wheel and holding on with one hand, he began scribbling with the other. He had barely finished and stowed the note away when a wall of water struck the starboard bow and spun the *Rainbow* like a top on the crest of the wave. The centrifugal force shoved Bo against the outside wall of the pilothouse and then out the door and into the storm.

Two hours later the storm had moved onto the Texas coast and into the Rio Grande Valley where its inches of rain were welcomed by farmers tending to their fall crops of lettuce, bell pepper, and squash. From Port Aransas, three shrimp boats followed a Coast Guard response boat out into the Gulf. Following the coordinates provided by the chopper, they came upon the *Rainbow* about five miles south of where it was last seen, southeast of Corpus Christi.

Allie, Louie, and Sam were all on the response boat— Allie to tend to her father and Louie to pilot the *Rainbow* home if she would go on her own power. And if not, the other shrimpers would tow her home. As they approached, Louie was relieved to see that the *Rainbow* was intact, her rigging still erect. But his relief was tempered by the fact that there was no sign of life.

"Best let us board her first and see what's what," said the response boat captain as they pulled alongside the *Rainbow*. He shot a glance at Sam, which Sam understood and answered by putting his arm around Allie's shoulder. "We better let them do their job," Sam said, drawing Allie close as he felt the muscles in her upper arms tighten.

The captain called Bo's name before stepping aboard. There was no answer, and he walked from the bow to the stern, around the back, and then entered the pilothouse from the far side. In Allie's mind he was taking too long, and when he came back out the door and back to the bow, she cried out. "Daddy."

"I'm sorry miss, he's not here."

Allie tore away from Sam's embrace and scrambled onto the *Rainbow* to see for herself. She entered the pilothouse and saw no signs of her father, which of course was not unusual since it was not Bo's boat. Staying at a respectful distance, Louie followed her inside and did see what was familiar to him, and he found everything where it belonged although a few items were scattered as would be expected in a big blow coming at the end of the hurricane season.

Allie stood in shock, her eyes frozen wide open, her hand over her mouth. The captain assured her a search was already under way. "He could be floating on the water or already drifted up on a beach by now."

Allie dropped her hands. "Gone . . . just like Momma."

"What are his chances?" Sam asked.

The captain gathered his words slowly. "There's just no way to predict these things. I've seen it go both ways."

"Oh Sam . . . I just never dreamed . . . ." Sam reached for Allie and pulled her head onto his shoulder.

"I know . . . I know . . ." What he knew was that Allie never dreamed that she'd lose both of her parents to the sea—her mother swept away in a hurricane, and now her father washed away in a squall.

In the fading evening light, the *Rainbow* chugged back to Port Aransas, followed by two of the shrimp boats. The Coast Guard boat stayed behind to begin the search with the third shrimper running parallel at a distance to form a grid. By nightfall there had been no sign of Bo, and while the search continued through the next day, nothing was found and the search was scaled back on the third day to flyovers and bulletins to local authorities to check their beaches.

Allie insisted on staying at the Dream Bean throughout the search—although she went home once thinking that maybe Bo had stumbled back on foot and was snoozing in his recliner. She was working behind the counter, her back turned to the door, when she heard a familiar clang of metal on the counter. She turned quickly to find Louie holding Bo's beat-up coffee mug. "I found it in the boat—the only thing that isn't mine."

Allie looked at it for a moment and then picked it up tenderly, as if it was the holy grail of legend. As she drew it near, she felt a little rattle from inside. "What?!"

"I don't know," Louie said. "I didn't think it was my place to look."

Slowly, Allie unscrewed the top and looked inside. Rolled up loosely inside the bone dry mug was a torn piece of brown paper. She turned the mug over and let the paper slide out onto the counter. She rolled it out flat and found a message written in Bo's clumsy, thick hand: "Don't be sad. Keep living. Love you always."

At that moment, Allie was no longer her father's daughter—strong as a piling, determined as a gull. Her shoulders slumped, and then her whole body collapsed onto the floor where she cried and cried.

~ ~ ~ ~ ~

On a calm, cool evening as the descending sun painted the puffy white clouds in pinks and violets, the people of Port Aransas stood on the beach and said goodbye to Beauregard Savoy. Since nothing of him was found to bury, they took turns telling stories, laughing at his irritating rants and heralding his loyalty and strength. Louie spoke on behalf of the shrimpers and sailors.

"We all had our fights with Bo at different times. I know I sure did, and I regret'm now. But we know that if he'd been in his right mind, Bo'd have checked the weather before going out. He'd never risk his boat or his crew in a storm like that."

"I'm sorry about your boat," Allie said softly. "Let me know if I can help with any repairs."

"Repairs? Your pa might have forgotten some things, but he hadn't lost what he was. He was a damn good captain, and from what I can tell, he did everything he could to save the *Rainbow* from sinking. I'll never . . ." Louie could say no more.

The talk continued for a while and Allie took it all in. Her only consolation was that with her father's death, she was still learning things about him that he would never have revealed himself.

When the last stories had been told and memories shared, Sam read a proclamation from the town council and unveiled a sign, hand-painted by Rosie. From that day forward that stretch of the pier would be known as "Bo's Landing." And then at the precise moment that the sun dropped below the western dunes, a lone shrimp boat sent its sorrowful wail across the water.

Chapter 7

Allie sat on the porch of the Dream Bean, staring at the bow of the *Cassie* jutting out from its eternal berth on the dry land next door. It was two weeks since Bo had been lost at sea and she somehow expected him to come walking back out of the pilothouse and onto the deck. She imagined him coming out, waving at her, and sitting in his chair like he did so many afternoons. And then she closed her eyes and shook her head. "No," she said with the whisper of a breath. "He's gone and that's that."

Allie felt a pat on her knee and opened her eyes to see Rosie's big face looking at her. "Oh, sweet girl, I know it's so hard, but you just have to . . . ."

Allie stood up and brushed past Rosie without saying a word. She walked down the steps and around the corner toward home. Frozen for a moment, Rosie walked into the Dream Bean where Shelly and Dave were cleaning up after the lunchtime rush.

"That girl needs to pull herself together," Rosie said.

"What girl?" asked Dave.

"Allie. I was talking to her and she just walked away."

"Well what did you say to her?" Shelly asked.

"I was trying to tell her that she needs to keep her chin up and keep pushing forward, but she walked away without saying a word."

Shelly tossed her rag into the sink and made a beeline to where Rosie was standing. "Who are you to be telling Allie or anyone else what they need to do," Shelly said, walking up so fast that Rosie had to take a step back. "You know nothing about that girl, just like you knew nothing about her father. How long have you been here, like a month? You have a lot of nerve . . ."

"That's enough, Shelly," Dave said, rushing from the back. "I'm sure Rosie was just trying to give Allie a little encouragement."

"Encouragement? She's telling Allie how to feel and nobody has the right to do that."

"I was just trying to help her move forward . . ."

"Lady . . . you're the reason she's grieving."

"Me?"

"Yes, you!" said Shelly. "If you hadn't been yapping at Bo about fishing, he would have never gotten it in his mind to go out on the boat."

"Now wait a minute," Dave said. "We have no way of knowing that had anything to do with it."

"Well where else did he get the idiot idea to go out there? None of the other shrimpers were talking about it."

Rosie began to cry. "I . . . I was just . . . making conversation . . . that's all."

"Well you shouldn't talk about things you don't know about with people you don't know."

"Now that's enough Shelly," Dave said. "You've gone too far."

Shelly pushed Dave out of the way and stormed back through the kitchen. Dave stood in the middle of the room—this woman he didn't know sobbing in front of him, and the woman he did know fuming somewhere in the back.

A few blocks away, Allie stood in front of her house. She looked at the dark windows and then looked away. She couldn't go inside. Bo's ghost was everywhere. She turned around and walked to the Pier Association office. She pushed on the door but it was locked. Without even thinking, she walked down the street and turned the corner and began walking down the road to Sam's trailer.

A short while later Allie turned through the weathered picket fence of the trailer park and stopped when she heard music—a sad, melancholy trumpet— coming from Sam's rusty trailer. A window was open, and she stopped outside a moment to listen. It was jazz, and it tickled a memory somewhere deep inside her.

Sam was sweeping the floor when he glanced out the window and saw Allie staring into space, her head moving gently to the slow melody coming from the old phonograph behind him.

"You like that one?" he called out to her.

The question brought Allie back. She turned toward the trailer just in time to see the door open. "You know that one?" Sam rephrased his question.

"My mother had that record. What is it?"

"Miles Davis . . . *My Ship.*"

Allie sighed. She closed her eyes; Sam stood silently in the doorway and let her have the moment to herself. When the song descended to its final quiet chord and then evaporated into silence, Allie's eyes fluttered open, as if she was coming up out of a long, deep prayer.

"Come in." Sam swung the door open and Allie slid past him. She stood for a moment, letting her eyes adjust to the dark, until Sam motioned for her to sit at the table.

"Something to drink?"

"No."

Sam sat at the table across from Allie. She lowered her eyes, and when Sam couldn't get her attention, he reached over and gently raised her chin.

"What's up?" he asked.

Allie looked up at Sam, and a shiver went up his spine as he looked into the saddest eyes he had ever seen. Not just sad, but weary beyond her years. He'd seen how she'd pushed hard through the shock and grief of losing Bo, but now she was sitting across from him exhausted and beaten. She looked the way he had felt when he first arrived on the island.

Allie rested her hands on the table, her fingers woven into a little basket. She looked at it like the basket held all that she had left of any value. "I was just beginning to feel like things were finally settling down, like I belonged. Bo . . . Daddy . . . and I were starting to really enjoy each other instead of just putting up with each other. We'd gotten past the awkward, forced family thing."

Sam searched deep but couldn't find any words of comfort. He'd been through much himself, but nothing compared to what Allie had endured. Yes, he had lost everything, but only because he had been careless and selfish. He had nobody to blame but himself. But Allie? She had lived well and done right, only to have the ones she loved taken away. It was different. It was cruel. It was heartbreaking. Sam reached over and put his hands on top of Allie's. All he could offer her was a vague promise that came from the tatters of his own experience.

"You don't have to go through this by yourself," he said. "And you don't have to be strong."

Allie looked at Sam now with eyes that he recognized. He'd seen those eyes before—when his wife Brenda came to take him home from jail after that horrible night when he drank too much, wrecked his car, and hurt Kayla. They were more than just weary, sad eyes. They were hungry eyes, and he knew them well. He'd seen that look in Brenda's eyes when he'd immersed himself in his schemes and conquests at the office. She was hungry for the loving affection they once shared.

Just then, Allie opened her hands to accept Sam's, and he felt that hunger in her fingertips. He stood up from the table, sliding his hands away from hers.

"What?" Allie asked.

Sam didn't know what to say, or how to say it.

"Just . . . let me stay . . . a while," she said.

Sam spoke slowly, carefully. "We can't do this. You and . . . me . . . we're vulnerable. We can't . . ."

"What, Sam?"

"I'm old enough to be your father."

Allie leaned back in her chair, threw her head back and let go a laugh that filled every corner of the trailer. And then when all the air and sound had left her lungs, she leaned forward and covered her mouth with both hands. She shook her head and then put her hands back on the table. "Oh Sam, you dear sweet man. I hate to disappoint you but I'm not thinking about you that way. I was just looking for a place to chill out a while."

Sam's face turned red, and then he slid back into his chair and let out a long slow, breath. "I'm so sorry," he said. "I don't know what I was thinking. I guess I'm just tired."

"I think we're both tired," she said. She patted his hand, but this time she didn't let her touch linger. "I'm going to walk to the beach and head toward home. You're welcome to walk with me."

"I better stay."

They both stood up and Allie gave Sam a daughterly hug. "See you tomorrow."

Sam didn't answer but watched as she walked out of

the trailer, the door springing shut behind her. He leaned forward to peek out the window but Allie was out of sight. Sam was disappointed . . . and relieved.

When Allie got out to the beach, she took off her sandals, rolled up her jeans, and waded calf deep into the surf. Even though it was late into the fall the afternoon sun was warm and the cool water felt refreshing. As Allie walked, she reflected on what had just happened. She was surprised that Sam thought she might see something in him, and that he might see something in her. She laughed a little again but then she felt herself blush when she realized she had liked that moment. Because it was true what Sam had seen in her eyes: she was hungry.

Chapter 8

The Christmas holidays came with the usual bustle on the island, but without the traffic jams that plagued the larger cities up and down the coast. Most of the locals drove down to Corpus Christi for their major shopping, which left the island relatively clear of any major congestion. Based on the success of the impromptu Christmas Eve party the year before, when Sam strung lights across the front of the Dream Bean, Shelly told her regular customers and neighbors around the piers that she'd be open again that night. Dave suggested that she might want to advertise and bring in some serious traffic, but Sam said the success the previous year had come from the fact that people just stumbled upon the opportunity to create an event where there wasn't one. "It's more about building community than it is about filling the cash drawers," he said.

"That's right," Shelly chimed in. "I don't need a big cash night; I just want to have people in." She looked at Dave and saw the frown on his face. "You weren't here last year, honey. You'll see what it's like."

Dave scowled.

"What?" Shelly asked.

"Nothing," he said, but he wasn't being completely truthful. Not if "nothing" was the little storm brewing in his head about his place in Port Aransas. And that storm lingered as Christmas Eve came and the party at Shelly's unfolded. It wasn't quite as big as it was the year before, but from all accounts the spirit of the night was just as strong, and when everyone had gone home to wait for Santa, Shelly's tip bucket was as full as it had been the first time.

"See!" Shelly said, showing Dave the bucket brimming with cash. "No advertising needed. Just turn on Sam's Christmas lights—the ones that you paid for, by the way—and they will come."

"Yep . . . you were definitely right about that," Dave said, trying hard to sound enthusiastic.

They all agreed to sleep in on Christmas morning and meet back at Shelly's at noon for sandwiches. "No gifts," Shelly had declared, and they took her at her word. All but Rosie, who couldn't resist unloading a few of her curios that she said she had "hand-selected" for each of them. Shelly's gift was a worn-looking metal sign that said, "Good Times With Good Friends Makes Good Coffee." She thanked Rosie and leaned it against a wall next to the counter.

A few days later, during a lull in the holiday week that was mostly a continuous lull, Dave told Shelly that he needed to visit Debby's family in Victoria.

"Oh . . . well, yes . . . of course," Shelly said.

"I hear some worry in your voice," he said.

"No, it's not worry, it's just . . . this is the first time you've mentioned them in a long time, and I'd sort of forgotten that you still have them as a family and all of that. It's good for you to keep in touch."

Dave put his hands on Shelly's hips and pulled her close. "Yes, they still are my family. But . . . the reason I need to see them is to tell them that you are now my family too."

Shelly cringed. "Ooh . . . is that a good thing to tell them? Will that upset them?"

"I don't know. It might, but I need to let them know what is happening with us. It wouldn't be right to say nothing and then just suddenly be married again."

"No, that wouldn't do." She looked him in the eyes. "Are you nervous?"

"Very."

"Do you want me to go with you?"

"No, this is something I need to do alone."

"You won't let them talk you out of it will you?"

"Of course not. Nobody could do that. And besides, that's not something they would do. They've always wanted the best for me."

"They sound wonderful. I would like to meet them some day."

"There'll be a time for that." He let go of her and turned away, not wanting to talk any more about it. He knew he would have to go slow. His fear was exactly as Shelly had said—that he would upset them. He hurt for them, knowing that while he could have another love in his life, they could never have another daughter.

"When will you go?" Shelly asked.

"I'm thinking New Year's Eve."

"Awww . . . I was hoping we could start the new year together."

"I'll be back soon enough. Besides, New Year's Eve has always been overrated if you ask me."

"That's just because you've never done it the right way," said Allie, who walked into the kitchen in time to catch the end of their conversation.

"And just what is the right way?" Shelly asked.

Allie just smirked and walked on by. She didn't want to let on that she didn't really know. Except for a few times when she and her teenage girlfriends had stayed out late and gotten a little rowdy, she too had no real expectations for the night, and certainly nothing like what she had seen in Times Square on TV.

"So how do you celebrate in Port Aransas?" Allie asked Shelly.

"It's actually pretty low key," she said. "There's no official celebration. Most of the action is in Corpus Christi. Most people around here stay home or they go to their favorite bar."

Sam came in the front door and was startled by Allie's immediate question: "What about you, Sam?"

"What about me?"

"What do you do to celebrate New Year's Eve?"

"Oh, is that coming up again?"

"Don't be coy. Surely you have some kind of celebration or ritual to mark the end of one year and the beginning of the next."

Sam stopped to think about it. In the time he had been on the island he had spent New Year's Eve either bussing tables somewhere or alone in his trailer. He certainly had never celebrated like he had in Dallas. "Nope, nothing comes to mind."

Allie sat down at the table across from him and leaned on her hand. "There's gotta be something we can do to mark the changing of the calendar. A new ritual, a new tradition."

"Traditions aren't just created overnight," Dave said, coming from the back. "You do something and then if you like it and do it again, it might become a tradition, but that can take years or even . . . ."

"Stop," Allie said. "I get it. So let's just do something. Anything."

Everyone just stared at each other a moment and then began offering ideas. None of them sounded too fun— and Shelly definitely did not want to have a mob at the Dream Bean again.

And then Dave's face lit up. "How about a cookout on the beach . . . at midnight."

"I thought you were going to Victoria?" Shelly said.

"And miss the chance to start a new tradition? No way!"

"Just us?" Allie asked.

"Sure," Dave said. "We won't advertise, and we won't turn anyone away, but yes, let's try to keep it small. Just family."

"What about Rosie?" Shelly asked.

"What about her?" Dave asked. "If she hears about it, she's welcome to come."

Shelly made sure she wasn't the one to mention it to Rosie, but Sam did, and she was among the small group that met on the beach near Sam's trailer at dusk. They cooked hot dogs over a pit that was dug into the dry sand and drank cold beer and chilled wine and watched the sun sink behind the dunes and the full moon float up out of the Gulf accompanied by its flotilla of silent stars. The conversation was light and pleasant, as they reflected on the year and their lives in general. A few toasts were raised including one to Bo who was the obvious missing link between the year ending and the new one to come. Rosie, who was still stinging from Shelly's rebuke of her attempts to cheer up Allie, kept her thoughts mostly to herself but did raise a glass "to my lovely new friends" and hoped aloud that she might learn more about how to live in this "lovely little town."

At midnight they welcomed the new year by breaking the county's ban on fireworks as Allie struck a match and touched it to the end of a Roman candle that Dave had bought at a stand on the highway. They watched in silence as each colored fireball whooshed up and out across the water and fell to a silent death in the dark Gulf. And that was the end of the celebration, and perhaps the start of a new tradition as Allie had wanted, or maybe not. It would take 365 days for New Year's Eve to come around again, at which time maybe they would gather on the beach, or maybe not.

Dave and Shelly loaded the car and drove back to Shelly's house on the first day of the year in which they were planning to marry. They said their goodbyes, but there was tension in the air because Dave was driving later that morning to Victoria to visit Debby's family. Dave was nervous about the whole situation, and Shelly was just anxious for him to get that done so that she could have his full attention again.

Rosie followed them off the beach and back into town in her Cadillac. She offered Allie a ride, but Allie declined and Rosie didn't push her. She drove back to her own home in silence and wondered if she would ever fit in and if her move from the city to this small seaside town had been such a good idea after all. As she drove she turned on the wipers before realizing that it was tears and not rain that was clouding her vision.

"And what about you?" Sam asked Allie as they stood alone on the beach.

"I'm going to walk home this way," she said, pointing down the long strand of dark sand that curved up the coast and back toward the piers and town. "I just want to be alone now."

"I can't let you walk back alone," said Sam. "But I can follow you and leave you alone with your thoughts."

Allie thought about it a moment. "Count to fifty. No, make that a hundred, and then you can follow me." She turned and began walking.

By the time Sam began to follow her, Allie was visible as nothing more than a small silhouetted figure moving away from him on the gray sand. He noticed several times that he seemed to be gaining ground, and he knew that meant that she had stopped for a moment. So he stopped too until her silhouette began to grow small again. He followed her for twenty minutes until he saw her turn back toward the land on the road leading into town. By the time he got to that same turn, Allie was two blocks in, and she turned to wave him off. He stood and watched until she was out of his sight.

Allie never told Sam the extent of her pondering that night and he never asked, but he knew. For as he walked back to his trailer under the full moon, he saw the musings of her heart that she had stopped to draw with her bare feet: a question mark, a heart with a jagged line through it, a dove, a round face with a frown. Sam stood for a moment at that last sand drawing, and then with his own bare foot he turned one corner of the frown up.

Chapter 9

"Glad I didn't end up here," Dave said to himself as he stopped at a busy intersection in Rockport. The town was larger and more prosperous than Port Aransas just to the south. It had the little pastel-painted shops like Port Aransas, only there were more of them. And more residential streets lined with more windswept bungalows. And more groceries and gas stations. And if you had more money than most people, it had Key Allegro with its mansions on stilts and boat slips and swimming pools overlooking the bay. Debby's family had rented a vacation condo in Rockport for a while, but even they had tired of the traffic and the fact that the town sat on the bay and not on the Gulf. Which meant they often slipped down to Port Aransas where the pace was slower and the beach was real. That's how he had come to know and appreciate his adopted island home.

Driving north out of Rockport, he crossed the entrance to Copano Bay on the two-mile causeway and skirted the western edge of the Aransas National Wildlife Refuge where cranes and pelicans rose and fell together in large white clouds above the table-flat marshes. From there the highway turned northward at Tivoli and crossed the rice fields and scrubby grasslands dotted with cattle. Shortly after that he was in Victoria, a town that you never saw from a distance but were always just suddenly in. He remembered how when driving in from the north, you could see the blinking red light of a solitary water tower and nothing else for twenty miles, and then when you finally reached the water tower you were in the thick of the town with all its traffic and strip centers and car lots.

The drive from Port Aransas to Victoria was less than ninety miles, but it always surprised him that it usually took more than two hours. He never could tell if the extra time required was just because of the small-town slowdowns and delays behind cattle trucks and combines, or if there was something in the heavy coastal air that actually slowed his progress as he crossed some of the flattest landscape he had ever seen. Nevertheless, there was little of real interest to see on the way, and that helped him to focus on what he needed to say, which was different from what he wanted to say. What he needed to say was that he was getting married and moving on with his life. What he wanted to say was that he had fallen in love and was getting married but that he would never stop loving their daughter, and he would always be grateful for their love and acceptance of him as a son.

He was still reviewing his lines as he drove into the heart of the old downtown district and pulled into the driveway of the great old house that Debby's brother had bought and restored to elegance for his family. Framed by tall palm trees, sprawling oaks, bright red oleanders, and wild confederate roses, the house was easily the most stately and noteworthy on Main Street. Inside, it was warm and welcoming like the family that had lived there for almost twenty years.

That history of hospitality did not keep Dave from feeling anxious as he turned off his car, grabbed his overnight bag, and walked through the back door into the kitchen. He had always carried a weight of regret and guilt with him on these visits to Debby's parents, as if he was somehow responsible for her death, and he always was put at ease immediately when he found them to be their usual gracious and loving selves. On top of that, they were always busy—so much so that he was reminded again that they had not stopped living their lives and neither should he. And that was the message that he hoped to convey on this particular visit.

That first afternoon and night with them was the same as nights and afternoons had always been in the more than twenty years that he had known them, the only difference being that Debby was absent. And that night, in the upstairs corner bedroom where he and Debby had slept so many times as a couple and where he had grown strangely accustomed now to sleeping alone, he had the sweetest dream. It was daytime, and he and Debby were there in the house and she was as lovely and vibrant as she had been on her very best days—with a smile that was luminous and full of life. But in the mysterious, unspoken language of dreams, there was an understanding between them that she would not be with him much longer, and there was no fear or sadness in that knowledge. And he looked across the room and saw Shelly sitting in a chair in the corner, waiting for him. He looked at her and she smiled, and in the same unspoken language of dreams there was the assurance that everyone was going to be okay.

So it was with a spirit of lightness and calm that Dave sat down with the family for breakfast the next morning, and as the meal came to an end, he quietly announced, "I need to bring you up to date on things." In phone talks and letters over the past year he had dropped hints that he was spending time with someone new, and now he was hoping to not just give her a name but also express his feelings for her, to the point of saying, "and we've talked about getting married." And he got through all of that fine, and they nodded their heads as he slowly turned over each card of his story, stopping short of revealing that they planned to marry in four months. He would keep that card hidden unless they called his hand, which Debby's mother did right away when she asked, "Have you set a date?"

Dave's face flushed red and the stuttering that he had known as a shy child began to show itself. "Well . . . we're looking at . . . at . . . May . . . maybe."

"May? So soon?"

Dave swallowed. "Well . . . we . . . we don't see a reason to wait."

Debby's mother looked wistfully out the window. Dave imagined what she was thinking and he ached for her. Debby's father cleared his throat and spoke in a tone that was firm yet gentle—the same voice he used when he was called upon to read the gospel passage in church. Dave understood that the man now was speaking on behalf of the family.

"We're very happy for you, Dave. Of course . . . we'll never be able to know and love Shelly like we loved Debby, but we'll enjoy getting to know her. We certainly support you in whatever happens."

Dave exhaled and swallowed back the lump of emotion in his throat. He was grateful for their compassion and understanding, and more than that he was relieved that they'd all gotten through the session with relatively little discomfort. But his relief was short lived because Debby's father had one more question to ask: "So, what will Shelly do in Dallas?" Dave had walked safely through one door and around the corner, only to find another door waiting that he had not prepared for. He paused to arrange his words carefully.

"Well, we're not going to live in Dallas. We're going to stay in Port Aransas. Shelly has her business there and I'm going to help her run it."

"But what about your career . . . and your

education?" Debby's mother was no longer staring out the window at some unknown object. She was back in the room, at the table, fully engaged. "Are you just going to walk away from that?"

"Well this is a career change for sure, but a lot of my experience will come to good use in running and growing a business."

"Well . . . I don't understand it. Seems like you're throwing a lot away, but if that's what you really want to do. . . ." Her sentence ended just there—somewhere between an endorsement and a rejection—and she got up from the table and went to the sink to wash the dishes.

Dave had said all he knew to say and wanted to say, and the rest of the day went on without any more mention of it. Dave told them he would leave the next morning, and he did with their well wishes and an invitation to come back soon and bring Shelly. He wanted to tell them that he would stop by the cemetery on the way out of town—as if to ease their sorrow with another declaration of his continued love for their daughter—but he stopped short of that for fear of muddying the water. He hugged them again and waved as he drove away. He did stop at the cemetery. Seeing Debby's name carved into the granite monument brought home the reality of how much his life had changed. He tried to cry but he couldn't; he wanted to scream at the top of his lungs but he didn't dare. So he simply got back in his car and drove back to Port Aransas under a funnel cloud of mixed emotions.

Dave's fear of sharing his new love was now replaced with a raw angst about the other change he had made and that he had slipped into so easily without much thought until now: leaving his career in a downtown Dallas office tower for a partnership in a small coffee shop in Port Aransas. "Have I totally lost my mind?" he asked himself as he drove onto the deck of the ferry and began the slow drift back across the bay to Port Aransas and to Shelly.

In contrast to Dave's unsettling visit to Victoria, a relative calm had settled over the Dream Bean, where all signs of the holidays had been stowed away for another year and replaced by the regular rhythm of business in the small island town. As much as Shelly enjoyed Christmas and always had since her earliest memories of racing to the tree to open gifts on Christmas morning, her practical nature had come to appreciate the predictable calm of the long stretch from winter into summer, with the only bump being the chaos that SandFest brought to town. Looking ahead into the new year, all she cared about was making a little more money than she spent and having a few friends around to keep her company. And Dave, of course. She did care for Dave—not just care for him, but love him—didn't she? She kept asking herself that, and she kept answering herself with, "Of course I do; I'm going to marry him on the beach in May." For someone who preferred the ordinary seasons of the year, planning a wedding and then going through with it—and playing a role no less than that of the grand queen of the day—well that was proof enough for her that her love for Dave was not just very real but was also deeply anchored.

She was in the process of reviewing that thesis in her head again—and sharing a part of it with Sam—on the same morning that Dave was driving back from Victoria. Sam had come in to the Dream Bean on his way to the Pier Association for an appointment and had started the conversation.

"Heard anything from Dave?"

"No. Wasn't expecting to. He was really wanting to stay focused."

"About?"

"This was the visit where he was going to tell the parents that he is getting married . . . to me." She smiled big at the sound of it.

"Hmm. That's a big one."

"Yes, it is. But he needed to do it and this was a good time to do it, so I expect him to come back in here later today with a clear head and ready to start making plans."

"That would be good."

"Well of course it would be good." Shelly looked Sam over, hunting for any signs of doubt or skepticism in his body language. "And . . . so you think he might have had trouble making the pitch?"

Sam took a sip from the cardboard cup that Shelly had just filled for him. "Oh, I'm sure he got through the talk just fine."

"But?" Shelly probed.

"But now that he's done with that, it makes the wedding and marriage and life with you very real. It's no longer just a dream."

"And you think he'll have trouble with that?"

Sam set his cup down on the counter and looked Shelly in the eye. "Remember that first day Dave and I came in here together? We had just met on the beach at sunrise. He wasn't there to fish or swim or sunbathe. He was there trying to mend his broken heart."

"Yes, I know that."

"Well," Sam stopped. He was tempted to tell Shelly about the broken heart that Allie had drawn on the beach on New Year's morning, but he didn't want to invade Allie's privacy. "Broken hearts aren't ever really fixed. Not completely." Sam looked at his watch. "Gotta go."

Sam tried to give Shelly a reassuring smile as he turned to walk out the door, but he wasn't sure that he had sold it very well. He was wondering about that when he almost fell over Rosie who was coming up the steps of the Dream Bean as he was walking down. She shuffled awkwardly to dodge him and dropped two brown paper gift bags she was carrying. He stopped to help her pick them up.

"What's this?" Sam asked as he handed over one bag and then the other.

"Just some little gifts for the girls," Rosie said.

"What's the occasion?"

"No occasion. Just . . . gifts for friends."

Sam gently took Rosie by her free hand and guided her down off the steps and out of view from inside.

"Rosie . . . you don't need to do this."

"What?"

"You don't need to . . . win their friendship."

"Is that what I'm doing?"

"Isn't it?"

Rosie exhaled and set the bags on the ground, and then in a total release of all her carefully practiced Southern charm school affectations, she plopped down onto the bottom step and let her panted legs spread apart like the tomboy that she might have once been. She shook her head and then lowered her face and began to cry.

Sam wasn't sure what to do. He reached out a hand but didn't know where to start in providing some sort of comfort—a pat on the shoulder, a touch on the hand, a brush of the hair? He couldn't decide so he stood awkwardly in front of her, like a coach standing before an injured athlete on the bench.

Rosie blubbered. "This was a mistake. I should have stayed in Houston. Nobody likes me. I don't fit . . . ."

"Stop," Sam said with an edge in his voice. Too much

drama for one morning, he thought, unsure if her emotions were real or just part of the show she seemed to be staging all the time. But then Rosie raised her head, and what Sam saw revealed that if she was just acting, she was indeed very good: black mascara streaked down her carefully rouged cheeks. Sam sat down on the step beside her.

"You're trying too hard," he said. "You can't force friendships. They either happen or they don't happen."

Rosie sniffed but didn't say anything. Sam looked straight ahead, not wanting to make eye contact. He could see out of the corner of his eye that she too was looking straight ahead. He continued.

"It may look to you like we're all longtime friends, but we're not. We're all very new to each other. I've been here three years, and I spent the first two of those years down there in that trailer by myself. Dave just drove into town one day, sort of like you. And Allie, that's the strangest story of them all. She's still pretty much fresh off the boat. Shelly's been here her whole life, but we seem to be the only people she really knows and so that doesn't say very much."

Rosie turned her head and looked at Sam. She blinked like a dog waiting to see what her master might do next.

"What I'm trying to say is that none of us woke up one day and decided to create this . . . this family . . . that we seem to have. It just happened. That's the way friendships usually go. They just . . . happen . . . or they don't."

Rosie sniffed and sighed and leaned over, resting her head on Sam's shoulder. Sam stiffened at the unexpected intimacy of the moment. And then realizing that his awkward posture might send Rosie over the emotional edge again, he relaxed his muscles and slumped a little. They sat quietly in that position for a moment, and then Rosie lifted her head and patted Sam on the knee.

"You're a sweet man, Mr. Sam."

Rosie stood up, gathered her bags, and walked back to her car. She climbed inside, started the engine, looked in the mirror, wiped the mascara from her cheeks, and drove away.

Sam stood up and paused for a moment, trying to remember where he had been going. Oh yes, he was going back to his office. He looked at his watch. "Darn," he said, and he rushed around the corner, down the street, and up the steps of the Pier Association.

Chapter 10

Sam was met at the front door of the Pier Association by a man in a dark suit and dark glasses to match. Sam noticed a dark SUV parked across the street.

"Good morning. Sorry to keep you waiting." Sam unlocked the door and walked inside. The man didn't say a word but stood on the porch until Sam turned on the lights and motioned him in.

"So, what can I do for you?"

The man opened a leather wallet to reveal a gold shield with large blue **DEA** letters on it, and then he spoke in a crisp, practiced manner. "We believe there is some new drug movement in the area."

The man looked Sam in the eyes, reading his expression to see if it revealed a question, a concern, or a clue. He saw the questions on Sam's face, and he answered them.

"We're touching base with individuals who may be in a position to see or hear something. You head the Pier Association."

"Yes. Most of our members own small shops and businesses and boats. I doubt seriously that . . . ."

"You might be surprised. We had a woman in Port Lavaca who was selling seashell wind chimes on the highway from the trunk of a fully loaded Lexus sedan. Turns out she was selling more than wind chimes."

"Okay . . . I see your point . . . but if anyone around here is making money on drugs, they're sure not showing off." Sam pointed out the window at the line of brightly painted but modest, ramshackle shops.

"Actually, it's not just the shop owners we're looking at. There might be dealers pretending to be high school or college students. And we're interested in what may be happening farther down the beach near your trailer park."

"My trailer park?"

The man took a photograph out of his coat pocket and showed it to Sam. "You live here."

Sam looked at the photo of the entrance to his trailer park, with his own rusty trailer visible in the back corner. The man continued. "You're in a good location to notice unusual activity: Small boats coming onto the beach, vehicles late at night, odd debris. Anything out of the ordinary."

Sam handed the picture back to the man. "Excuse me, but nothing around here is particularly ordinary, so how am I supposed to know the difference? But on top of that, people around here like to mind their own business and not ask questions."

"We're not suggesting you play detective on your own

and start snooping around and asking questions."

"Well that's good because I'd never do such a thing."

"Sir, all I'm asking you to do is be observant and let me know if you see something unusual." He handed Sam a business card and then turned and walked out the door.

Sam sat down at his desk. For a man who had built a new life based on minding his own business, this was not a good development. Sam dropped the card into his desk drawer, shoved it shut, and turned on his computer. He didn't know what else the day would bring, but he was sure he wasn't going to waste it spying on his neighbors.

~ ~ ~ ~ ~

Dave rolled off the ferry and back onto the island with his head still swimming from the notion that he had thrown away his career. As much as he wanted to wrap his arms around Shelly now and celebrate his newly unfettered romance, he didn't want to do it at the Dream Bean. Yes, he had helped build its success, but now it represented the loss of who he was and who he could be, or at least that's what he had been told in Victoria.

Turning the corner from the ferry landing, Dave drove past the piers and the town center and continued down the highway to Pete's C-Stop where he bought a Dr Pepper and the Sunday edition of the *Corpus Christi Caller-Times*. He thumbed through it in the car, pulling the thick employment section out and putting it on top.

He turned back down some side streets to the house he was renting, took the paper and his bags in, and checked his mail.

And then he gave in to the fuzzy feeling between his eyes and decided to lie down for a few moments. The emotion of the trip and the rhythm of the road had made him drowsy, and a short power nap seemed like a sure cure.

Dave had just closed his eyes, or so he thought, when he was startled by a banging at the door, and when he sat up on the edge of the bed his eyes caught the clock. "Damn," he said and slid to the front room in his socks and looked out the window to see Shelly's car parked out front. "Damn."

He rubbed his eyes and combed his hair with his hands and swung the door open so fast that it banged against the wall. "Hey you," he said loudly, trying to mask his fatigue.

"Hey you too," Shelly said through the screen door. "I thought you might come straight to the Bean. I've been dying to hear how it went."

Dave unlatched the screen door to let her in. "I just stopped here a moment to check on things," he said. Shelly walked past him into the den and didn't see the blush that was drawn to his cheeks by his lie: The clock said he had been sleeping for three hours.

Shelly turned, expecting an embrace, but instead she found Dave sitting on the arm of the sofa. She sat down on the cushion below him and wrapped her arms around his waist.

"Tired?"

"A little."

"Well why don't you catch a nap and then I'll come over later and make us dinner."

"Sounds great," he said.

Shelly stood up. "I'll just check your pantry to see what I need to get." She walked toward the kitchen but stopped when she saw the newspaper on the table. She picked up the section resting on top. "What's this?"

Dave winced, realizing he had left the employment section sitting on top of the paper.

"I was just looking . . . seeing what's going on in the business world."

"In Corpus? Seems to me like you're looking for a job. Does your boss know?" She smirked and dropped the paper back on the table.

Dave got up and started to walk toward her, but Shelly continued. "We're doing so good at the Bean now, better than I ever imagined. I thought you were enjoying it."

"I have been, but now I'm starting to feel like I've done all I can do. Allie has become more of a partner with you at the counter. And I know you can find a better cook and dishwasher than me."

Shelly shook her head. "No, I can't," but she knew she couldn't just coax him back with sweet talk. Her way was more blunt. "I'll have to admit that I'm surprised by this. I didn't realize you weren't happy."

"I'm just feeling . . . I don't know . . . like I'm standing still. So I thought I'd see if there were other opportunities nearby."

Shelly was listening, but in her mind she was measuring the impact of what she was hearing. Port Aransas was all she knew, and all she cared to know. She'd been to big cities and enjoyed the visits but had no desire to live there. She reached for Dave's hand.

"You know, I'm all for you being happy and at peace with yourself. If you find a good opportunity, then I think you should pursue it."

Dave brightened. "Really?"

"I just have one question, though: How often do you plan to come back and see me, because I won't be going with you."

And in one sentence Shelly had managed to raise Dave's spirits and then crush them. She let go of his hand and walked to the door, waving over her shoulder as she walked out. Dave hung his head, knowing he'd walked right into her trap. But he also knew that he was stuck. Unsure now whether dinner with Shelly was still on, Dave knew he couldn't let the situation fester. He walked to the Dream Bean and found it locked up. He made the short walk to the Pier Association and found Sam sitting on the steps.

"Hey, Dave, how was the trip?" Sam said lazily.

Dave climbed the steps and sat next to Sam. "It was fine. Great actually. It's the coming home that hasn't gone so well."

Sam didn't speak, but that didn't stop Dave from spilling out his troubles. "I've let myself go, Sam. I've become nothing more than a dishwasher and busboy. I might as well move down to the trailer park with you. Is there a vacancy?" As soon as he said that Dave realized the insult of his comment. "Oh gosh, I'm sorry."

"Don't worry about it."

Dave sat silent for a moment. "I better go see if I can find Shelly. Good night." He stood up and walked around the corner and out of sight.

Sam sat on the steps until the sun slipped below the horizon, turning the white lapboard walls of the old hotel across the street from orange to dark blue, and then he started the walk toward home. He'd heard everything Dave said, and he might have asked for more details, but he had purposely held himself back. He was growing weary of being the father confessor to everyone who sought advice or just wanted to unload. And now, as he walked back down the beach toward his trailer, he cursed the agent who had stepped into his office that afternoon. Because now, every twinkling light out on the Gulf, every lone person walking on the fringe of the water, every car parked up on the dry sand with its engine running and windows fogged had a sinister, suspicious air.

Chapter 11

"Oh . . . yes . . . I see it!" Rosie giggled as she dipped her brush into the orange and red pigments and mixed them into the pinks and melons that she hadn't expected to see on such a gray day. Looking out across the horizon and then down at her palette, she worked the paint until she had what she was seeing and then brushed the colors horizontally across the canvas. "Yes," she told herself, and then she worked on another color, this time adding some green to the mix. She was feeling very pleased with herself when a large raindrop splashed onto the middle of the palette and sent droplets of color across her white blouse. "Well that's not very nice," she said, and as if to answer her rebuke the low-hanging clouds released a scatter shot of more large raindrops on top of her bare head and the canvas. She pulled a dishtowel from out of her kit and lay it across the canvas and then the bottom fell out and she was quickly soaked to the skin.

Rosie grabbed the canvas, easel, and chair, but when she ran to her car she couldn't find the keys. She was standing there, shivering like a soaked dog when she heard her name and looked down the beach to see Sam with an umbrella, motioning her to come his way. More cold than embarrassed, she let go of everything but the canvas and trudged through the clumpy wet sand. Sam sighed heavily as she got closer, not sure that inviting this woman in was a good idea. But his better self took charge and he stepped forward with his umbrella and ushered her around the corner and into his trailer.

"You're a dear," she said, "but how did you know I was out here?"

"I didn't. I was just out here hanging some clothes and I saw you." He pointed out the window to some shirts hanging in the rain on a line between his trailer and the fence.

"Does that really work?"

"Yes, if you don't mind wrinkles." Sam saw a shiver roll across Rosie's shoulders. He stepped quickly to a cupboard and pulled out some towels. "Sorry I can't offer you something dry to wear."

"I'm just sorry to get everything wet."

"Not a problem. Everything in here is plastic. You can't possibly hurt anything."

Rosie laughed, but she caught herself and kept it small as she was teaching herself to do.

With no place to go for privacy, Rosie set down her canvas and any River Oaks modesty she held onto and vigorously toweled off her wet, curly hair.

"How about some coffee or hot tea?" Sam asked, squeezing past her into the little corner kitchen.

Rosie stopped scrubbing her head and let the towel fall down across her shoulders as she sat down at the table. "I'd love a cup of hot tea."

Sam lit his tiny stovetop and moved a teapot onto the burner. He put two mugs and a basket of tea bags on the table.

Rosie was surprised. "You too? I thought coffee was all you salty islanders drank?"

"Not everyone here is so salty, and we're not all islanders. I came from the city too." Sam tilted the basket toward her and she picked out a mild English breakfast tea and dropped the bag into her cup. He selected a black tea and then brought the teapot to the table and filled their cups. He sat across from her and they made small talk about the weather, she noting that the weather in Port Aransas was not so different from Houston. As Rosie picked up her spoon to remove the teabag, Sam noticed her fingers were smudged with the same colors that were splashed across her blouse.

"How's the painting going?"

Rosie lifted her small canvas up on the table and peeled off the dishcloth to reveal a stork standing on one leg in the foam.

Sam turned on the light above the table and leaned the canvas against the window. "That's really nice," he said with genuine surprise in his voice.

"Thank you, but you get the credit. You were right about the colors."

"Maybe so, but you definitely know how to use them." He took a sip of tea and looked at the painting again. "This is what you should be selling in your gallery. How's it going down there anyway? Haven't seen much of you lately."

Rosie took a long slow sip. "It's been okay. After the dust-up with Shelly I decided I might best focus on the shop, and that's been good. I've had some good traffic; sold some of my old treasures . . . and had a couple of local artists bring in their paintings."

Sam leaned forward and pointed to the canvas. "Curios and antiques are fine, but this is where your future is."

Rosie set her cup down and put her hands to her cheeks, trying to hide an unexpected blush. "Oh, you're just talking."

Sam didn't reply. He took another long sip of tea. They talked about the state of business in Port Aransas and the coming of SandFest and what that might bring to a shop such as Second Chances. They didn't notice that the rain had stopped, and when a bright ray of sunshine came washing across the table from the window, Rosie leaned back in her chair.

"Well, I guess that's my signal to let you get back to your doings," she said. "I'm almost dry, and the sunshine will take care of the rest."

Sam helped her cover her painting and offered to walk her back to the car and look for her keys.

"I can manage," she said.

He opened the door and watched her walk across the drive and out the gate. He noted that she didn't shower with him thank-yous and compliments. She just walked away like a native—with the understanding that hospitality was freely given and taken without fanfare. Sam closed the door, feeling that progress had been made.

Back at the car, the rain had patted down the fluffy sand, and Rosie's key ring shone in the bright sun on the ground just outside the door. She loaded her gear on the floor and then stopped to look back out at where she had been painting. She uncovered the canvas, held it up, and compared the scenes. "Finished."

When she got back to the shop, Rosie cleared out a front corner and placed her new seascape on an easel in the window where it could be seen. She collected the half-dozen paintings that she had taken on consignment and spread around the shop and she hung them together on a blank wall closest to the door. Then in the back of the shop, where she had set up her studio, she put brush to wooden plank and hand-painted a sign to hang in the window: "Gallery Open."

Rosie sat behind the counter and celebrated her accomplishment with a glass of wine from an old bottle she had brought from her collection in Houston. And then she had another, and another, until her head got heavy and she just had to lay it down. She was resting there—her heavy breathing causing the papers on the counter to flutter—when she heard the door open and she lifted her head and opened her eyes. As she focused, she recognized one of the two figures walking toward her.

"Well, hello Martin. What brings you around? Shouldn't you be in school?"

"Uh . . . we get out early sometimes. We were wondering if you needed any help moving anything?"

Rosie tried not to draw attention to herself as she sat up straight and then stood up, but she couldn't hide a wince at the sudden throbbing in her forehead.

"Are you okay, Ms. Chase?"

"It's just these bad migraines. They'll pass." She looked at Marty and then at the taller, older-looking boy standing next to him with the flaming red hair. "And who is this one?"

Marty started to talk but the other boy stepped forward and held out his hand. "I'm Justin. I know Marty from the high school. We were looking for Allie. I heard that she works here sometimes."

Rosie walked around the counter, her foot bumping the empty wine bottle that she had set on the floor. Marty nudged Justin, and the older boy whispered, "be cool."

"Allie hasn't been around here in a while," Rosie said. "She's been keeping to herself more ever since her daddy passed so suddenly last month."

"Yeah, that was really sad," said Marty.

Rosie walked to the front door and looked out, noticing that the sun was beginning to cast its last low rays on the Port Aransas streets. She turned to face the boys.

"You're too old to be in high school, aren't you?" she asked, looking Justin in the eye.

"Yes ma'am, that's right. I graduated in December from Stephen F. Austin, and now I've started taking classes at the UT Marine Institute over on the beach. I met Allie last year during SandFest and just wanted to look her up and reconnect."

"So you're going to be a marine biologist? That's so interesting," Rosie said, forcing interest behind her raging headache.

"Yes ma'am. Well actually, I'm just looking into it. Taking a couple of winter courses to see if it's for me."

Rosie walked back to the counter and leaned against it. "Well if I see Allie, I'll tell her I saw you. But you'll probably see her long before I do. The Dream Bean's your best bet."

"Yes ma'am. We've already been there but we'll check back tomorrow. Thank you," Justin said.

"Hope you feel better," said Marty, and the two boys stepped outside and started walking toward the institute.

"Wow, I've never seen an old lady blitzed like that," said Marty.

"That's harsh," said Justin.

When they got to the corner of Station Street and Channel View, they stopped.

"Well, I guess I'll see you around," said Justin.

"Tomorrow?" Marty asked.

"Maybe so."

Marty turned back up the street and toward home.

Justin stood for a moment in the growing darkness, making sure Marty didn't look back, and then he trotted away from the direction of the institute and back toward the piers.

By the time Allie arrived at the Dream Bean the next morning, everybody had seen Justin except her. "What did he want? What did he say? What's he doing here?" Allie's questions came rapid-fire, and she couldn't hide the grin on her face as she asked one final question: "Was he looking for me?" Little by little, from the answers she got, she pieced together that Justin was taking some classes at the Marine Institute and would be in town through the spring. Some of his work was related to classes at the high school, and that's how he had met Marty. His classes were in the morning, so afternoons were the best time to find him. And the best place to find him was on the beach. And yes, he did want to see her.

All that morning Allie was in a zone, talking fast and moving fast as if she could speed up time. "Careful girl," Shelly told her several times as she rushed across the room with a tray load of food. To her credit there were no spills, but there were some close calls. And when the business slowed down, Allie jumped into odd jobs.

"I like this new boy energy Allie has," Shelly whispered to Sam when he stopped in during the early afternoon. "She's cleaned up the freezer, and the storeroom has never been more organized. Maybe we could keep Justin out of sight for a couple more days until Allie has scrubbed down the restrooms."

"It's nice to see her in such a good mood," Sam said. "Wish I could say the same for Dave."

Shelly heard the comment but said nothing about it. After the night of the blow-up, Dave had sought Shelly out and not found her at the Dream Bean or at her house. He went back to his own place but she never showed up. He found her the next morning back behind the counter at the Dream Bean, but she gave him the silent treatment and he didn't push her that day or the next. She still needed a cook and a dishwasher, so he didn't leave her without the help, but they settled into a rhythm of working together but going their separate ways at night. Since they weren't having any personal conversations, neither one of them knew if the wedding was still on or was off, and more than that they didn't know if there was a relationship left to warrant a wedding.

Allie was oblivious to all of this. Sam knew the relationship was strained, and he knew to not inject himself into it. And he hoped most of all that Rosie would stay away and not feel the negative vibes and insert herself again. As luck would have it, she continued her exile at her own shop.

Everybody was tiptoeing on eggshells except for Allie, who was like a teapot on the stove. By two in the afternoon, she couldn't stand the pressure any longer. With no customers to serve, the dining room swept and scrubbed, the kitchen cleaned and everything else organized and put away, she declared herself done for the day. Shelly, Sam, and Dave pretended not to notice, but all rushed to the windows to watch as Allie practically ran out of sight down the street toward the beach.

"Careful girl," Shelly whispered again.

Chapter 12

When Allie walked out from between the dunes onto the beach, she was hit full in the face by the blustery, February wind. It was never very cold in Port Aransas, at least not for very long, but the wind coming off the water could still raise a chill, and Allie was glad she wore her heavy jacket and knit hat. She looked southward down the beach and saw just a few people walking, none of whom looked familiar in the midafternoon sun. Turning to the north, she could see the rooftops of the Marine Institute. Thinking that Justin would probably come from that direction, she sat down on the edge of a shower platform, drew her knees up to her chest and pulled her jacket down over her legs. Resting with her head on her knees, she stared blankly out toward the horizon where a tanker seemed to hover on a thin line of silver just above the water. She remembered learning about mirages in school—how light rays bent by warming air caused distant objects to appear to float above the ground. She wished she had gone on to college, even just a community college, and wondered if she might someday have enough extra money for tuition. Her mother hadn't left her anything but the possessions she owned, and Bo had left her even less except for the empty shell of the *Cassie*. And then she thought about Shelly and how she had made a good life and living for herself without going to college, or at least she didn't think she'd been to college. The fact was, Allie didn't know that for sure and she made a mental note to ask her about that.

Feeling dozy, Allie turned her head sideways on her knees and closed her eyes. She was sitting like that when she heard a rustle and opened her eyes to see a tall young man standing about ten yards away, hands in pocket, looking at her. She raised her head and immediately noticed the bright red hair poking out of the sides of his gray stocking cap.

He smiled at her. Her heart jumped and she masked her excitement with a big stretchy yawn as she stood up.

"Hello," he said.

"Hi stranger." They both stood there for a moment, neither knowing what to say next.

"So they told you where to find me," Justin said

"Yes. How long have you been in town?"

"Just a couple of days. Getting settled in and all of that."

"Where are you staying?"

"I'm in an apartment . . . over there." He pointed back over his shoulder. "You wanna walk a while . . . try to warm up a little?"

"Sure."

Allie and Justin walked side by side down the beach, easing into conversation that revealed what they had been doing during the past ten months. Allie talked about Bo and the *Cassie* and how her father had been lost at sea. Justin said he took some time off after graduating in May, and now he was taking a couple of courses at the institute.

"That's cool," Allie said. "Do you think you'll like it?"

"I don't know. We just started this week."

"How'd you end up here . . . I mean, going from the pine forests to the Gulf?"

Justin laughed. "Yeah, it's an odd journey. I went to SFA because it was close to home and we could afford it. But after growing up in the trees I wanted a new perspective—a bigger sky—and it doesn't get any bigger than this." He stretched out his arms as if holding the entirety of the coastal sky.

"I wouldn't know about that. I've been on the coast my whole life," Allie said. That led her to give a short version of her life story, beginning in Freeport and finding her way to Port Aransas. "But it's really different here, not at all like Freeport."

"How so?"

"Well, less industrial for sure, and more laid back. People here leave you alone if you want that," she said.

"Do you want that?" Justin turned toward Allie as they walked.

"Well . . . not completely. I do have friends here and

we get along pretty well." She talked about Shelly and Dave, and the Dream Bean. And Sam. "He lives right down there," she said, pointing down the beach to where they could barely make out the silvery reflections from the tops of trailers shining in the sun.

Justin craned his neck. "Oh really? That's interesting." He stopped walking and looked back northward toward town and the institute.

Allie noticed that he seemed distracted. "What's up?"

Justin hesitated. "Just wondering . . . how far we've walked . . . and how much farther till we get outside of town?"

"Why do you ask?"

"Oh . . . we're going to do a beach study in one of my classes, and we're supposed to find a location that is not so populated."

"It thins out past the trailer park. Do you want to go see? We could see if Sam is home."

"No, that's okay. I need to get back. This is enough research for now."

"Is that all this was . . . research?"

Justin smirked. "Silly."

By the time they got back to where they had met, Allie had gathered the nerve to ask Justin a question. "Got plans for dinner?"

"No. Got something in mind?"

"Well, I don't have Daddy to cook for anymore, and I'd enjoy some company at my table."

Justin hesitated.

"What . . . too aggressive?" Allie asked.

"No . . . it's just . . . sure, why not. What time?"

~ ~ ~ ~ ~

Allie was working on stir-fry chicken when she heard the knock on the door. She thought it was Justin and was startled when she opened the door and found Marty instead. She looked past him to see if he was alone.

"What's up?" she asked, unable to mask her mix of confusion and disappointment.

"Justin asked me to come tell you he's not going to make it."

Allie's shoulders slumped. "What happened?"

"He said he had a meeting he had to keep. He sent me with this." Marty handed her a small white envelope. Allie looked at it, and then not hiding anything from Marty, she opened it to find a simple white note card. Unfolding it, she recognized Justin's handwriting from the note he left her after the previous SandFest:

"So sorry to miss our date. I'll make it up to you. Promise! J."

Allie sighed.

"Well, I guess that's it. See you later." Marty turned to walk away.

Allie stood at the open door for a moment and began to close it but then she had an idea. "Hey wait. You had dinner yet?"

Marty stopped. "No. My mother's working late so she

told me to get something to eat in town."

"Well . . . come on, then. There's no need for dinner to go to waste."

Marty bounded back up the sidewalk and past Allie into the house where he found the table laid out with place settings for two. The sound of a sizzle on the stove nearby drew him into the kitchen, where he lifted the lid off the frying pan and inhaled the sweet aroma of teriyaki sauce. "Nice!"

Allie watched him from the doorway—the way he just made himself at home like a big puppy with no boundaries. "I hope I have enough," she said out loud.

Marty came back to the table and slumped into a chair. He pulled his ever-present head phones from over his shoulder and piled them and his phone on the table next to his plate. He looked up and caught Allie watching him with a big smirk on her face. "What?"

"Oh nothing. You just remind me of a big goofy Labrador I had when I was a kid."

"What's that?"

"It's a dog."

"I never had a dog."

Allie brought the frying pan to the table and pushed more than half of its contents onto Marty's plate with a wooden spoon. She gave herself part of the rest and then put the pan on a hot pad on the table. "Eat up," she said.

Marty dove in while Allie started floating questions across the table.

"So . . . what's a high school kid like you doing walking around town on a school night?"

Marty munched a moment and then took a big swallow of the iced tea that Allie had set out. He sighed and then covered his mouth, stopping a belch that he might otherwise let out. "I worked at the market late this afternoon and then Justin stopped in before I left and gave me that note."

"Hmm." Allie thought about that a moment. "And you said your mother works late."

"Yeah, she's a nurse."

"What about your father?"

"Don't got one . . . at least not anymore."

"Hmm . . . me neither." Allie stopped talking and stirred the food on her plate. She looked across the table at Marty, sitting where her father used to sit, and sitting where she thought Justin might sit.

"So . . . tell me about you and Justin. Why's he hanging out with a high schooler like you?"

Marty held off his answer to gather up one last big bite and shovel it into his mouth. Allie took a small bite herself and chewed while Marty answered.

"Oh, Justin came to the high school and asked for some help with a project at the institute. He said it would be a part-time job through the end of the school year, and it would pay."

"That's interesting. What's the job?"

"He didn't say yet. He's still lining people up."

"So how many of you are there so far?"

"Just me, I think."

"Nobody else in the class was interested?"

"He wasn't in class. He talked to us on the parking lot after school."

Allie's forehead scrunched up. She thought she had more questions but she wasn't sure. She hadn't been to college, so she didn't know how it worked. But deep down inside somewhere she had an innate distrust of school parking lot business.

Marty wiped his mouth and looked at his phone. "Gotta go." He stood up brusquely, and it was all Allie could do to keep up with him as he walked swiftly to the door. "Thanks," he said without turning around and then he was gone.

Allie closed the door and went back to the table. She looked at where Marty had been sitting and wished it had been Justin. If he had been there, they might have had a nice conversation. Instead, Marty left her hungry for food and the answers to more questions.

Chapter 13

Sam looked around the Dream Bean and what he saw made him tired . . . and even a little sad. His three closest friends were near him, but from where he sat in the middle of the room, it looked as if they were complete strangers.

The coffee shop had just enjoyed a nice Tuesday morning rush and things were quieting down, which normally would have had Shelly, Allie, and Dave gathered at the counter or even sitting around a table and taking a collective breath. But on this morning, they had all moved to opposite corners, like boxers in the ring. Dave was standing at the back counter, having just settled things down in the kitchen, and was staring down at the screen on his smart phone. Shelly was in the opposite corner, her back turned to everyone, cleaning up the condiment bar. And Allie was standing at the front windows, looking out across the town toward the piers and the Gulf.

Sam, of course, knew exactly the nature of the centrifugal forces that had pushed everyone to the outer edges. Shelly and Dave had continued to maintain a chilly distance from each other in the days since Dave returned from Victoria and revealed that he was thinking about looking for a full-time job. They worked shoulder to shoulder as business required, but as soon as the shop emptied they spread themselves out. Allie was constantly glancing toward the windows ever since she learned that Justin was in town, and when there weren't customers to serve, she was drawn to the glass like a bird seeking a way out into the sunshine.

There was one corner of the room still not occupied, and Sam considered going to that spot and seeing if the others would notice. But in keeping with his growing desire to stay out of the confessional booth as the listening priest, he decided to leave the others to sort things out themselves. So without saying goodbye, Sam stood up from the table, walked slowly to the door, opened it gently so as not to rattle the bells, and closed it quietly behind him. And he didn't look back to see if Allie was watching him from her lookout post. He just walked down the steps, turned left down the sidewalk and walked past the lonely hulk of the *Cassie* to the Pier Association two blocks away.

At the office, Sam found nobody waiting on the porch for him, as was sometimes the case. Business was so informal that local shop owners tended just to walk in or leave a note stuffed in the gap in the doorframe rather than call or make an appointment. He checked the mailbox and it was empty except for some flyers from the usual roofers and plumbers down in Corpus Christi, and the light on the answering machine was not blinking—not even for a recorded message from a telemarketer. Standing at his desk, Sam picked up his calendar. While he had some meetings scheduled regarding some fresh ideas for SandFest, those were still a couple of weeks off.

Feeling restless, Sam sat down at his desk and considered his options for the day. He could make the rounds of local businesses, which he had done a time or two just to check in with them and see if there was anything they needed. After all, they were the ones paying his salary. But the extended chill at the Dream Bean had put him out of the mood of even being superficially friendly with anyone. And he knew too that a round of the shops would require a visit to Rosie's Second Chances, and he just was not at all in the mood for her overzealous personality. So he decided to walk back to his trailer by way of the beach. It had been a while since he had walked the sand in his bare feet, and the mild January weather might even allow him to get his feet wet.

Five minutes later—after threading the needle on a route that kept him out of the sight of his constituents—Sam was walking south down the beach with his pants rolled up and his shoes crooked in his fingers. He noted a few "winter Texans" who were out walking and gave them a friendly-enough head nod as they approached and passed on the sand. About halfway home, the remnants of a typical foggy morning broke away and the sun lit up the sand as if someone had thrown on a floodlight. The deep warmth on his shoulders brought a yawn and a stretch to Sam's body, and he found himself fighting against the growing weight of an irresistible mid-morning nap. He looked down the beach and in the hazy distance saw the corner of the fence that held his home. For a fleeting second he thought he could make it, but the next thing he knew he was sitting cross-legged in the light brown powder. And then a moment later, he was flat on his back.

~ ~ ~ ~ ~

Rosie had just set up her stool and easel and was arranging her painter's box when she looked out to scan the horizon and was startled to see seagulls swooping down and poking at the legs of a body stretched face-up on the dry sand. "Oh my," she said, and then quickly decided that what she saw was none of her business, but the shrieks of the gulls kept drawing her attention and when she looked again she began to think the worst— that perhaps this was a water-logged cadaver that had washed onto the shore after a tumble off a cruise ship or a drilling platform. She looked up and down the beach to see if someone else might also see the body and make the appropriate call, but seeing that she was alone, she knew she had to do something. So anchoring her easel against the breeze, she began to take a slow, circuitous walk toward the body, moving around so as to approach it from the feet. As she came closer, the gulls scattered but continued their cat-like shrieking from overhead. Stepping forward and seeing that it was a man, she nudged the sole of his bare foot with her own sandaled foot and stepped back when she heard a moan and saw his fingers move. She jumped back another step when his head lifted and his eyes fluttered open. And then she saw his face.

"Sam?!"

Sam sat up and rubbed his neck. He looked around at where he was and then he looked up at the silhouette of Rosie's head, which had blocked the sun like an eclipse.

"Oh . . ." he said, and then he instinctively reached for his shoes, which had fallen out of his hands and were laying at his sides.

"What are you doing here?" Rosie asked.

Sam drew his legs up and looked around some more, still clearing his head. "I must have dozed off."

"Well I was about ready to call 911. I thought you were a corpse washed up from Mexico. Here . . ." She held out her hand to Sam, who took it, and she leaned back against his weight to pull him onto his feet. Still disoriented, he dusted himself off and then looked at his wrist as if he wore a watch, which he never did. "Any idea what time it is?"

"I left the shop at about eleven, so it's probably twenty after or thereabouts."

Sam sighed. "Well, that's one way to lose an hour."

"Or worse. You better check your pockets. The gulls were getting ready to pick you clean, and I don't know who was here before I arrived."

"I don't have anything anyone would want." Sam looked across the sand and saw Rosie's easel. "How's it going today?"

"I was just getting started," she said, and began walking back to her easel with Sam following. "I'd offer you a chair but I only have the one."

"That's okay. I probably should go home. That's where I was headed anyway."

"Well now that you're here, why don't you stay awhile." She laughed. "And since you don't mind sleeping in the sand, I think you'll be okay just sitting."

Rosie gave Sam a teasing look that drew a smirk across his face. "Well, when you put it that way . . ." he said, and he sat back down in the sand.

Rosie sat down on her stool and began arranging things and then she looked out toward the water and saw nothing that caught her interest. Sitting on the sand beside her, Sam sniffed a little at the gusty wind, and that gave her an idea.

"Actually . . . it might be nice to have a human in a painting for a change," she said. "Would you mind posing for me so I can at least sketch in some rough details?"

Sam swallowed down a grumble and inhaled a deep

sigh. "Be nice," he thought, and then he said, "So . . . where do you want me?"

"How about just sitting the way you're sitting now, but maybe five yards out in front of me."

Sam moved out to where she pointed, and then when he had sat down for the second time, she slowly turned him with her voice until she got the profile she wanted. "And . . . hold still. That's perfect right there."

Sam sat with his knees drawn up under his cupped hands and his head tilted back a little. The wind coming from the south swept back his sandy-gray locks. Sitting in that position, he closed his eyes to drink up the warmth and his head bobbed slightly.

"You're not going to sleep again, are you?" Rosie asked as she worked on the outline of Sam's head and shoulders.

"No, just soaking up the sunshine."

Rosie looked and painted, looked and painted, roughing in the details of Sam's face: the bushy eyebrows, the stubbly chin, the crow's feet pointing toward his silvery blue eyes. Without Sam knowing it, she took the opportunity to study and learn his grizzled looks. And that led to questions that she wanted answered.

"So, Mr. Sam, looking at you sitting there, I'd say that you were probably born and raised on this very beach. I'd say that, except that when we first met you said something about how so many people in Port Aransas, yourself included, have come over on the ferry and never gone back. So . . . you care to elaborate on that?"

Sam dropped his chin, let go of his pose, and slumped into himself. Wasn't this the reason he had avoided all the shops and most certainly hers this morning, he thought. Wasn't he trying to steer clear of conversations and interrogations? But, again, he told himself to be nice. He took a deep breath and offered a small serving of his story.

"You're right, I'm not from here. I came over on the ferry just like you. I came from Dallas looking for something new or at least different. This is home now, and I doubt seriously I'll ever take the ferry back across other than just for a visit."

Rosie continued to paint as she talked. "Dallas, huh? That makes us birds of a feather doesn't it?"

"Only if you're talking about us not being from here. I don't think your life in Houston and mine were much the same . . ."

"That's all I meant," she interrupted, the irritation rising in her voice. "Everyone in Texas knows that Houston and Dallas are big cities but they're worlds apart. And . . ." Rosie's voice trailed off as she went to work painting the corner of Sam's eye.

"And . . . what?" Sam probed, and then caught himself as he realized he'd extended a conversation that he didn't want to have.

"Oh . . . I was just going to say that everyone has

different reasons for running from those different worlds."

"Running?" Now it was Sam who was irritated.

"Running, leaving, it's all the same. Could you . . . could you just go back to your pose for a moment. I've almost got what I need."

Sam raised his head again and Rosie noted how the sun had moved in just the few moments they had been talking. She reached for new colors to bring out the brighter highlights on his brow and the darker shadows under his chin. She noticed, too, how the sun lit up the filaments of hair that could be seen at the top of his loosely buttoned shirt. She felt herself blush at the sudden wave of unexpected intimacy. She'd painted feathers on birds, but never before the hair on a man's chest.

Sam cocked his head a little. "Did you say something?"

"Oh, no, just pondering the change of light and colors." She ducked behind her canvas to hide the red in her cheeks. "It just keeps changing and it's hard to keep up, but . . ." and Sam didn't hear anything else for a few moments until she said with a finality in her voice, "There."

Sam cocked his head again. "Done?"

"For now," she said, and started putting things away. "I'll fill in the rest with my memory and imagination."

Sam stood up and dusted himself off. "Can I see?"

"Yes, but only when it's finished. A painter never shows her unfinished work, and especially not to her subject."

Sam let out a long sigh of false dejection. And then taking a more honest tone, "Help you to your car?"

"That'd be delightful," she said. "I'm just over there."

"Oh, you mean that big red Cadillac over there? The only one on the beach, and the only one in town, for that matter?"

Rosie laughed as they walked toward her car that indeed was impossible to miss, especially parked up against the dull face of the dunes. "You're a sly one, Mr. Sam. And a good sport to sit for me." She popped open the trunk and loaded everything in, including her canvas that she had covered loosely with the remnant of a bed sheet. "I'd love to repay you in some way. Perhaps buy you a cold drink at your favorite watering hole?"

Sam stood quietly for a moment. "I appreciate the offer, but that's one of those things I had to leave back in Dallas."

"Good for you." Rosie fiddled with her keys. "That's one of those things that came across with me on the ferry. I'm working on sending it away . . . but it's hard."

In those words, Sam heard again the vulnerability and hurt that Rosie carried—and that she tried so hard to hide with her enthusiasm. Sam saw her shiver a little.

"Instead of a drink, how about a cup of hot tea in the trailer?" he asked.

As Sam poured two cups of hot tea, Rosie thumbed through his small stack of records. "Oh, can we listen to this one?"

"Sure." Sam set the cups on the table and then took the record that she had selected: *The Greats of Classical Music*.

"So you like the classics?"

"I do," she said. "My parents started me out early going to the symphony in Houston."

Sam set the tone arm down on the first track, Barber's "Adagio for Strings," and then sat down across from Rosie. She had already mentioned her parents, so he asked about her childhood.

"I grew up in River Oaks, and basically I was raised to be just like my mother. That meant taking all the lessons—music, ballet, art. I was a total a flop at ballet—and I do mean flop, as in falling all over the floor. My teacher didn't know whether to pick me up or just leave me there and use me as a dust mop. And while I love music, I didn't have the patience for piano. I wanted to be outside, and that's how I came to love painting. I'd see something and want to copy it, and before I knew it I was making little pictures, giving them as gifts to friends and strangers."

As she talked, the first plaintive notes of Debussy's "Clair de Lune" filled the trailer. Rosie set her teacup down and rested her chin on her hands.

"You like that one?" Sam asked.

"Yes, very much." She looked down at the table, trying to hide the moistness in the corner of her eyes.

"What . . ." he started to ask her, but she touched his arm and whispered, "wait," to pause his question. She closed her eyes and listened. He watched her for a moment, making note of the natural beauty of her face, brought out by less time spent in front of the makeup mirror and more time in the sun painting. He hadn't noticed that before and that intrigued him. And then feeling like a voyeur he turned away and looked out the window.

When Debussy was finished, Sam let the next track play, but he turned down the volume.

"That was nice," she said. "Thank you."

"Where did you go . . . just now?" he asked.

"Oh . . . just back about thirty years, when I was young and in love. We were on our honeymoon, driving up through the Piney Woods to Hot Springs, and that song came up on the cassette player. With the sunshine lighting up the tops of the pines, it was dreamy. We held hands like we'd never let go, and that became our song."

Sam nodded.

"Somewhere along the way we quit holding hands and we forgot the song."

Sam exhaled. "I know how that goes."

"Care to tell me more?" Rosie's voice was empathetic and not at all nosy as it might have been when they first met.

"Not especially," Sam said.

Rosie gave him a come on look, but Sam didn't budge. "I'm sorry, I can't."

"Can't . . . or won't?"

The phonograph needle slid into the center of the record, and Sam stood up to lift it up and turn it off. He sat back down across from Rosie. "Dave knows the whole story. It's why I'm here. You can ask him, if you wish, but . . . I can't tell it again. I'm through talking about it."

"Okay, Sam . . . okay." Rosie looked at her watch. "I suppose I better go home. Got an artist from Rockport coming early tomorrow. Wants to show some paintings in the gallery."

Sam perked up. "That's terrific, but don't give up all your wall space. Save some room for your own work."

"Gotta finish 'em first," she said, "but I appreciate the encouragement."

Sam walked Rosie back to her car. "Bye," she said as she climbed in.

As Rosie pulled slowly away from the dunes and rolled down the hard-packed sand of the beach road, Sam acknowledged her right to make her own place on the island. She, too, was a refugee.

Chapter 14

"So . . . just what is it you are doing?" Allie stood across the Dream Bean counter from Justin, trying to hide her disappointment at being stood up for dinner two nights earlier—and being left without an explanation or any contact at all except for the odd visit from Marty.

"I'm . . . I really am sorry for not showing up."

Allie tried to be angry, but something about Justin's blazing red hair and big smile just didn't permit anger. He was so unusually handsome, in her eyes, like a big Airedale terrier. He wasn't pale and freckly but instead tanned and ruddy. And he stood straight and tall, not slouchy and lazy-looking like most of the college boys she had seen around town. He had a confidence and energy that she found intriguing if not completely irresistible.

Still, she poked at him again. "You're not going to answer my question?"

"Oh, it's not so exciting. I'm more interested in getting to know you."

"You'd know more about me already if you'd shown up," she said.

"Okay, okay, I get it. Then what about tonight?"

Allie's forehead wrinkled.

"Oh, no, I'm not asking you to cook for me again. I was thinking we'd go out somewhere. Maybe down to Corpus Christi."

"You mean, like on a date?"

"Not *like* on a date. I mean a real date."

Allie thought about it a moment, teasing him.

"Well . . . sure. My calendar is clear. What time?"

"6:30 . . . and be casual."

"I can do that."

"See you then," Justin said, and Allie watched him as he walked out the door.

She spent the rest of the day in a fog, making conversation but in a superficial way because her head was someplace else. And mostly her head was at home in her closet, trying to figure out what "casual" meant. Allie knew what that meant around the Dream Bean: jeans and a top of some sort, even just a clean T-shirt, depending on the weather. But when she put the word "casual" next to the word "date," that was a compound idea she'd never entertained before. By the time she and Shelly finished closing up the coffee shop, she had taken a mental inventory of her closet and had determined that she had nothing that was really "casual date" worthy.

"Shelly, where does a girl shop around here?" she asked finally.

"What do you need, honey?"

"Something to wear . . . on a date."

"A date? Really? Justin?"

"Uh huh. But nothing dressy. He said casual."

"Hmm, . . . " Shelly thought about it. "There's the Walmart in Rockport."

"No," Allie said.

Shelly leaned against the counter and thought some more. "There's Emeralds to Coconuts. They have some cute stuff."

"He said casual. I'm good with that, but I'm not so good with cute," Allie said.

Shelly looked at the girl standing in front of her—part tomboy, part wild child. "I'm thinking you can do cute really well if you have a little help. Come on, I'll go with you."

They closed up the coffee shop and climbed into Shelly's Beetle and drove a half-mile down the highway to a little strip center painted in peeling aquamarine.

Allie followed Shelly inside to what looked at first glance like a typical tourist shop, with racks of T-shirts and swimsuits and dusty glass shelves crowded with baskets of seashells, rubber sharks, and snow globes.

"Follow me," Shelly said, leading Allie to a back corner with some large round clothing racks. "First thing is to get you out of those jeans."

While Allie shuffled with a pained expression on her face, Shelly turned the rack and spread out the hangars until she found several pairs of capri pants in various shades of khaki. "These are fun. Why don't you pull out a few in your size and try them on. No need to come out and show me. I'll pull some tops."

Allie did as she was told, and then Shelly pointed her to a back corner that was sectioned off by curtains that ran from the ceiling to the floor. As Shelly poked around at the tees and blouses, Allie rustled around behind the curtain.

"How's it going in there?" Shelly asked.

"I don't know."

"Don't know what?"

"What guys like."

"Doesn't matter what guys like. You get what you like, and they'll like what you like." Shelly passed some tops through the gap in the curtain. "Try these."

After another period of rustling behind the curtain, Shelly asked, "Well . . . what do you think?"

A moment later Allie came out, still wearing her jeans and T-shirt, with a pile of rejects in one hand and one pair of pants and a pale green top in the other. A few minutes later, they were back in the car and in front of Allie's bungalow.

"Thanks for the help," Allie said. "It's been a while since I've been shopping. And never for a date."

"Never . . . really?"

"Yep. Just wasn't part of my scene in Freeport."

Shelly looked straight ahead. "Hasn't really been part of mine here in Port A, either."

"I guess we both have some catching up to do."

"Maybe so." Shelly continued to look straight ahead. Allie saw the squint in Shelly's eye and made an educated guess at what was on her mind.

"Don't worry . . . you'll figure it out."

"What's that?" Shelly turned and looked at Allie.

"You and Dave . . . you'll figure it out."

"Maybe so." Shelly perked up. "Meanwhile, you have a great time tonight."

"Thanks!" And Allie was out the door and up the sidewalk.

As Shelly drove to her house, she thought about Allie and Justin and quickly realized that she and Dave had never actually had a date. They'd worked together, hung out together. They'd talked about life and love and a future together. But in all this hanging out, talking and planning, smooching and cuddling, there had been something missing. They'd never been on a real date together. In her usual way she began to think about how to remedy that, and then she came to a stop sign and hit the brakes hard. "No . . . I can't do it all by myself."

~ ~ ~ ~ ~

Allie was sitting on the arm of the sofa, watching out the window when the dark car pulled up. She jumped to her feet, and then stood frozen when nothing happened for a full minute. And then she saw the car door open and Justin get out and walk to the front door. There was another long pause, and when she couldn't bear the wait any longer, she pulled the door open, startling Justin and causing him to toss his cell phone into the air. He juggled it back into his hands, and when he saw the questioning look on her face, he turned the screen toward her so she could see the exact time: 6:00 p.m.

"I said six and I was just trying to be precise," he said.

"You goof," Allie said, as if talking to someone she had known for years. "I'm ready."

She stepped out onto the porch, pulled the door shut, and checked the lock on the doorknob.

"That's cute," Justin said.

"What?"

"Your ensemble. Really cute."

"Ensemble? Does anyone really say that?"

"I do . . . or at least I just did. It was supposed to be a compliment."

Allie stopped herself, knowing she was nervous. She took a deep breath. "Well, thank you. I picked it out for tonight. I was hoping you'd like it."

"I do . . . very much." For his part, Justin was dressed in khaki pants and a polo shirt with boat shoes and no socks, which Allie knew to be typical college fraternity garb. And she wasn't surprised to see that the dark car she saw out the dirty windows was actually a deep blue BMW coup. "Nice," she said as Justin opened the door for her. In her mind she concluded that Justin came from a wealthy home. She knew that could be a problem—that their interests and outlooks might not match—but she took another deep breath and resolved to not rush to any judgments.

"So, what's the plan?" Allie asked as they pulled away from the house and headed toward the highway.

"We have reservations for seven o'clock at the Omni in Corpus. And then we'll see what happens after that," Justin said.

Allie was silent, and before she could think too much about what he meant about "after that," Justin filled in the blank. "We might go to a fun bar I know on the beach for a drink before coming back."

As they drove south down the length of Mustang Island toward the Kennedy Causeway that leads to Corpus, Justin whistled through his teeth.

"What's that about?" Allie asked.

"I still can't believe I'm down here. After growing up in Tyler, this is still so foreign to me."

"So how did you get interested in marine biology anyway?"

"I think it's what you joked about last year when we first met—that I had spent my entire life in the woods. I guess I was primed for something different, and it can't get any different than this." Justin gestured toward the open Gulf and whistled again.

"Well it's sort of different for me, too," said Allie, "The refineries in Freeport might as well have been pine forests. And I never got to the beach much."

"Hmm," Justin said.

"What's that?"

"I was just thinking about how we're going to learn about these things together. Have you been to Corpus?"

"This is my first time. But it sounds like you've been here before?"

"With the family once, and then another time since I've been in Port Aransas."

By the time they got to their table at the Republic of Texas Bar & Grill on top of the Omni Hotel, they were both tired of talking and ready to eat. Justin made sure they had a table near the windows, and after they made their choices they watched as the setting sun coaxed up the glitter of lights from the streets below.

Allie sighed. "It's beautiful. The highest I've ever been in my life is on the Ferris wheel at the county fair. How 'bout you?"

"I've been to the top of the Empire State Building and the Eiffel Tower."

"You've really been around."

"Just school trips. But I've not been anywhere like this with someone like you."

Allie blushed.

Dinner came and they continued talking over steak and lobster. Justin told how his father was a doctor in Tyler and encouraged him to go to medical school too, but his grades weren't good enough.

"That explains your hot wheels," Allie said, "but you said you went to SFA because it was affordable. I thought a doctor's kid could go anywhere he wanted?"

"He can, if his father works in private practice and not at a public clinic, and if he has good enough grades to get scholarships, which I didn't," Justin said. "As for the car, I bought that myself. I've been working at something since I was thirteen."

"I'm impressed. Any brothers or sisters?"

"An older sister. She married out of college and is living in Baltimore. What about you—any other family?"

"Not blood family, but I have Sam, Shelly, and Dave. And now Rosie too."

"You mean the lady at the gallery? I thought she was a native—and a bit of a lush at that."

"Really? What makes you say that?"

"Marty and I saw her when we were looking for you. She was a little wavy if you know what I mean."

"I don't know about that. She comes off a little nutty sometimes, but I've never seen her buzzed."

"Maybe you're right. So who is she in this family of yours. The mother?"

"More like the crazy aunt. Nobody could be a mother to me. I already had the best. So . . . are you going to tell me about the research you're doing?"

Justin set his wine glass on the table and leaned back in his chair. He looked into Allie's intense eyes and knew he couldn't avoid the subject any longer.

"Well . . . I'm not supposed to talk about it, but . . ." Justin paused and looked out the window. Then he turned back to Allie, his gaze now as intense as her. He spoke just above a whisper.

"Okay, here's the deal: I can't tell you anything unless you promise you won't tell anyone else. Not even family—and I'm talking about your friends."

Allie leaned forward, her tone and volume matching Justin's. "Gosh, when you put it like that, I'm not sure I want to know."

"Well, you keep asking, and even though I don't know you well, I know I can trust you, and I like that . . . very much."

"Well yes, you can trust me. Except if you're breaking the law. Then of course I'd have to turn you in, but . . ." She stopped when she saw Justin look down at the table. "Oh, please, don't tell me you're doing something stupid."

"No, it's just . . . it's not illegal, but it's a little dangerous."

"Well you've already told me way too much now, so you better go all the way. And yes, you can trust me, no matter what it is."

And so he explained: His father, along with working at a public clinic in Tyler, had worked as a relief doctor in Latin America. Most recently he worked in Cuba but was banned from going back after he openly criticized the government. He'd stayed in touch with doctors there who were struggling with a shortage of supplies, including medicine.

"So, he's been shipping supplies to Cuba by way of Mexico, because they're not as tough on exports. And I'm helping him by staging the supplies down here. Boats pick up the supplies here and carry them to Mexico and then they're shipped to Cuba. I got the idea after coming last spring during SandFest."

Allie leaned across the table. "I'm shocked . . . and impressed . . . and scared, too, for you."

"I think I'm mostly okay, as long as I keep playing the part, and if you play the part with me now."

"Does Marty know what's going on?"

"He still thinks I'm doing research. He knows the island well and has helped me know what happens on the beach—when there are people, when it's clear, when the police might be patrolling. It's all pretty simple. He's a good kid and I wouldn't do anything to put him at risk. And I have the same feeling about you, so if you want to walk away from this, I'll understand."

"No . . . I'm okay. I can handle it." Allie paused and poked at her food. "So, where are you hiding every day?"

"Oh, I'm not hiding. I'm really enrolled at the institute, and I'm learning a lot and even making good grades for a change. The only part that isn't real is the research, although there'll be some of that next semester."

Allie laughed. "Well, it's good to know what is fact and what is fiction. Is there anything I can do to help?"

"Just keep my secret and continue to play along. Except for the you-and-me part of it. That's for real."

It was late by the time they finished eating and left the restaurant, and by the time Justin had crossed the causeway back to Mustang Island, Allie was asleep in the passenger seat. The next thing she knew, they were coming to a stop in front of her house. Allie yawned and stretched and looked out the window.

"Oh . . . I guess I made us miss the bar. I'm sorry."

"We'll go some other time. Let's get you inside."

Justin opened the car door and walked Allie up the sidewalk, holding her hand and steadying her with his other hand placed gently on her back. When they got to the door he held on to her hand as she turned to say goodnight.

"I had a wonderful time," she said.

"Me too. When will I see you again?"

"That's up to you. You know where I am."

"Great. I'll come by the Dream Bean sometime tomorrow afternoon. I have classes in the morning."

He leaned forward and her eyelids fluttered shut. Their lips touched softly for just a moment and then he let go of her hand and backed away. "Good night."

Chapter 15

Allie's feet barely touched the floor as she moved around the Dream Bean cleaning tables, taking orders, pouring refills, talking to customers. The sparkle in her eyes added to the morning sunshine coming through the windows from off the Gulf. Shelly watched the dance with a mixture of pleasure and envy. It wasn't so long ago that she had performed that same dance, but now the music had become faint and she longed to hear it again. She looked back into the kitchen and saw Dave, his back turned, scooping a mound of scrambled eggs from the griddle onto a plate.

Shelly turned and jumped when she found Allie standing right behind her, watching her looking at Dave.

Allie leaned forward and whispered. "You know, one of you is going to have to make a move."

"I know." Shelly whispered back. "He's in a funk, and it's not just about us. He's knotted up with some kind of male ego thing, and I don't think I can help him with that." Shelly raised her voice to a more normal volume. "So, you've been here for an hour and you've not told me anything about last night. But judging from the way you've been dancing around this place, I'm guessing you had a nice time."

Allie smiled. "Yes, we had a very nice time."

"Care to share?"

"We had a nice drive, a great dinner, and good conversation."

"And?"

"What? You expect me to kiss and tell? I'm not that kind of girl." Allie pretended annoyance, and Shelly thought she was serious.

"Sorry to pry." Shelly started to walk away but Allie reached out, grabbed her hand, and pulled her back.

"Hey . . . I was just kidding. It was nice. We had a great time. I fell asleep on the way home, we kissed goodnight at the door, and that was it."

Shelly sighed again and squeezed Allie's hand. "Good for you. I'm glad he didn't rush you." She looked back toward Dave. "Gentlemen are in short supply."

"And so you shouldn't let go of that," Allie said. "Like I said, somebody's got to do something, and maybe he's too much of a gentleman to argue with you. You're in a tough spot but playing at friends won't fix it."

Shelly sighed again. "You're right." She looked back at Dave and then at Allie. "You mind sticking around after lunch and closing the shop?"

"Sure."

After the lunchtime crowd had thinned out and Dave had cleaned up in the kitchen, he came out into the dining room and Shelly took him by the hand.

"Come with me."

"Huh?"

Shelly turned Dave around, untied his apron, pulled it over his head, and tossed it onto the counter. "As your employer, I'm informing you that you will spend the rest of the day on a mandatory field trip."

Shelly took Dave by the hand again and led him toward the door. Dave looked over his shoulder at Allie and shrugged a question toward her. Allie waved at him and mouthed, "Just go."

Out on the porch, Dave balked, pulling away from Shelly's grip until their hands released.

"What?" Shelly asked.

"I don't know what you have in mind, but I'm not sure I'm up to it."

Shelly grabbed his hand again and this time it wasn't a playful grasp. It was a firm, tight hold. Without saying a word, she pulled him around the side of the building and to the back. She opened the passenger door of her Beetle, pushed him in, and slammed the door shut. She walked around, got in the driver's seat, turned the key, and stepped on the gas, causing the engine to race for a moment before lurching forward.

"Now," she said, "this is what's going to happen this afternoon. We're going to get away from the Dream Bean and the town and people, and we're going to figure out what to do about you and me."

Dave said nothing as Shelly maneuvered the few blocks to the ferry landing and then rolled aboard for the brief float back to the mainland. He rolled down his window to let in the sounds of the ferry horns and the sloshing of the water and the shrieks of the gulls that accompanied every crossing. He wanted to get out and stand for a moment, but by the time he had thought about it they were almost across. In a few more minutes they rolled off and headed north.

"Do you have a destination in mind for this torture session," Dave asked, halfway serious.

"Yes. Aransas National Wildlife Refuge."

"Why there?"

"Because it provides plenty of options."

"Options?"

"If this doesn't go well, I have the option of leaving you there to find your way home, or of pushing you into the marsh and waiting for a gator to drag you away."

Dave thought about that in silence as they crossed the causeway into Rockport.

"You ever think of moving over here?" he asked.

"No."

"Why not? You could probably make a killing."

"It's not real," she said.

"It looks pretty real to me," he said as they passed the entrance to Key Allegro.

"Rockport is on the bay. Port Aransas is on the Gulf. It doesn't get more real than being on the Gulf."

Dave looked out past the houses and boats, across the wide expanse of water, and there, shimmering on the horizon in the heat waves, was a greenish-brown line marking the land on the other side of the bay. The water between them and the other side was placid, save for the ripples pulled up by the southeasterly wind.

A while later Shelly pulled off the highway and into the wildlife refuge. Driving past the visitor center without slowing down, she cruised down the blacktop road, passing several turnoffs until they came to a circle and the entrance to a raised boardwalk that disappeared into the marsh.

"You obviously know you're way around here. Is this where you dump all your boyfriends?"

"I've only been out here with one other man."

"What happened to him?"

"He was my father."

Shelly turned off the motor, got out of the car, and started walking toward the boardwalk. Dave followed her. There was nobody else around. They walked a thousand feet or so to the end of the walk and onto a flat observation platform that looked out over the bay and up the marshy shoreline. Shelly sat down on the warm wood planks and stretched her legs out in front of herself, leaning back on her hands. Dave sat down beside her, and he couldn't help but appreciate the quiet.

Shelly enjoyed it too, but then that was not why they were there, so she broke the silence.

"So, Dave, what are we going to do about you and me?"

Dave was jarred by the bluntness of the question, and his answer was not prepared.

"Is there still a you and me?"

"Of course there is, but the question is, what are we? Are we friends, are we coworkers, or are we something more, something that will last?"

Dave was silent for a long moment. He watched as a lone crane took big steps in the tall grass on the edge of the water, bending its long neck down and dipping its black beak into the dark water, bringing it up, and plunging it down again. Dave admired the bird's persistence as it fished for something it couldn't see.

Dave pulled his own legs up and crossed them in front of himself. He sighed, and Shelly spoke again.

"Listen, if you need to go work somewhere else to feel whole and complete, I'm okay with that. I can find another cook."

Dave looked up at her and smiled. "I appreciate that, but it's not that simple. I'm having trouble resetting myself. When I first started off on my own out of school, a big part of that was starting my career. That anchored me; it steadied me. Now, here I am starting off on my own again, but I don't have a big job to focus me."

"Well you had more than just a job back then. You had Debby, right?"

"Yes."

"And she was an anchor, too, right?"

Dave nodded.

"So you had two anchors then. And now you have just one?"

Dave nodded again.

"Well, I'm thinking the relationship anchor was stronger than the job anchor. After all, you said you followed her to Dallas."

"Uh huh."

"So, isn't it the same now?"

He looked at her.

"Dave, I want to be that anchor, but I'm not going to force myself on you."

Dave leaned forward and kissed her. When he leaned back, Shelly saw tears in his eyes.

"Now what?" she asked.

"You are a treasure, you know it?"

"No, I'm just a girl who loves a guy and doesn't want to lose him because he has some stupid idea of what he's worth. And if I have to tie a chain around you, then that's what I'll do."

Dave laughed. "Oh, I see, you're that kind of anchor."

"No, you can go work wherever you want to work. But at the end of the day, I want you at home with me."

Dave took her hands. "I'm warning you, it may get a little stormy."

Shelly smiled. "Remember what I said when we were

driving through Rockport—about how I prefer living on the Gulf and not on the bay? It can be stormier on the Gulf, but that's why I like it. It's more exciting. It's more alive."

Chapter 16

Allie walked into the Dream Bean the next morning to find Shelly setting up the counter and Dave in the kitchen, just like she'd seen them the day before.

"What happened?" Allie asked.

"We're good. Worked it out."

"So, what's he going to do?"

"What he's not going to do is leave."

"Hmm . . . but what's he going to do?"

"That's up to him. He can stay here and cook, he can open his own business, he can go to Corpus every day. Hell, he can go back to Dallas every day if he wants. He just has to be home with me every night."

Just then, Dave turned and looked at them both, waved with a spatula, and smiled.

Allie smiled back and then whispered to Shelly, "Any idea which way he'll go?"

"Don't have a clue—but that's okay. He's here."

Allie took Shelly's hand and gave it a squeeze. Just then the bells on the door jangled. "Back to business," Allie said, and walked back to the counter to greet the day's first guest.

"Good Morning, Louie. The usual?"

"Yes, Miss Allie. And I need it strong today."

"Well, you know that's not going to change. Bo would come back and haunt me."

Louie sighed. "We really miss him, you know. He could be a real pain in the ass sometimes, but there wasn't a better man down at the pier. How long's it been now?"

"Six weeks. Seems longer to me." Allie filled Louie's mug, snapped on the lid, and pushed it across the counter.

"Nothing's ever been found, has it?" he asked.

"No, it's almost like he was never here."

"Well at least you still have the *Cassie* out there. That's something. Have a good day."

"You too." Allie followed Louie out the door. "Where you going today?"

"Down off Padre Island."

"Be safe." She watched him walk down the steps and down the street toward the piers. She turned to go back inside and her eyes stopped at the *Cassie*. Yep, she still had the boat, but it was a lifeless hulk without Bo bumping around on its deck. Just then a gust of wind rattled her mast and Allie jumped a little. And then she jumped again when she felt Sam walk up behind her.

"Whoa, sorry, didn't mean to spook you."

"Oh, Sam, I was just looking at the *Cassie* and I thought I saw something . . ."

"What? A ghost?"

"No . . . well . . . yes. . . . Oh maybe, I don't know. I really miss him."

"We all do."

"And now the *Cassie* seems empty and out of place without him."

"I've been thinking about that," Sam said. "Wondering what we might do with her. But it's really your call."

"I'd definitely welcome your ideas. Hey, Dave seems to be looking for something new to do. Maybe the two of you could come up with something together. Need some coffee?"

"Definitely."

They walked back into the Dream Bean together.

"Morning Sam," Shelly said. "Thank you for bringing my girl back. With any luck I might need her this morning."

Allie stepped around the counter to pour Sam a cup. "We were just talking about the *Cassie*—what to do with her."

"Right now she's a great billboard," Shelly said. "If someone asks where we are, I tell 'em we're right next to the boat on the street corner, so you better leave her alone."

"She may become a rat hotel if we don't keep an eye on her," Allie said. "I don't think anyone's been in there in weeks. I know I haven't." Allie looked at Shelly and then back at Sam. "When things slow down here why don't you grab Dave and go over there and look her over. Maybe you'll have a brainstorm about what to do." She pulled a key off her key ring and handed it to Sam. "The pilothouse."

Early that afternoon Dave and Sam walked next door to check things out. They didn't find any rats, as Allie had feared, but they also didn't find much of anything else. Bo had never really spent any time in the pilothouse, and all they found inside was his rod and tackle. And there was nothing on the deck but his chair.

"What do you think, Sam?" Dave sat in Bo's chair, and Sam sat across from him on the gunwale.

"She's a unique space, that's for sure, and she needs a unique use."

Sam realized it was the first time he had been on the boat since it had been pulled out of the water. Last time he sat there was when he and Allie sailed with Bo back from Freeport before the storm. Even just sitting in her slip, she was buoyant, almost alive, but now she felt hard and lifeless.

"She's as dead as Bo as she sits now," Sam said. "It was Bo's energy that gave her life. She needs a new spark."

"Well . . . it's not gonna come from me." Dave stood up. "I know what you and Allie are doing. Trying to find me something to do. I appreciate that—I really do—but it has to be more than just a job."

Dave walked back across the lot to the Dream Bean, leaving Sam sitting on the boat. Sam stood up from the gunwale and then sat down in Bo's chair. He put his feet up on the gunwale as Bo would, leaned the chair back, and tried to look at the world as Bo might have seen it.

And that's when he saw it, or more accurately, felt it. Dave would never be at home on the boat because he wasn't a boat man. He was an office man. He was accustomed to square corners and low ceilings. The unpredictable curves of the horizon and the endless sky were not his natural habitat—or at least not yet. But there was someone else, new to the island like Dave, who had proven she couldn't be boxed in. As full of life as Bo. He hadn't seen her in a while, but it was time to visit Rosie.

~ ~ ~ ~ ~

Sam looked through the glass door of Second Chances and saw Rosie talking to a trio of women who looked to be about her age. He quietly pushed the door open and stood just inside where he heard one of the women explain they had come down from San Antonio for some shopping and rest while their husbands fished on a chartered boat.

"Are you ladies sure they aren't going on down to Mexico to catch some pretty little senoritas?" Rosie laughed loudly, and the three joined in, and then one replied, "They do that and they can just stay down there.

We have everything in our names already."

Rosie looked up to see Sam standing inside the door. "You girls look around and just shout if you need something. I'll be pleased to help you spend your husbands' money." Rosie approached Sam and offered her hand. "What brings you to my end of the street?"

"Just thought I'd check on you and see how business is going. Looks like you have a little early traffic."

"Yes, and that may be all I see today. It's pretty slow around here now that the tourists have gone home. I'm not sure I gave that enough thought."

Sam rubbed his shoe against the bare concrete floor. "That's what I came to talk to you about. What would you think about a change of scenery—or maybe a broadening of your horizon is a better way to put it."

"What do you have in mind?"

Sam explained the concerns about the *Cassie* and the need to have someone there more often.

"You know I love that crazy boat, Sam, I told you that the first time I saw it, but I just don't know if there's anything I could do with it. She's too small for a shop, although I suppose I could put some samples over there and a sign that points people back over here, but it's not like anyone is beating down Shelly's doors either."

Sam thought a moment. "Yeah, I think you're probably right." He sat down in an antique chair next to the counter and let out a long sigh.

"What's this really about, Sam?"

"Allie's missing her father, and seeing the boat sitting there empty just makes it worse. And Dave is bored and looking for something to do. And . . ."

"And you want to fix it all but you can't," Rosie said.

"Just want to help if I can."

Rosie leaned against the counter. "Those three women—they're about as bored as they can be down here while their husbands are out there on the water having their fun. I'd like to help them too because I know where that boredom leads, but all I can really do is sell them a trinket or two if that's what they want."

Sam rubbed his palms on his knees. "You think I should butt out, huh?"

"Isn't that what you all told me I should do when I first got here?"

Sam looked down at the floor and shook his head.

Rosie put her hand on his shoulder. "That was good advice for me, and I'm just passing it back. However," she paused and watched as the women milled around the back of the shop, each holding an item in their hand, "there's a difference in wanting to fix things and just offering some help—and you've done that by coming down here to talk to me."

Sam stood up. "Maybe so."

"And you've put an idea in my head."

"Uh oh . . . what's that?" Sam tried but failed to hide his misgiving, and that brought a big laugh from Rosie.

"Don't worry, Sam, it won't hurt you at all."

Chapter 17

Sam was awakened by a faint whining noise and leaned up on an elbow to look at the clock. It said 2:37. Hearing the noise again, he pulled on some shorts and a T-shirt and stepped outside into the warm, dewy air. The whining had gone away, but now he thought he heard muffled voices. He looked over the fence, and on the dark, moonless beach he saw a light bobbing on the edge of the water. Sam pulled the trailer door shut and walked out the gate and the few yards down the road to the dunes that separated the beach from the trailer park. As his eyes grew accustomed to the darkness, Sam could see that the light was attached to a small, flat boat sitting on the edge of the sand. And then he saw movement and his eyes focused on the silhouette of a figure moving from the boat onto the beach, carrying a dark object to where a dark car was parked with its trunk open. And then the silhouette moved back toward the boat carrying something else.

When the figure turned back toward the car, Sam dropped down onto the backside of the dunes and watched as the movement repeated several times. Then he heard the whining sound again and saw the boat move away from the beach, turn out into the water, and fade into the darkness and silence. And then he heard the trunk of the car slam shut and he watched as the driver's door opened, with just enough glow coming from the dome light to illuminate a shock of bright red hair blowing in the breeze. When the car door shut and the engine turned over, Sam lay flat against the back face of the dune and waited as the car rolled past him with headlights off and turned out toward the highway.

Sam stood up and all was quiet again for a moment, and then there was a rumble across the water and the faint flashes of lightning that revealed thunderstorms on the Gulf. Sam turned to walk back to the trailer and a shiver ran through his body, not so much from the chilly damp air as from the realization that Allie's friend Justin was up to something. And the chill grew deeper as he recalled the conversation with the DEA agent who had visited his office in early January. While Sam had not gone out of his way to watch for "suspicious activity" as had been the agent's wish, he had not forgotten the dire warning. And now that he had seen what was at least unusual activity and that it seemed to involve Justin, Sam was troubled. He climbed into the trailer and, as the rumbling got louder outside, he reheated a cup of old coffee in the microwave, sat down at the table, and stared out the window. As he sipped the hot, bitter brew, he studied his options. Based on his brief visit from the agent, Sam knew that to tell the agent what he had seen would unleash a heavy-handed interrogation that might not be warranted if Justin was in fact just doing some sort of research. Likewise, telling Allie might raise suspicions that weren't necessary. Then again, if he remained silent, he might be enabling something bad that might hurt others and especially Allie. Sam looked at the muddy grounds floating at the bottom of his near-empty cup and pushed it away.

By now the storm had overtaken the island, shaking the trailer on its concrete footings with the raindrops sounding like pea gravel thrown against the aluminum shell. Sam lay down on his bed and drifted off to sleep until a sharp crack of lightning jolted him awake and seemingly implanted yet another option in his mind: There might be safety in numbers, and a new perspective, if he told Shelly what he had seen.

In the growing light, and with the rain subsiding as the storm pushed further inland, Sam walked to the Dream Bean. He sat at a table on the porch and was almost dozing again when he heard footsteps. Shelly was climbing the steps, and when Sam stood up she jumped backwards and tumbled onto the gravel and shell parking lot. Sam rushed down to help her and was met with a fist on the jaw, which caused him to fall backward in a different direction.

"Owww . . . why did you do that?" Sam lay flat on the ground, holding his cheek.

"Why did you jump out at me?" Shelly sat up and rubbed the back of her head, shook the dirt out of her hair, and then checked her hands for signs of blood.

"Jump out? I just stood up."

"What the heck?" Sam and Shelly turned to see Dave running up, and then he crouched down between them, looked around, and whispered, "Who did this?"

Sam and Shelly pointed at one another, each rubbing their wounds and Shelly groaning for emphasis. Dave reached out a hand and pulled her to her feet, leaving Sam to help himself up.

"I hope there's a good story behind this . . . but it'll have to wait." Dave nodded in the direction of the piers, and they turned to see Louie and some other shrimpers walking toward the shop.

Shelly gave her hair another shake and then walked up the steps to unlock the door. "Give us a moment," she growled at the half dozen men who were climbing the steps behind her. Dave turned on the lights and pointed the men to a table, and then disappeared into the kitchen. Sam, stretching his neck and shoulders and brushing the grit off the back of his shorts, sat down at a table next to the shrimpers. Louie looked at him and grinned.

"Oh, that?" Sam nodded toward the parking lot. "Just a little accident in the dark. So . . . how are you men doing this morning?"

"OK. Hoping the storms clear so we can go out."

"That was quite a storm, wasn't it?" Suddenly, Sam had a new thought and leaned forward. "Any reason for a boat to be out on the water in that mess last night?"

"Not for a fisherman."

"Maybe drug runners," said one of the other men. "Afraid of nothing. They're more loco than us."

The men laughed, but Sam was thinking seriously. "You ever see any of them?"

Louie answered. "From a distance. We don't get too close. Don't want to get shot up."

"Big boats?" Sam asked.

"No, usually small."

"And fast," said another.

Shelly arrived at the table with a carafe. "Line 'em up," she said, and those with mugs in hand put them up on the table. She had cups for the two that didn't. When everyone was topped off they all thanked her and walked toward the door.

"Careful out there," Sam said.

"Always," said Louie, looking at Sam and then at Shelly. "And you too." He grinned and then turned and was out the door.

Sam turned to Shelly expecting more grief from her about the parking lot crash but she had something new on her mind.

"Since when did you become so interested in boats and fishing?"

Sam swallowed. He hadn't realized Shelly had been

listening so closely, but now he had an opening.

"Since I saw Justin on the beach unloading a boat," he replied.

"No . . . really?"

"At two in the morning, and just before the storm."

"Are you sure?"

"Mostly sure."

"Allie will be here in an hour and we can tell her then."

"Not so fast." Sam hesitated. "That's what I came to talk to you about."

"What's there to talk about? We need to let her know Justin may be bad news."

"But we don't know for sure," Sam said. "I don't want her to get her heart broke and I certainly don't want her to get into trouble. She's been through enough already. But I don't want to raise red flags either if there's nothing to it."

Shelly rubbed the table with her rag. "So . . . what do you propose?"

Sam leaned back. "I don't know. I'm stumped."

Shelly turned toward the kitchen, looked at Dave, and then back at Sam.

"Sure, let's ask him," Sam said.

Shelly called for Dave, and before Sam could finish his first sentence, Dave interrupted. "This isn't another project to keep me busy, is it?"

"No . . . and we're sorry about that . . . but this is

something serious," Shelly said, and then she explained what Sam had just told her. And then Sam told them both about the visit from the agent.

Shelly snapped. "And you waited till now to tell me that part of it? That pretty much says it all. We've got to tell Allie, and Sam . . . you've got to tell the agent."

The two men were quiet. "Well . . . don't we?" Shelly asked.

"I agree—it does look bad—but Sam is right too. We don't know for sure what is going on. We don't need to get Allie worked up over nothing. We need more information."

Shelly exploded. "This kid is definitely into something bad. And the people he is running with could be dangerous. I'm not worried about her heart getting broken. I'm worried about her life."

"Yes . . . yes . . . but let's don't rush anything just yet." Dave took her hand, hoping to calm her. He was quiet a moment and then turned to Sam. "What about this: Let's see if there is a pattern. Try to see if there's a particular night of the week when this is happening. We can take turns at night and see what happens. We should know in a week or two. In the meantime—not a hint of this to Allie. We can't let our concern for her cloud the fact that Justin's innocent till we know otherwise."

"But wouldn't the DEA do the same thing if we tell them?" Shelly asked.

"I don't think so," said Sam. "That agent seemed the

type to arrest first and ask questions later. He might grab Allie for just being near Justin. Speaking of which . . ."

They all heard the clumping of footsteps on the porch and then Allie walked through the door.

"Did I miss a meeting?" she asked, seeing the three standing in the middle of the room.

Shelly calmed herself. "Nah, just yapping about the shrimpers who came in early. They were a handful this morning." She walked back toward the counter. "Looks like a good day out there. You okay?"

"Couldn't be better." Allie hung her jacket and purse on a peg and then grabbed an apron. "Ready for action."

The morning went by as usual with most of the regular customers coming in and a few strangers who had come to the island for a winter break. Shelly and Dave were helped by the fact that Allie didn't spend any time gushing about Justin, so there wasn't the temptation to prod her with questions. Sam was able to clear his mind of any worries with an appointment with a prospective new tenant for one of the downtown storefronts, although he paused and caught himself when he was asked about crime in the community.

Dave and Sam began their sentinels that night, beginning after midnight since the first incident had occurred after midnight. Dave volunteered to take the first watch, and while Sam invited him to hang out in his trailer until he heard something, Dave said he'd sit in his car on the road outside the trailer park so he could watch and not just listen.

As the time dragged by, with the sound of the breakers rolling onto the beach one after another, Dave's mind began to leaf back through all the changes that had come to his life. He had gone from a corporate job and a warm house in Dallas to working as a short-order cook and sitting in a cold car on the beach, watching for drug runners or pirates or whatever it was that was going on. It was all very real and yet it felt like he was watching someone else's life. He even wondered if he were to close his eyes for a moment he might wake up and find himself back in Dallas. While not really wanting to test that notion, Dave's head got heavy, and when he leaned it back on the headrest his eyelids fluttered shut. The distant rhythm of the surf took him back to the cruise that he and Debby had taken, when the best they could afford was twin beds in a cramped cabin right above the waterline. Laying alone in his bed, he looked up to see the spray hitting the porthole, and he was both comforted by the cradle-like rocking of the ship and terrified by the thought of the hull giving way and all that dark water rushing in and consuming them forever.

A moment later—but it was actually a couple of hours later—Dave was awakened by a tapping sound. He sat up straight and was disoriented for a moment, and then he heard the tapping again and he looked to his left to see Sam standing outside the car. Dave fumbled for the switch to lower the window. "Sorry, I'm not very good at this."

"I don't think you missed anything. Go home," Sam said.

Dave didn't argue. He nodded at Sam, cranked the engine, and drove away. Sam walked down to where the road met the beach and stopped to look around. All was quiet. There was a sweetness in the air that he knew was the morning dew. He turned back to his trailer to get a few hours sleep.

Dave and Sam continued their watching through the rest of the week, making sure they got some rest before they started each night. They didn't see anything unusual, but they understood that if there was a pattern of activity it could be from week to week or even month to month. Or there could be no pattern at all. They agreed to keep watching until they saw something.

On the fourteenth night their persistence paid off. Sam was in the trailer sleeping lightly when he heard the thin whine of a boat motor. He put on his sandals and stepped outside to find Dave kneeling beside the front fender of his car. They nodded to each other and crept down the road to the dunes where they observed a boat bobbing silently on the edge of the beach, a car rolling up with lights off, movement from boat to car, the boat disappearing back out into the dark, and the car crawling away down the beach. And just as Sam had seen, the man getting into the car had a blaze of red hair.

When the car was out of sight, Sam and Dave walked out onto the beach where it had been parked, and then out to where the boat had rested on the sand. There was nothing left behind from the meeting so nothing had been proved except that Justin had been on the beach twice now in the wee hours of the morning, and he had been seen unloading a boat. There was nothing bad about that, but it didn't look good either.

"I think it's time to talk to that agent," Dave said.

Sam kicked at the sand. "I don't know . . . I think we need more information."

Chapter 18

"Okay, so here's what I think." With a theatrical swoosh, Rosie pulled the wrinkled bed sheet off the easel and everyone leaned forward to see the splashes of bright color that she had flung across the large canvas.

Having learned the ways of Shelly and her friends at the Dream Bean, Rosie had stopped at the market the day before and sent word by way of Marty that she wanted to call a meeting to consider the future of the *Cassie*. It had been a couple of weeks since she had told Sam that she had an idea, and then it took her that much time to mull it over and then put it all down on canvas. She even closed her gallery for two days so she could give it her full attention. When she walked into the Dream Bean that afternoon with the canvas in hand and Marty following her with the easel, she still had some splatters of paint in her hair.

"I have trouble with words, so I decided to show instead of tell you." Rosie stepped back and made room for Shelly, Dave, Allie, Sam, and an assortment of others from the Pier Association to come forward and give her work a close inspection. With chins on hands and cocked heads and elbows poking at each other and a fair number of grunts and sighs and "hmms," they considered the scene that Rosie had painted on the two-by-three-foot canvas: A bright day-glow rendering of the Dream Bean and the *Cassie*, and instead of standing side by side like siblings that never talk, they were connected from the roof of the coffee shop to the top of the pilothouse and mast by strings of colorful lights. And below those lights were people sitting around tables strewn with bottles and glasses, as well as a few people leaning on the rail of the Dream Bean, watching, and over on the deck of the *Cassie* were more people sitting on the gunwales all the way up to the peak of the bow. The windows of the pilothouse were open and you could see the silhouettes of people inside.

Shelly scrunched up her brow somewhere between a question and a frown. "I'm not sure I'm understanding."

"It's beautiful. It's a party garden," said Allie, bouncing on the balls of her feet.

"It's a venue," said Dave.

"A what?" asked someone near him.

Dave turned around and faced Shelly. "There's a place I used to love in Dallas, called Ozona, and they had an outside garden that became a bigger deal than the restaurant. Eventually they moved the main door from the restaurant to the garden because that's where everybody wanted to be."

Shelly huffed. "Well, I don't want people going to the

garden and not coming here. I'm already living on the edge. I need all the business I can get."

"And you'll get even more," Dave said. "The Dream Bean would be the focus in the morning and early afternoon just like it is now, and then in the late evenings people would start to move over to the *Cassie* and the space in between—like Rosie has it painted. You could tie it all together with a deck. And see there in the back," and Dave pointed to a spot in the background between the coffee shop and the boat, "you could have a small stage and feature local bands or even groups from Corpus or wherever. Not noisy rock and roll; just good music—jazz, folk, stuff to listen to while you're hanging out with your friends."

He turned to Rosie. "I think you nailed it." Rosie grinned and clapped her hands like a little girl.

As Shelly, Dave, and Allie looked and talked it through, and others took their turn and stepped up for a closer look, Sam motioned Rosie to the side and whispered, "How did you know Dave would get so excited about this?"

"I didn't, and that's not what I was working on. I told you how much I love that crazy boat, and you all said it needs new life. Well the best way to bring life is to bring in people, and the best way to bring in people is to throw a party." Rosie let out a laugh that cut through the murmurs; people turned to look and she waved them back toward the canvas. "Don't mind me."

And then speaking louder, "It's just a rough idea. You all will have to work out how to make it happen—if these two gals think it's a good idea."

Rosie motioned to Shelly and Allie, and when Allie hesitated, Dave spoke: "It's Shelly's coffee shop and your boat, Allie. We can get it done if you two want to do this."

Shelly looked across the room. "Sam?"

Sam rubbed his chin, wary of looking the guru. "I think Rosie has a terrific idea here. There's really not much money needed—putting in a deck, patio furniture, stringing some lights. You'll want to get a liquor license for the *Cassie*, some other details like that. But I think Dave and I can take care of that. Mostly Dave since I have my work for the Pier Association."

Sam chanced a quick little look at Shelly, and she saw it and understood. This was not just a plan for the Dream Bean and the *Cassie* but a new project for Dave to jump into. He could be construction contractor, handle the permits and licensing, and even be the booking agent for music or whatever else might take place.

Shelly looked at Allie, who was grinning from ear to ear, and she knew there was only one good answer. "Okay . . . I'm in. We'll do it. But I have just two rules."

"What's that?" Allie asked.

"Dave is going to be the point man for getting it all set up so that Allie and I can continue running the Bean."

"I can do that," Dave said.

"And we're going to have to make it clear in writing who's running things when it all gets going."

"We know who the boss is," came a voice in the crowd. Everyone turned and laughed but when they turned their attention back to Shelly, there were tears in her eyes.

"There's not going to be any more boss," Shelly said. "From here on out it's going to be partners." She pulled Allie and Dave beside her.

There was applause and hugs and then people left to go back to work. Rosie started to move the painting and easel, but Shelly stopped her. "Mind if that stays here for now?"

"Well sure, honey, that'd be just fine."

"I can't wait to show Justin," said Allie.

"Where is that boy of yours anyway?" Rosie asked. "I haven't seen him around lately."

"Just been busy with school and all," Allie said.

Dave and Sam looked at each other and Dave gave Sam a nod.

Later, as Shelly and Dave cleaned up the kitchen and got ready to close the coffee shop, Sam walked to where Allie was cleaning the glass on the front door. He watched her clean the inside and pointed out a spot she missed. When she rubbed it and there was no change, she walked outside and he followed her.

"Allie . . . I'm not so sure about Justin."

"What do you mean?" Allie kept working, with the

glass squeaking as she wiped away the dirt and the streaks of blue cleaner.

"It seems like he's always running off at odd hours."

Sam watched Allie's body language, and when she turned, he looked in her eyes for anything that might signal worry or distrust. His stare startled her, and she was the one with a question. "What is it, Sam?"

"That's sort of what I wanted to ask you . . . about Justin. What's he doing? He seems to come and go a lot, and especially at night when most people are settling down. Everything okay with him . . . and with the two of you?"

Allie turned away and swallowed back her nerves before answering. "Sure, he's just working on some research, like he said. Makes sense to me."

Sam gently took her shoulder and turned her so he could look her in the eye. "I wasn't going to tell you this, but I had a federal agent in my office recently. He said there's been some drug activity in town. Said it might be someone pretending to be in college."

"That could be anyone."

"It could, but then I've seen Justin on the beach, at two in the morning, meeting a boat, carrying boxes to his car."

Allie stepped back out of Sam's reach and put the bottle and rag on a table. "You've been spying on him?"

"No, in fact the agent asked me to keep an eye out and I've refused. But then I heard noise on the beach one night, and it was Justin. Dave has seen him too."

"You pulled Dave into this?"

"I just wanted someone else to look, too. I didn't want to make a judgment on my own."

"Have you told the agent?"

"No, not yet. Shelly thought we should but . . ."

"Shelly? She's in on this too?"

"She knows about it."

Allie picked up the spray bottle and the rag and thought a moment about what Sam had seen and what Justin had told her. As she pretended to work on a dirty spot on the window she considered the two stories like pieces of a jigsaw puzzle and found that they could fit together and create a picture that made sense—that the activity Sam and Dave had seen was the exact same activity that Justin had described: He was sending medical supplies to Cuba for his father and was doing it at night. It all made sense to her, but she had promised to not tell anyone. Still, she had to defend Justin somehow.

"It's not what you think, and if you speak to the agent, then you're not only going to hurt Justin but you're going to hurt a lot of innocent people. And if you do that, there's not going to be any business partnership."

Allie handed the spray bottle and rag to Sam, stepped down off the porch, and started walking down the street.

"Where are you going?" Sam shouted after her, but there was no answer. Allie had raised the warning with

Sam to not do anything with the agent, and while the story pieces seemed to fit, she knew deep down that her reasoning might be biased. She knew Sam and Dave well enough to know that they wouldn't do anything on purpose to hurt her. And what did she know of Justin? She knew that she liked him. And that he was smart and polite and seemed to care for her more than just like her. And she knew that his father was a doctor and . . . she stopped in mid-thought because she only knew that because that is what he had told her. And then she slowed her steps and realized that she was walking herself to the beach and that was because that is where they usually met if not at the Dream Bean. And then she remembered that the reason they always met at the beach was because that's what he always suggested. And now, sitting down on the sand, she realized how little she actually knew about Justin. And the biggest thing she needed to know right now but had no way of knowing was where he lived.

Chapter 19

"How could I have been so stupid?" Allie moaned. "How?!"

She sat in the sand, her head hanging with her hair blowing across her face. And then just as quickly as she had fallen to the ground, she stood up, put her clinched fists on her hips, and looked out at the water. Having steadied herself, she turned to walk and a few moments later she walked through the front doors of the Marine Institute and up to an information desk where a middle-aged woman was sitting at a computer.

"I need to see Justin . . ." She stopped when she realized she didn't know his full name.

"I'm going to need more than that," said the attendant.

"I don't know . . . he's a graduate student, that's all I know."

The attendant moved her mouse on the desktop and clicked a few times. "You're lucky because we only have fifty grad students . . . and . . . yes, just one named Justin. Justin Campbell."

Allie's shoulders relaxed. She not only knew his full

name now, but she knew he was a student. That part at least was true.

"And you are?" The attendant stared at her.

Allie hesitated. Sister or girlfriend? She wasn't sure which would get her past any security questions. She settled on the truth: "Friend . . . acquaintance, really."

"Well, it says here he is only taking six hours of credits and," she looked at the clock, "the last classes get out in about twenty minutes. You can wait over there if you wish." She pointed to a lounge in a corner of the room.

Allie thanked her and went to sit down. She was alone at first until three girls with backpacks came and sat on a sofa across from her. They talked and laughed; she tried to not eavesdrop but couldn't help but hear them talking about plans for a happy hour. Allie's thoughts went back to Rosie's painting and for a moment her spirit was lifted by the thought that soon they could hang out at the *Cassie*. And then one of the girls said they couldn't go because they had to go out on a boat that night. That lightened Allie's spirit even more because she knew that these kids really were doing research as Justin had said.

"What about Justin? Is he coming?" asked one. "Don't know. Haven't seen him all day."

Allie's face flushed with the thought that she had fallen for a boy and she didn't even know his full name until now. She had gone all the way to Corpus and back with him. How much further would she have gone with him if they had spent more time together? She looked at the three girls and wondered how much they knew about Justin—and how far they had gone with him?

Allie was mulling that when the three girls got up and began to mingle with others that spilled into the room from the hallways. She stood and leaned against a wall and watched for Justin but he didn't appear, and as the tide of students ebbed she knew she wasn't going to see him.

She walked to the desk again, and the attendant looked up from her computer. "Didn't see him? Sometimes their classes meet at the field study areas."

"You wouldn't have an address for where he lives, would you?"

"No, and even if I did I couldn't tell you. But . . . some of them live at the apartments on Beach Street or the brick cottages on Cotter. It's just a short walk." She pointed over her shoulder.

"Thank you," Allie said. She walked back down the road and noticed the small brick buildings tucked back off a drive, and she noticed, too, that there was a parking lot and there she could see Justin's blue BMW. There was a row of mailboxes but no names. She looked at the half-dozen buildings and knew immediately she wasn't going door-to-door looking for him, nor was she going to stand out on the lawn in front of them and call his name like a dumped girlfriend in a bad movie. Besides, he might be out in the field like the attendant had said. Or he might have gone straight to the happy hour.

Allie started back down the drive, and when she heard voices she locked up to see three boys walking her way, including Justin. They were dressed in jeans, T-shirts, and jackets, each with a backpack. She stood still with her arms crossed and waited till he saw her, and she continued to stand still until he broke from the others and walked toward her.

"Hey, I was planning to come see you after I got cleaned up a little." She could see the caked mud on his shoes and jeans. At least that wasn't a lie.

"Yeah, well that would have been interesting since your girlfriends are expecting you at happy hour."

"What?"

"So is that where you are when you tell me you have to go and then you run off?"

"I've been there, yes, but no, that's not where I go. Can't afford it. I usually go home and rest so I can go out later and work on that other project I told you about."

"Well that project is . . ."

"Hush, not here," he said, and he pulled her by the hand to the second cottage, where he let go of her hand to unlock the door, waved her in, and dropped his backpack on the floor. "Now . . . what's up?"

Allie stood in the room and was struck by how empty and sterile it was. She'd always heard about how some college students and especially freshman girls create nests in their dorm rooms—homes away from home—but this was nothing like that. Aside from a well-worn sofa and chair, a coffee table, a dinette, and a chest with drawers, there were no personal touches at all. She walked across the Saltillo tile floor and looked into a bedroom that was as spare as the den and open kitchen.

"Do you really live here?" she asked.

"Yes, just barely, and that's why I never invited you over. There's nothing here. This is what they call student housing, and it's all I can afford."

He walked to where she was standing. "So, there was something you were saying about my project."

She looked around the room again. It didn't look like the lair of a drug dealer. It looked like what it was: the room of a broke college student. "The project you told me about—sending the medicine to wherever it is—you may need to change your plan. You've been seen . . . by Sam and Dave."

"They don't know what I'm doing . . . do they?"

"Of course not, I wouldn't tell them anything. But that's the problem. They don't know the good you're doing so their imaginations are running wild."

"What do you mean?"

She told him about the drug agent that put Sam on notice, "And then he sees you at two in the morning—and only because you woke him up; there are people at that ratty trailer park by the way—and naturally he starts connecting the dots. It's not a stretch to see someone on the beach unloading a boat at two in the morning and think that drugs are coming in."

Justin looked puzzled a moment. "Wait a minute, did you say he saw me unloading a boat?"

"Yes."

"Well that's ridiculous, because I've been carrying boxes of medicine *to* the boat." He stopped a moment. "Oh . . . he must have seen me bringing back the boxes of fruit."

"Huh?"

"Yeah, they've been repaying us with fruit. It doesn't cover the costs, but they're more willing to accept aid if they pay something back. By the time it gets here it has a short life so I've been giving it away."

"Where . . . to who?"

"That's what I've got Marty working on. He's helping me find families in need or agencies that work with the poor and . . ."

Before Justin could finish his sentence, Allie wrapped her arms around him and hugged him so tight he couldn't speak in more than a whisper.

"What's this?" he asked, and when he felt his shoulder getting damp, he looked at her face. "Why the tears?"

"I was afraid. For you, for me, for us. I was afraid that you . . ."

"Were part of a Mexican drug cartel? Come with me." He led her into the bedroom where he opened the closet door and took a small brown box off the top of a stack of boxes. It was wrapped heavily in waterproof tape, but he took a box cutter out of a desk drawer and slit the box open. He brought a small white box out of that box and opened the lid to reveal sixteen vials. He took one out and handed it to Allie. She read the label: Penicillin.

"I'm sorry, I didn't want to doubt you, but Sam started talking and I became worried that maybe all of this was too good to be true."

"Well I'm not a drug dealer—not that kind of drug— but I'm still probably breaking the law in some way and I don't need to get caught."

"Why don't you just tell Sam and Dave so at least they won't turn you in based on a misunderstanding. I'd tell them myself but they probably think I'm too hooked on you to see the truth."

Justin sat on the sofa. "Even if I don't tell them and they don't do anything, that agent is sniffing around. He'd probably jail me and ask questions later."

Allie sat down beside him. "Well at least make me one promise: Stop the shipments for a while . . . until you figure out another arrangement."

Justin shook his head. "All those boxes in there are scheduled for next month. I don't have any way to tell them to quit coming until I see them on the beach again. That's the only way we communicate."

"What if you just don't show up?"

"I won't do that. These supplies are dated like the fruit."

Allie sighed. "Then you need to make that delivery so

you can tell them it's your last for a while. We just have to make sure nobody is watching."

"How are we going to do that?"

Allie was quiet for a moment, and then she stood up. "You just do what you need to do and let me work on that." She held his hand and started to let go of it, and then she leaned down and kissed him, and turned and walked out the door.

Allie walked back to the Dream Bean in the gathering dusk, and when she found the coffee shop dark and locked up, she walked next door to the *Cassie* and sat on the deck in Bo's chair. She tilted it back like he did and when she got it safely balanced she began to think about the trouble at hand. Sitting in Bo's chair, she wondered what he would say, what he might do. No doubt he would not approve of this boy named Justin, not because he might take away his little girl but just because Bo never approved of anyone. Then again, he might have appreciated the way Justin seemed to go against the tide, and—she laughed aloud—the fact that he seemed to have a bit of the pirate blood in him with this risky business he was in. And then she remembered the time she had warned Bo to not buy a boat when his health and his mind began to fail him. He had taken her advice and indeed had not bought a boat. Instead, he stole a boat—or at least he borrowed one without asking permission. Allie wondered now if it might be time to borrow a boat.

Chapter 20

Allie paced outside the door of Second Chances, trying to get in her mind what it was that she wanted to ask Rosie to do. She knew what the outcome needed to be: to draw attention away from the beach near the trailer park while Justin made his last delivery. And mostly she just needed to draw Sam and Dave away from their stakeouts and especially the federal agent if he was lurking. But after spending a part of the previous night pacing in front of the boats on the pier, she had concluded that she wasn't going to steal a boat. That idea was too big and too dangerous, and she might end up in jail instead of Justin, or even risk injury to others. She needed a lighter touch—something that was natural and fit the location better. She didn't know what that might be, but she knew that Rosie had a good head for dreaming up schemes.

Allie pushed the door open and found Rosie at her easel, fluffing the feathers of a pelican sitting on the top of a piling at sunset.

"Well how are you, Miss Allie," Rosie asked, putting her brush down and wiping her hands on her oversized white shirt. Allie wondered why painters always wore white when everything they did was in colors that would just show how messy they were.

"I'm okay. Came down to pick your brain on an idea," and then Allie explained what Justin was doing and why she needed to protect him one more time. She ran through all her crazy plans including stealing a boat, and Rosie took it all in, letting out a "my-oh-my" and a "gracious" and a few odd chirps at different points of the story. And then when Allie was finished she laughed out loud as she often did before making what she thought was an obvious statement.

"Well that's easy enough. Now what time did you say he needs to make his connection?"

"Two o'clock."

"Well that's perfect because people are easily up till that hour for a party."

"A party?"

"Yes, the party that's going to celebrate the grand opening of the new *Cassie* garden or whatever you and Shelly are going to call it."

"But we haven't even started making changes there."

"Yes, so you better get going on that. Just set the date for the opening to line up with Justin's connection and everyone in town will be at the *Cassie* and nowhere near the beach. And you can count on Sam and Dave to stay late to help clean up, so they won't be anywhere near the trailer park."

"But what about the agent?" Allie asked.

"We'll get Sam to invite him too. He's been looking for drug business, and there's no better place to look than a big ol' party—especially if Marty and Justin invite some of their friends. And then when the time comes Justin can slip away and go take care of his business."

Allie stared at the pelican a moment, admiring the pink and orange highlights on the pelican's white head and noticing the same colors on Rosie's shirt. She'd never quite noticed how a white bird was not really so white. And then she looked up at Rosie and realized there was so much more to this woman than anyone had noticed.

Allie gave Rosie an unexpected hug, which brought a sort of yelp of delight from the older woman, and then she was out the door.

The next morning Allie told Shelly and Dave that she wanted to open the *Cassie* on that specific night. When they asked why, she told them, "It's Bo's birthday," even though she didn't have a clue about his actual birthday. They all looked at each other and Dave said, "That's doable." Over the next two weeks the space between the *Cassie* and the Dream Bean was transformed. Shrimpers from the pier pitched in to grade the lot flat and design the deck, and others put in some landscaping, which was mostly a few small palm trees moved from some donor's lot. Dave and Sam made a run down to Corpus and hauled back a trailer load of metal patio furniture. Sam worked with Shelly and Allie to file the documents for a liquor license and a temporary permit for the party. And Dave put on his promoter's hat and signed a cover band from Rockport that he'd heard good things about. All the work was done on the promise that they'd get paid from the first month's receipts from the new venue.

Everything went smoothly and on schedule, except for a delay with the concrete contractor that had been hired to pour sidewalks and piers to support the decks. They were already coming late—at six p.m. to take advantage of the cooler evening weather—but a problem at another job backed them up and they couldn't come until eleven.

"That's no problem for us. It pours in and sets better when it's not so hot out," said the contractor, but Allie was furious. She had gathered some volunteers to help smooth out the mix and now she was embarrassed that they'd be working past midnight. But nobody else was worried about it; in fact, there was a party atmosphere while they waited for the truck. Shelly kept the coffee and cold drinks coming while everyone worked to shake the concrete down into the holes and smooth out the walkways. Within a week the wood deck was on and stained, and the last touch was to string lights across the garden from the Dream Bean to the *Cassie*. Because it was Sam who had first lit up the Dream Bean on that Christmas Eve two years earlier, Shelly insisted that he have the honor of flipping the switch.

"Now that's what I call a party garden," cackled

Rosie. Sam put an arm around her shoulder. "It's just like you painted it," he said.

The night of the party arrived and it was everything that Allie and Shelly had imagined and more. Shrimpers shared beers and stories until time to go home because they were to sail with the dawn. The band took their request for a rousing zydeco rendition of "Jole Blon," which they ended with a hearty "To Bo!" Marty and his high school buddies came and a few stayed late but most were gone before midnight. Justin entertained his college friends well past midnight—Shelly gave Allie some time off so she could get to know some of the crew. And instead of being treated rudely like she was that SandFest when she first met Justin, she was bathed with respect when they learned that Allie owned the *Cassie*.

"That's so cool—a business woman at twenty-something."

Allie blushed and covered her mouth when the truth of that sunk in, and then for the rest of the night she bustled and visited with a self-assurance that was well beyond her normal confidence. Sam saw it and nudged Rosie and whispered, "You see what you've done, don't you? You've helped turn a girl into a young woman."

Rosie squeezed his hand. "That's kind, but it really does take a village, you know."

At 1:30 a.m., Justin found Allie and told her he needed to go. "I'll see you tomorrow." He hugged her and held her hand a moment, and then Allie pulled him close again and kissed him, and whispered, "Be careful out there." She watched as he walked around the stern of the *Cassie* and slipped into the dark alley beyond.

The agent, who had been posing as an acquaintance of Sam and who had been watching the party with a keen eye, saw Justin leave and he did the same, slowly backing off the bow of the *Cassie* and turning into the street to follow Justin back to his apartment. He watched from a distance as Justin unlocked his door and walked inside. The agent leaned against an oak tree for a while and then looked at his watch when the lights inside the apartment went off. It was two thirty.

Confused and irritated, the agent walked quickly back to the *Cassie* to find the party was over, the band was packing up, and some of the neighbors were helping clean up. He walked to where Sam was picking up beer mugs. "What was that about?"

"I don't know what you're talking about, but at the moment I'm cleaning up here so I can go home." Sam stared the agent in the eyes. The agent stared back and then shook his head and walked away.

~ ~ ~ ~ ~

Allie was fumbling nervously with the top of a sugar shaker when Justin walked into the Dream Bean the next morning. She set it down hard on the table, grabbed him by the hand, and pulled him back out onto the porch.

"So, everything went as planned?"

"Yes, I went home and studied and then went to bed."

"I'm talking about your connection. Did it go okay?"

"Oh that, yes, it went fine. But . . . that was two weeks ago."

"Two weeks ago? No, it was last night—during the party."

"No, it was two weeks ago."

"What?"

"Yes, I made the connection two weeks ago."

"But you said you had no way to tell them not to come."

"I lied. So, just as you've suspected, I'm not as honest as I pretend to be."

Allie was quiet a moment. "So you did it two weeks ago? But when . . . how did you keep Sam and Dave away?"

"I think it had something to do with a late batch of concrete." He smiled at her and watched as the understanding slowly lit her face from within.

"You mean . . . you arranged that?"

"No, that was Sam's idea. He just had to sell it to everyone else. He really does have a good handle on the businesses down on the pier."

Allie was silent again, and then a new realization washed over her. "So, everyone knew what was happening except me?"

"Everyone had a piece of the story . . . everyone

except the agent. But it started when you told Rosie, and of course she can't keep a secret. She told me what you were thinking about—stealing a boat, I mean, really?—and I changed the connection date. And she told Sam and Dave and Shelly, and they agreed to hustle on getting the *Cassie* ready, and Sam had the concrete batch timed just right, which had everyone down here, including the agent who Sam saw watching from across the street."

"But how did you change the date? You said that was impossible."

Justin pulled Allie close. "Impossible for me, yes, but not for my father, and when I told him what was at stake he worked his contacts."

"And what was at stake?"

"I told him: There's a girl I've met and care the world about, and if something bad happens to her or her friends because of what we're doing, then, well, I just can't let that happen. And he understood completely. He told me, 'You're standing on sacred ground. You need to protect that with all you've got.'"

"Sacred ground?"

"Yes, that's what my father calls the ground that two people stand on when God is turning them into something new together."

Allie leaned her head on Justin's shoulder. "So, it's over for now."

"No, it's over for good. He'll find another way to do

his work. Meanwhile, he told me to focus on school and to not let go of you—at least not until he's had a chance to meet you. He said a girl who would steal a boat for a man is one in a million."

Chapter 21

Like the coming and going of the seasons, life at the Dream Bean settled back into a familiar pattern after the opening of the Sea Garden, which is what the *Cassie* came to be called. Shelly and Allie had tried to brainstorm a name but Sam suggested they wait a while and see what the public started to call it. In just a few months it evolved from the *Cassie* to *Cassie's* Garden to the C Garden. And then a reporter from the newspaper wrote a review and got the name wrong; it showed up in the paper as the Sea Garden instead of the C Garden and the name stuck. Allie was furious at first that the name of her father's boat had been lost in translation— and with it, her mother's name—but Shelly advised her to just go with it.

"It's been a long time since anyone's called my place 'Shelly's' Dream Bean but they keep coming and that's all that matters."

With the Dream Bean's kitchen cooking for both venues, Shelly decided it was time to hire more help. Gone were the days of everyone just pitching in; this was a real business now. But change brought headaches, the biggest one being Winston, a large man who answered the ad for a cook. He quickly proved he could do the work, but his opinions and his mouth were as big as his belly. At the end of his first week, Winston pulled off his apron and declared, "Now that I've got your kitchen organized, I'm gonna write up a menu so we don't have all this flailing around."

"No, you're not going to do that," Shelly answered. "We have our way of doing this, and if you can't do it that way then we'll find someone else."

Winston wiped the grease off the soles of his shoes with his apron and tossed it in the corner. "Good luck with that."

Dave was back in the kitchen the next morning, but by that afternoon Shelly was shaking hands with Angelita, a tiny woman of about sixty-five who not only understood the concept but in a matter of days took it to a new level, adding some ingredients that were not always asked for. She did it based on asking a simple question, "What's he look like?" Depending on the answer, she'd add jalapeños to an omelet or diced tomatoes to grilled potatoes. If the answer came back, "He's a big'un," she might add another egg. "Don't want anyone leaving hungry," she said.

A week into Angelita's occupation of the kitchen, Shelly saw her chopping onions and said, "Good morning, Angelita. How are you today?" There was no answer as the chopping continued, but then she heard,

"Good morning, Shelly" coming from the walk-in freezer, and out stepped Angelita. And then the woman who was chopping onions turned and the two stood side-by-side.

"Huh . . . twins?"

"This is Bernita. I called her in to help. Need to catch up on the prep to speed things up. Need more bins for storage, too."

"Ah . . . okay . . . but . . . I can't pay for two of you." Shelly stood with her arms crossed.

"No . . . no . . . you pay for just one but some days you get two."

"Or maybe three," said Bernita, and the two snickered like schoolgirls.

Shelly's arms fell to her sides. "What?"

"Sure, if we get real busy I might call in Carmelita. You still just pay for one."

"There's another one?"

"Triplets. Surprised you never heard of us. We were sorta famous back in '50. We were born at home. Big storm came and Momma floated us to safety in three bushel baskets she tied together. Made the front page of the *Caller-Times*. They called us the Florez Flotilla."

The sisters giggled, but Shelly shook her head and walked back to the counter. She started wiping it hard with her rag, staring out into the full dining room, when her hand was stopped by Dave's hand.

"What are you doing?"

Shelly looked down at the counter—spotless and shining—and back up at Dave. "Don't know."

She shook her head again as if to clear the cobwebs. "What are you doing this morning?"

"Going to Victoria to interview a band. Come with me."

"The place is packed. Wouldn't be fair to Allie. Why this morning?"

"They all work at Home Depot. Gonna catch them on their break and pick up a CD."

"What are they called?"

"Demolition Crew."

"That sounds a little dangerous. Are you sure they're right for us?"

"I heard them on YouTube. Sounded like folkies but need to make sure."

Just then Allie hustled back toward the counter with a stack of dirty dishes. "A little help?" she asked.

"You bet." Dave grabbed an empty dish tub and went out to clear a table. Shelly watched it all and felt something for the first time: Business was good, but it was swallowing her whole. She walked back to where the twins were working. "How would the three of you like to work full time? Not paying one for three, but two for three. Three for three if business keeps up?"

Angelita and Bernita looked at each other. "Sí," they said, and Angelita added, "Carmelita comes with us tomorrow." And they returned to their work.

Shelly's shoulders relaxed, but now she felt two distinct aches that caused her to wrap her arms around herself as if to keep her insides from coming out. One, a slow throbbing just above her right hip, seemed to correspond with a new fear that she had just overextended herself with the Florez triplets. The other, a pressure up under her breastbone, was a counter punch to the pain in her side, brought on by her fear that she was destined to live and die in the coffee shop having never done anything else her entire life.

Shelly sucked in a huge breath of air and turned back to Dave. "Can Victoria wait till tomorrow? I can go with you then."

"Sure. I'll give them a call." He took her hand.

"This is business," she said and gently slipped her fingers out of his grasp.

"Maybe."

The next morning, with the Florez triplets in place—including Carmelita, who was an exact duplicate of the other two and was dispatched to the dining room and wherever else Allie needed her—Shelly and Dave drove northward away from the coast. The sun was bright and the breeze light. Shelly tapped her fingers on the armrest.

"You're in a good mood," Dave said.

"Just glad to get out of town for a few hours . . . and away from the beach."

"The beach?"

"Yep, all that open water and clear sky and endless

horizon makes me a little drifty sometimes."

At the Home Depot they went straight to the garden department and found the Demolition Crew sitting on a row of cinder blocks. One of them stood up, wiped his dusty hands on his orange apron, and stuck one out for Dave. "Sorry, we've been unloading fertilizer. I'm Chip, the one you spoke to. This is Tom and Gary." The other two nodded. "Nancy couldn't make it. She has a real job. But she's the poet. She writes our stuff."

"This is Shelly, my . . ." Dave paused. "She owns the Dream Bean and is partners with Allie at the Sea Garden. That's where you'd be playing."

Chip reached into the pocket of his apron and pulled out a CD case. "Here it is. We could've zipped it to you."

"This is good," Dave said. "We can listen on the way back. We wanted to meet you in person anyway."

There was another long pause, and then Shelly stepped in.

"Can't wait to hear what you've got. We're new at this . . . trying to figure out the best music for our crowd. How do you describe yourselves?"

The three guys looked at each other. They shared shrugs, and then Gary spoke for the first time. "Mostly folk, I guess. We play whatever Nancy has going on."

"So . . . what about the name of the group? Doesn't really match the cut I've heard," said Dave.

"We started out just us guys and we were playing

some heavy stuff, really shredding the sound," said Chip. "Nancy was our favorite teacher in school, and after we invited her to one of our gigs she asked if we'd accompany some of her tunes for a demo, and we did. We've been regular with her ever since."

"We get more gigs with her and people actually listen," said Gary, "but she let us keep the name. In fact, she insisted; she said it was ironic."

Chip looked over his shoulder. "Well . . . we better get back to the truck."

"I'll call you tomorrow," Dave said, and he and Shelly watched as the three walked around the side of the fenced garden area to where a semitrailer was parked.

"They seem okay to me," Shelly said. "Typical tattoos but no piercings."

"At least not off stage," Dave said. "We'll see what they sound like. That's the main thing. But first, how about lunch? I know a place."

"Sure. But only if we can take it out somewhere. I'm tired of sitting at tables in square rooms."

"I thought you said you were feeling, what did you say, drifty? I thought that meant you need walls?"

"That was a metaphor. I was talking about the big picture—spiritually."

They drove a few miles to The Corral and picked up barbecue sandwiches and then went downtown to the square. They sat on a bench under the canopy of an ancient live oak tree and ate. Shelly looked around.

"So this is where she lived?"

"Uh huh."

"You went with her there to get barbecue?"

"Yes, but we never did take-out. And I've never eaten here before."

"Well, that's something."

"Awkward, huh?"

"Not so much. You have your past. I have mine too and it's all around us in Port A. It is what it is."

They continued eating in silence, but Dave's heart sank. He knew he should have made the trip alone. And then he felt the top of his ears burning as he realized how awkward it would be if Debby's parents came walking by. He was desperate to leave, but when they gathered up their trash Shelly wanted to walk around the square and read the historic markers.

"It's a pretty town. I can see why you liked it here."

"I never lived here; we never talked about living here. Dallas was home. And now my home is Port A. We better head back and check on things."

Shelly stopped walking and faced Dave. "I need you to make me a promise."

"What's that?"

"We don't get so busy with the business that we never have time for anything else."

"Agreed."

"And one more thing: Let's take a different way back; let's go someplace neither one of us has been before."

Dave thought a moment. "I've never been to Goliad. Have you?"

"No. Heard about it all my life but there's never been time. What's there?"

"One of the old Spanish missions . . . I think."

"Let's go."

Driving across the coastal plains that alternated between neatly furrowed sorghum and pastures dotted with the silhouettes of cattle, they listened to the Demolition Crew sing through a collection of likeable folk songs about love gained and love lost, with Nancy's lilting soprano leading the way. Dave especially liked a tune about two lovers trying to work things out, with a refrain that said:

"Nobody thinks we can, everyone doubts us still,
We know it won't be easy, but we will."

When the CD played through Dave looked at the handwritten playlist on the jewel case and saw the tune was titled "We Will." He pushed the buttons on the dash, and as the song played again, he reflected on how Shelly had said "we" when she talked about making time for other things. They'd not been close in recent weeks, and the business had become the glue of their relationship. But now she was speaking in words that hinted at something more once again. He shook his head. "What a fool I've been," he thought, and then he looked over at Shelly to make sure he hadn't said it out loud. Shelly was looking sideways out the window, her head back against the seat. Dave looked forward and suppressed a sigh. The words of the song played again: "We know it won't be easy, but we will."

Chapter 22

Sam frowned as the invitation rolled around in his head. It was blunt, as would be expected from Rosie, but what put him off was that she issued it in front of a crowd.

"Go with me to Round Top," she bellowed while they were sipping coffee at the Dream Bean. Business was slow at the gallery and Sam didn't have any pressing appointments, so she had called him and said, "I have a proposition for you." He thought she had another big idea about how to "spruce up Port A," as she liked to say, but instead she wanted him to go with her on a road trip to Round Top, the state's biggest antiques fair, to pick up some stuff for her gallery and maybe "get some more business ideas for this crazy little town. And besides, it'll be a hoot."

She had already planned it all out. It was a drive of a little under two hundred miles, which meant they could go and come back in one day. But she figured they would need time to look around, so she planned a two-day trip with a motel stay. "In separate rooms, of course," she said, watching Sam blush as the others looked on.

Rosie didn't leave much time for a decision with the

fair just two days away. Sam stumbled for an answer but Shelly piled on with glee.

"Come on, Sam, it'll be good for business," she said. "You need to get out and see what's going on in other towns. And besides, you need some time away. It's good to get off the island every now and then." Shelly glanced at Dave. She was still feeding off the energy from their daytrip together.

Rosie slapped the table. "Whadayasay, Mr. Sam? It'll be great fun. I'll do the driving and all you have to do is follow me around and help me fill up the trunk of the Caddie. So?"

"Okay . . . okay." Sam sighed. "But on one condition."

"What's that?"

"No tea rooms. I won't waste a minute of my life in a tea room."

Rosie laughed. "Do I look like a woman who likes to eat off doily tablecloths?"

She stood up. "So, do we have a deal?" She held out her hand. Sam was slow but he finally shook it, with Allie patting him on the back. And then Rosie abruptly headed for the door.

"Where are you going?" asked Allie.

"Gotta clean up the car. Wasn't going to waste my loose change on a car wash and vacuum if Sam wasn't going."

Allie waited till Rosie was out the door. "You're a

good man, Sam Barnes. I think she's still a little lost and some time with a kindred spirit will do her some good."

And then she laughed a little. "You're a brave man too."

"What makes you say that?"

"Let's just say that I think she might be looking for more than a kindred spirit."

"Nah," Sam said, standing up. "She's let it be known she doesn't care for that anymore."

"She might have said that, but saying and doing are two different things."

Allie and Shelly walked back to the counter and left Sam to chew on that awhile, and he did, all the way back to his trailer where he recalled when Rosie visited him there and they listened to music and she unloaded some of her burdens, including her wrestling with alcohol. Sam shook his head. "I should've just said no."

The drive to Round Top was easy enough, traveling north on Highway 77 up out of the coastal plains to La Grange, the town on the Colorado River made infamous by the whorehouse that ZZ Top sang about. The Chicken Ranch, as the house was known, was long gone, and the cozy little town remained. Rosie and Sam pulled into a diner for sandwiches, and as they ate Rosie asked him if he'd ever been to La Grange—"For business or pleasure?" she asked with a wink.

"I've been through a few times, but this is the first time I've actually gotten out of the car."

"Well I'll just have to take your word for it, but you hold a secret better than any man I've ever known," Rosie said.

"It's pretty easy when you keep to yourself."

"That's what you did before you met Shelly and the others?"

"Pretty much."

"What changed you?"

"Nothing really. But the more time you spend with people, the more they pry and the more you tend to let your guard down."

"Is that what I'm doing now—prying?"

"It's okay," he said. "You ready?"

"Sure." Rosie got the check when the waitress came by and they split the bill at the register. Sam went back to put a tip on the table while Rosie stepped outside to freshen her lipstick. Thirty minutes later they rolled into the heart of Round Top and out the other side to the Big Red Barn, which was ground zero for the state's antique and crafts market. They spent the afternoon strolling in and out of the pavilions there and the tents and shelters scattered up and down the highway for several miles.

It didn't take long for Rosie to start snatching up knickknacks and collectibles, while Sam followed with a box to stow the purchases. The only exception was when they came to a tent with a rack full of old vinyl LPs. Sam put Rosie's box on the ground and started thumbing through the titles. He left the tent with five records.

"See, this trip isn't a bust after all," said Rosie. "You'll have to invite me down to the trailer again to give them a listen."

"We might do that," Sam said.

At a gallery tent, Rosie talked up a few of the artists and handed them her business card. Back outside, Sam asked, "I thought you were going to focus on *your* art?"

"I am, but I need to boost up the gallery. It's like at Shelly's: The more food she has, the more coffee she sells."

Their next stop was a tent full of oak furniture, and the smell of wood and lemon oil sent Sam's thoughts drifting back to another time when he and Brenda would spend the better part of a Saturday in Forney just outside of Dallas, walking up and down the aisles of the antique malls. Over time they furnished their home with old chairs and tables and desks that were added to the beds and dressers they'd gotten from their families. That last time he visited Brenda in Dallas he sat at the kitchen table they stumbled on at one of those shops, but he didn't make that connection until now. He had become so disconnected that he wasn't sure if he'd ever be that connected to anything or anyone again.

Sam looked up from a cane back rocking chair and, as if to emphasize the point, there was Rosie, looking perfectly charming and at ease in her jeans, yellow blouse, and wide-brimmed straw hat. She wasn't what some might call pretty, but she definitely was what many would call a handsome woman.

"What?"

Sam's thoughts were interrupted by Rosie's question. "Huh? Uh . . ."

"I turned around and you were staring at me. Everything all right?"

"Oh sure." Sam turned as if to look at something else.

Later that night, as they sat down for dinner at a steakhouse, Rosie pressed Sam. "Were you thinking about her today?"

"A little. Not so much about her but doing things with her. Shopping for antiques, mostly. We did that a lot."

Rosie patted his hand. "You'll always have those memories. Nothing wrong with that. I still think about my ex sometimes too. It was good before it was bad. Anyway, I'm glad you came with me on this adventure. Besides the old records, seen anything else you need?"

Sam shook his head. "No. There's no room in the trailer anyway."

"Tell me about that. How long you plan on living in that overgrown sardine can?"

"Hadn't really thought about it. Don't feel any urge to move."

Halfway through dinner Rosie called the waiter to the table and asked for a glass of red wine. "A nice vintage from earlier this year, perhaps," she cackled.

Sam waited till the waitress was gone. "Is that a good idea—considering what you told me?"

"Just one glass with dinner. No harm in that. Won't you join me?"

"I'll stick with iced tea," he said.

Sam didn't know how important his choice was until the wee hours of the morning when there was a soft tap at his motel room door. At first he ignored it, thinking it might be a large bug fluttering against the door. But then he heard it again—this time a rhythm of five knocks. He pulled on his pants and shirt and opened the door a little to find Rosie standing outside, still dressed as she was at dinner.

"Huh?" he asked, and instead of answering she just walked in. She sat on the edge of the bed and in the dim lamplight Sam saw that her cheeks were streaked with tears. He sat on the bed beside her and noticed the sickly sweet smell of wine as she exhaled heavily. "What's happened?"

"Please, Sam, just hold me a little while."

Sam put his arm around her shoulders and noticed for the first time that she was more frail and boney than she appeared.

She spoke softly. "Remember what I asked you earlier—do you see anything you need? Well—I see something I need." Rosie kissed Sam on the cheek and then she put a hand on the side of his stubbled face and pressed her lips to his. Taken by surprise he didn't resist at first, but then he felt himself awaken fully and he pulled away.

"No," he whispered.

"Please." She tried to pull him closer and he stood up. "No, Rosie . . . no."

Rosie burst into tears and drew up into a ball on the end of the bed. Sam stood over her a moment, not sure what to do: Sit down beside her again and risk more turmoil, or retreat?

Rosie's sobs eased into whimpers and then into heavy breathing and then she was asleep, or maybe she was passed out. Sam couldn't tell for sure. He sat in the chair in the corner and leaned his head back. He awoke later to the sound of the door closing and looked up to see that she was gone.

Exhausted, Sam moved to the bed. It was still warm and his hand lingered for a moment in the bowl her body had wallowed out in the tired mattress. He pulled the spread over the tangled sheets and slept in his clothes until he was awakened by the sunlight peeking through a gap in the worn curtains. He was brushing his teeth when he heard the opening and closing of car doors. He grabbed his bag and went outside, and as he started to get into the passenger seat, Rosie spoke softly from behind the protective barrier of her oversized sunglasses. "You better drive."

Sam drove them to the Red Barn where they stopped to pick up a couple of items Rosie had bought the day before but had left behind for packing. Sam noticed how she was a completely different person—not chatty and effusive but clipped and deliberate with her voice a full octave lower. By mid-morning they were headed back toward the coast, riding in total silence except for the occasional mention of a broken-down barn or a weathered house. When they rolled onto the ferry at Aransas Pass, Sam stood outside the car and watched the island draw near. He'd never craved its cloister more than now, and more than that he craved the isolation of his trailer, but first he had to get Rosie home.

As he got back behind the wheel, he noticed that Rosie stared straight ahead out the window. Driving off the ferry and onto the road, Rosie said, "The gallery, please." When they arrived a few minutes later, there was no talk about helping unload or anything at all. Sam shut off the engine, left Rosie's keys hanging in the ignition, grabbed his records off the back seat and then walked around the corner and was gone.

At the trailer, Sam opened the door and stood a moment admiring its simple, built-in comforts. There was no room for the trappings of a bigger home, and there wasn't the need. Sitting on the edge of his own narrow bed, he confirmed in his heart there was no place in his life for someone like Rosie other than just as a friend. It wasn't that he was embarrassed or shocked by her. He wasn't turned off by her emotions. And it wasn't that he didn't feel some affection for her or even a sort of love for her. He did, but it wasn't the type of love she desired.

The day was just half over but Sam was exhausted. He thought about putting on one of his new records, but instead he opened the windows and fell asleep to the soft music of the surf.

Chapter 23

After the drama of Round Top, Sam kept to himself for a few days. He had, as Rosie suggested, seen a few things in La Grange and Round Top that he wanted to look at doing on the pier, such as hanging banners from light poles and across walkways. So he used that work as an excuse to stay in the office and research vendors.

A dozen blocks away at Second Chances, Rosie was in the same mode. The gallery was open and she greeted and welcomed customers with her usual flair, but she didn't dare stick her head out the door for fear of being seen. And where in the past she would park her Cadillac out front to look like she had customers, now she parked in the alley and practically dashed in and out the back door.

While Sam and Rosie both thought they wouldn't be missed, they underestimated the curiosity surrounding their two-day trip. It didn't take half a day for everyone at the Dream Bean to start wondering and asking where they were.

"You don't reckon they decided to spend more time on the road?" Allie asked. "You don't think . . ."

Dave laughed. "What? That they fell into a passion pit and can't get out?"

"Well, unexpected things can happen," said Allie.

"And I warned Sam," piped in Shelly. "I told him to be careful."

"No, you didn't," said Dave. "You didn't warn him. You told him what you thought Rosie was up to, but it wasn't a warning."

"Well that's how I meant it." Shelly huffed away.

When Louie and Paco came in early the next morning, Shelly asked if they'd seen Sam.

"Sure, I saw Sam on the pier with a tape measure," said Louie. "He was pacing and measuring. I shouted at him but he kept walking. I think he didn't hear me."

"That's not like him not to answer. Are you sure it was Sam?" Shelly asked.

He looked at Paco, who shrugged. "Not completely," said Louie.

That evening, curiosity turned to concern and search parties were sent to the trailer park, the Pier Association, and Rosie's gallery. Sam wasn't at the office, but Dave found him outside his trailer, running the tip of a caulk gun along the edges of his windows.

"Hey Sam, hadn't seen you since you and Rosie left. Just making sure you're okay."

"No worries here. Just catching up on some chores."

"So . . . how was the trip?"

"Good." Sam kept his back turned.

"And everything went okay with Rosie?"

"Uh huh."

Sam continued to work, caulking and dabbing the excess with a white rag. Dave stood a moment and waited to see if Sam would break the silence. He didn't.

"Well, okay. See you around."

"See ya."

Sam listened as Dave drove away and finally stole a glance when he knew he was safe. But he also knew that Dave's questions meant there were plenty more to come.

Across town, Shelly and Allie pushed on the door at Second Chances and found it locked. Allie leaned forward to look in the window. The gallery was dark and seemed strangely empty. She cupped her hands and strained to see more, and what she saw caused her to step back two feet. "Oh my gosh . . ."

Shelly leaned forward and saw it: At the back of the dark shop, a pair of legs and bare feet stuck out from behind a wood partition. "Call 911!"

A few moments later a police car screamed up to the curb and two officers jumped out. They looked in, then ran around to the back with the girls following. They tried the door, they knocked and waited for an answer, and then with guns drawn they kicked it in. "Wait here," one said, and then they walked into the darkness.

They were gone for just a minute, but that was more than enough time for Allie and Shelly to consider the worst.

"Do you think . . . her heart . . . or maybe the bottle?" Shelly asked.

"Or an intruder. She's always here by herself," said Allie. "She drives that big red Cadillac like she has money."

And then they heard the scuff of shoes on the concrete floor and one of the officers stuck his head out the door. "Come with me."

Shelly could hardly breathe as she and Allie followed the officer through the dark of the back room to the partition where the body was laying.

"Is she . . . ?" Allie asked.

"She's . . ." The officer paused. "She's plastic."

"What?"

The second officer pointed the beam of his flashlight down on the cold, hard, pale skin of a plastic mannequin.

Shelly leaned back against the wall, relieved, but Allie walked out into the shop and found new cause for questions: The room was mostly empty.

"She left in a hurry," Allie said, pointing to a tall trashcan in the corner filled to the top and surrounded by trash and inventory that Rosie had left behind.

Sam was not prepared for the knock on the door of his trailer later that night, but when he found Shelly, Dave, and Allie standing at the bottom of his steps, he wasn't surprised to see them. When he heard that Rosie was gone, he sat down on the steps.

"What happened?" Shelly asked.

"Nothing, really. We had a small misunderstanding, that's all."

"What about?" Shelly pried for more information. "Must have been more than small for her to leave in such a rush."

Sam held tight. "It was nothing. . . . I'll check with her landlord tomorrow and see if he knows anything."

Even Sam was surprised by Rosie's sudden departure and he used his position as president of the Pier Association to ask the landlord about her. The man had no news about where she went, only that she left without notice and violated her lease both at the shop and at her apartment.

"I thought she was more levelheaded than that," Dave said when he heard the news later.

"There's more to this than Sam is telling us," said Shelly.

"And we'll never know any more than we know now. Better just let it go," said Dave.

A few days later Sam got a small box in the mail. It was postmarked from Rockport, and Sam guessed that Rosie had dropped it in the mail as she headed north away from the island. Sam reached into the box and pulled out a wad of newsprint. He unwrapped it to find a small, carved wooden box, which he recognized as one of the items Rosie had bought in Round Top. Inside of that was a folded piece of paper, and on that was a handwritten note:

Dearest Sam,

So sorry to leave without saying goodbye, but it's better this way. Tell the others whatever you wish. I know you are a man of honor and will do what's best. I want to wish you all the best of luck in everything. Tell that sweet Allie to hold on tight to that redheaded boy. And give Dave a kick in the pants—he'll never do better than Shelly.
Love to all,
Rosie

Sam's eyebrows furrowed with the thought that he had pushed Rosie into an unknown future. But then his head cleared with the knowledge he had done no such thing. Rosie had thrown herself on him in a drunken fit, and all he had done was save them both from a night that would have caused embarrassment and turmoil for no telling how long. No, he had no reason to feel guilty. Rosie was a grown woman and could take care of herself as she had before coming to Port Aransas. And Sam decided he would take care of them both in the best way he knew how: silence. If anyone asked him again if he knew why Rosie left, he would simply say, "No."

Sam secured his resolve in the matter during a late evening walk on the beach. Kneeling in the muddy sand just inside of where the water sizzled into foam, Sam dug down a foot with his bare hands and then took the small wooden box out of his pocket and dropped it in. He was going to refill the hole but the sand that he removed had already washed away. So he sat in silence as wave after wave slowly filled the hole with sand.

As he watched, Sam thought about the confusion of the motel room in Round Top and how he had handled it. And he thought about how when he first arrived in Port Aransas, he was incapable of making decisions at all, and how over the next three years he had come out of the shadows but was mostly bending toward the expectations of others. But the moment he said no to Rosie was the moment he said yes to himself and a future that held promise and interest. Saying no to Rosie meant he was going to be choosey about his relationships. Nothing would happen out of carelessness or loneliness or wanting to please anyone. It wasn't that he no longer cared what others thought; it was that he cared more about his place in the world. He still had no desire to go back to being a business "somebody," nor did he care about moving out of the trailer into a bigger home. It wasn't the size of his life that mattered; it was the quality of his life and the focus of his heart.

When the hole was completely filled, Sam stood up, brushed himself off, and walked home.

Chapter 24

"Is this them?" Allie watched as the black SUV pulled up beside the Sea Garden.

Dave held his answer until he saw Chip climb out of the driver's seat and Tom and Gary follow from the other side.

"That's three of them." Dave stepped down from the deck of the *Cassie*. Allie followed. "Hey guys, you found us okay."

"Yep." Chip stopped to shake hands but Tom and Gary walked on by and around the bow of the *Cassie* and stopped at the entrance to the Sea Garden.

"This is wild," said Gary. He walked toward the stage with Tom following.

"What about the girl?" Dave asked.

"Nancy'll be here in time for the gig," said Chip.

Dave looked in the back of the SUV. "Need some help?"

"We got it," said Chip, and then shouting toward the garden, "Gary, Tom . . . quit gawking and let's get set up."

An hour later the Demolition Crew was ready to go

except they didn't have their singer. Chip made a call and reported that Nancy was running late but she would be there on time. "We can do some covers till she comes."

Dave asked if they were hungry and when Tom nodded—the first communication he had made since arriving—Dave had one of the Florez triplets—he wasn't sure which one—make some burgers. They sat at a table near the stage and ate as other customers started to come and sit around them.

"You get good crowds?" Chip asked.

"We do okay," said Dave. "Between the locals and the tourists, it's a little hard to gauge what people want to hear. I liked your demo, of course, and especially Nancy. Speaking of which . . ."

"I'll give her another call." Chip stood up from the table and walked behind the stage with his cell phone. Gary and Tom continued eating. Tom didn't say anything, but Gary looked around and then asked between chewing and swallowing, "So what's the story on the boat? Did it wash up here in a storm?"

"It's a long story," Dave said, and then he looked around and looked at his watch. "Guys . . . it's show time."

It was eight o'clock and the garden was buzzing with several dozen people ordering food and drinks. Allie had hired some of Justin's friends from the institute and they were taking orders and serving from the Dream Bean and the *Cassie*. Without introduction, the band started playing some instrumental blues that floated over the scene as the sun began to set and the strings of lights stretched overhead took over.

Two blocks away, Sam locked the door of the Pier Association, and hearing the music, he walked down the street toward the Sea Garden. He found a vacant table near the back and was just settling into a chair when one of the college girls came to take his order. A few moments later he was startled to find himself staring at a mug of cold beer and realized it was the first time he had ordered anything stronger than coffee since he had been on the island. He had quit drinking for obvious reasons—the trouble in Dallas and then his lack of money for anything other than water during his first months in Port Aransas—and with the passing of time, abstinence had become habit. But now, as if a forgotten memory from his youth had been tickled by the strings of lights and the music and the murmurs of the crowd, he had ordered a beer.

He was thinking about that and staring at the mug, feeling its coldness between his two palms, when a woman's voice entered his ear: "Can I sit here a moment?"

"Oh sure." Sam stood up instinctively and pulled out the other chair. When he looked at her for the first time, he looked into the face of a woman roughly his own age. She smiled and sat down and then sighed.

"Can I get you something to drink?" Sam asked.

"A bottle of water will do fine. Gotta go to work soon."

Sam walked to the bar on the *Cassie* and brought back a bottle of water.

She twisted off the cap, took a big swallow. "Thanks."

"Busy day?" Sam asked.

"Always . . . and now this on top of it."

Sam was curious about what she meant and might have asked her, but Chip's voice bellowed from the stage, "Thanks everyone. We're the Demolition Crew and this is our first gig in Port A. We've strung you along with some familiar covers, but now it's time to bring up the real reason we're here."

"That's my cue," the woman said to Sam. She walked to the stage and turned to face the crowd.

"Well, hello everyone. Great to be here tonight. My name is Nancy." And then she stepped back from the microphone and lowered her head as the band began playing a soft melody that belied their edgy appearance. And then she stepped forward and slowly unfolded a song about a girl and a boy that settled in Sam's head like poetry. For the next forty-five minutes he was transfixed as Nancy sang one beautiful ballad after another, each one telling a story that was received as a gift by his weary soul. And as beautiful as Nancy's voice was, Sam was equally intrigued by her slim figure in blue jeans and blouse that she wore as naturally as the sandy blonde hair with touches of gray that fell around her average but pleasant face.

When the band took a break, Sam watched as Nancy talked to Chip a moment and then to Dave and Allie. And then he watched as she walked through the crowd, pausing and smiling when someone stopped her to offer appreciation. And then finally she was back at his table. He stood up again and wanted to say something—like, "that was wonderful"—but the words wouldn't come. Instead he just smiled and she sat down next to him.

"Beautiful place," she said. "Nice to be outside where you can breathe."

Sam nodded. His eyes and his mind were trying to figure things out. She was a total mismatch for the three men in the band, who he guessed were ten to fifteen years younger. And as she clutched her water bottle he noticed she wasn't wearing a ring or any other jewelry. And then he realized he was gawking and cleared his throat.

"Dave told me you all are from Victoria . . . so how do you know the guys?"

She smiled. "I had them in my English comp class at the high school. They were good writers, but they were more interested in music." And then she told Sam more of the story that Chip had told Dave—that the guys had graduated and had forgone college to work by day and play music at night, but they hadn't gone far as a metal band and were on the brink of quitting when she asked them to play on her demo. That was a year ago and they'd been together ever since. "I thought I'd never get them to quit calling me Ms. Belacek." She laughed softly.

"What about the demo? Anything happen with that?"

"No, it's just a silly dream. Ever watch 'The Voice' or any of those shows? You've gotta be under twenty-five to get noticed."

"I don't have a TV so I'll have to take your word for that."

"No TV? That's remarkable . . . inspiring really. I need to cut the cord a little myself." And just then Sam heard a buzz and Nancy pulled a phone from her hip pocket. She looked at the screen and then turned toward stage. "Looks like they want me back."

Sam's disappointment that the conversation had ended was washed away when Nancy began singing again. For the first time in a long time, he didn't feel the urge to go see if Allie, Dave, or Shelly needed help. He was content to be just one of the crowd, alone, listening. Was it the words she was singing, so beautifully chosen and paired so well with the melodies? Or was it watching her? She stood still at the microphone seemingly without an ounce of vanity or showmanship. When she began to sing she would close her eyes as if to hide from any sign of acceptance from the audience. She was there for nothing but the poetic stories told through the music.

Midnight came and the bar closed and the people went home. Sam sat quietly at the table in a sort of content daze when he heard the shattering of glass on concrete and looked over to see the aftermath of a collision between a server and Tom from the band. And that's when he saw that the band and Nancy were packing up their gear, and he decided that would be where he would help out. They carried guitars, drums, and amps to the SUV and then Sam stood by and watched Nancy wish her mates a good night.

"I'll walk you to your car," Sam said as the SUV drove away, and she motioned down the street. They walked in silence to her car, which was parked across the street from Sam's office. He thought about mentioning that but stopped himself for fear it might be taken as some kind of invitation.

"Well thank you for the escort," Nancy said, and then stuck out her hand, which Sam shook gently.

"Anytime," he said, and then watched as Nancy got into her car, cranked the engine, and slowly rolled away.

Sam was wide awake, and for a moment he considered going back to the Sea Garden and helping with the cleanup, but then he told himself that he was not on the payroll and Allie and Shelly had hired plenty of help. So he set off on a route back through the neighborhood and toward the highway to the trailer. But it was well past one in the morning and he didn't want to be walking down the shoulder of the highway when the bars that closed at two started spilling their patrons out onto the streets with droopy eyes and fuzzy heads. He crossed the highway and walked past the seaside houses and sand dunes to the beach and turned south toward the trailer park.

The moon was just a sliver rising above the horizon, barely illuminating the dark but familiar path. The only obstacles along the way were a bag of trash that someone had left behind after a day at the beach, and a strange flat object moving in the darkness in front of him. He angled toward the water to walk around it, and as he passed by he realized it was a blanket covering a pair of writhing lovers.

Closing in on the trailer park, Sam took off his shoes, rolled up his pant legs and let the water fizz around his feet. It felt cool and tickled as it climbed his ankles, and before he could talk himself out of it he dropped his shoes, peeled off his shirt, and walked straight into the water, extending his arms to welcome the embrace of the rushing breakers. And then he plunged head first into the deeper water and pulled himself through the darkness until he could hold his breath no longer and came back to the surface. He turned back toward the shore and waded back out onto the beach. He sat down on the sand and, facing the dark expanse of the Gulf, watched the lights of a tanker drift by.

Chapter 25

Sam awoke the next morning with his thoughts spinning. Perhaps it was the music, or the night, or the ambiance of the garden. It might have been some of that or all of that. But most certainly it was Nancy. Her voice, her easy way, her simple smile. She had the quiet calm and natural beauty of Grace Kelly, but without the fancy gowns and jewelry. Compared to the bluster of Rosie, Nancy was a gentle breeze.

Sam kept these thoughts to himself as he went about his work and mingled with the others at the Dream Bean, but he couldn't help wanting to know when Nancy and the band would be back in Port Aransas. He broached the subject a couple of days later with Dave.

"Looks to me like things are going well. Great crowd the other night," Sam said.

"Yes, we're gaining ground," Dave answered.

"How's the music working out?"

"I think we're on our way to a good rotation of bands. You were there the other night—what did you think of the Demolition Crew?"

"Very nice. Not sure what the crowd was expecting

with that name, but I liked them. That Nancy . . ."

"Is a nice-looking woman," Dave offered.

"I was going to say she can really sing," said Sam.

"That too."

"So are they coming back?"

"If they want to. It's a long way for them to come, but I'd take them several nights a week. The crowd definitely liked them."

Sam didn't press further, but every night for the next two weeks he stopped by the Sea Garden to see who was playing. A few times he walked on in, stayed and listened, but most nights he would peek around the corner, see it wasn't the Demolition Crew, and go home without being seen. And then on a Monday night, he left his office and was walking toward the Sea Garden when he heard music and that voice that had not left him since he'd first heard it. Sam stopped in mid stride to make sure he wasn't running, and then he took a deep breath and walked slowly up the street, turned the corner into the Sea Garden, and sat at a table at the back. He glanced at the stage to see if he had been noticed and then jumped a little when Shelly suddenly dropped into the chair next to him.

"Hey Sam, what brings you out tonight?"

"Uh . . . worked late and just stopped by on the way home."

"That's nice. Need something to drink?"

Sam looked around at the other tables. There were

pitchers of beer, bottles of wine, other beverages. He was tempted but he knew better. "I'll take a cup of coffee, but I can come get it."

"No, stay here. You'll want to be here when the band takes a break."

"Huh?" Sam was startled.

Shelly laughed. "Yeah, I've seen the way you're staring at her. And besides . . . she asked about you."

Sam blushed. Shelly squeezed his arm. "I'll be back with two coffees."

Sam shrank in his chair. He hadn't wanted any attention. He thought about getting up and leaving. The old Sam would have done that. No, he thought, the old Sam wouldn't have come here in the first place. The old Sam would have been at home in the trailer.

"Join you?"

Sam looked up and there was Nancy. "Please." He stood and pulled out her chair. A moment later Shelly delivered two cups of coffee. She winked at Sam and walked away without saying a word.

Nancy took a long slow sip. "That's better," she said. "This damp coastal air is hard on the pipes sometimes."

Sam raised his cup to his lips and took a sip too. "Yes, it's taken me awhile to get acclimated."

"You're not a native?"

"No, I'm one of those snowbirds who forgot to fly home."

Nancy cocked her head, ready to hear more. Leaving

out the ugly details, Sam gave her a short version of how he came to Port Aransas, got to know a few of the locals, and took the job at the Pier Association.

"Well it's nice to see you again. Are you here a lot?" Nancy sipped the hot brew.

"No, I was working late and just stopped by on my way home."

"Where's home?"

"Down the road a ways."

Sam changed the subject and they talked about the Demolition Crew and the drive from Victoria until it was time for Nancy to go back to work.

"Will you stay a while?" she asked.

"Sure."

As the band played, the music coming from the stage became the soundtrack for a long journey back in Sam's memory to when he was in high school and got caught up in a dance of conversation and flirtations with Janet— he knew she was beyond his social rank and yet she floated around him like a butterfly who might land on his shoulder if he just stood still long enough. And now, as then, he didn't have a clue what he might do if this lovely creature were to finally land. It was thrilling and yet frightening, and for the second time that night he found himself wanting to slide out of sight and run back to the trailer. But he didn't, and after the last set Nancy came back and they talked again while the band packed up.

"This is a fun place. I've never seen a boat sitting up

out of the water like that," Nancy said.

Sam told her the story of Bo and the *Cassie* and how she got battered in the storm and crawled back to port and eventually up onto dry land.

"Bo sounds like quite a character and a good sailor to bring her back like that."

"Bo didn't." Sam and Nancy turned to see Allie standing nearby. "Bo was hurt. Sam brought us in safe and sound. He's the best." She hugged Sam's shoulders from behind and scooted away to clean up tables. Sam blushed and looked down at his hands.

"True?" Nancy asked.

"Just that first part. I steered the boat. Can't speak for that other part."

Nancy smiled. "Well, I think I'd better help the boys load up. I rode down with them tonight so I better earn my seat on the bus."

Sam walked with her and helped the band load up the last of their gear.

"When do you play here again?" Sam asked Chip.

"Looks like Dave's got us scheduled for Friday nights pretty regular. We'll do it if we can pull Nancy away from her busy social life."

"Busy? Ha," Nancy said. "I'm no longer your teacher but I can still call you out for lying." She looked at Sam. "These boys have been pulling my chain ever since they were in my class. I keep hoping they'll grow up some day."

"Grow up? Where's the fun in that?" said Gary.

Everyone shock hands and Sam watched as they climbed into the SUV and rolled away. He was standing with his hands in his pockets, watching the tail lights get smaller down the street when Shelly stepped up beside him.

"What are you thinking, Sam?"

Sam turned and looked Shelly in the eye. "I'm thinking I need to go home before I say anything."

"It's okay to talk if what's in your heart is honest."

"That's the problem: I don't know what's in my heart."

Shelly took his hand. "No hurry. You'll figure it out. Meanwhile . . ."

"Meanwhile what?"

"She's a good singer. You can still enjoy the music."

"Yes she is . . . and I will."

Chapter 26

Allie sat cross-legged on the beach, her bare feet resting on the warm sand. She looked right and then left and then out at the open water. She expected Justin to come from the left as usual, but then again he might come from the right. And after sunset, well, he might even come from the sea. It all depended on what he was up to. Left if he was coming from the institute, right if he was coming from town. And the Gulf? He promised he was not running medicine anymore, and while she trusted him, she still worried. She knew that the truth was sometimes tailored to fit expectations.

She opened her hand and looked at the scribbled note that she found under her wiper blade at noon.

"Need to talk . . . 3:00 . . . usual place."

Those words "usual place" made her smile. She'd never had a "usual place" with anyone before. She'd also never had a usual guy, so meeting a usual guy in a usual place—well, she couldn't help but sigh along with her smile.

She also smiled because when she first saw the slip of paper fluttering in the wind she thought it was a parking ticket. She was in a hurry that morning and had left one tire up on the curb and hadn't taken the time to correct it. The Port Aransas police were spending more time around the piers because of the crowds coming to the Sea Garden, and Allie was pleased that she wouldn't have to pay another $64 fine that she really couldn't afford.

Allie looked out at the water and blinked sleepily. As much as she looked forward to seeing Justin, she appreciated time alone. She was working split days—mornings at the Dream Bean and evenings at the Sea Garden—and mid-day was hers. She pulled her legs up, leaned her chin on her knees and closed her eyes. The sound of the surf lulled her into a quiet bliss until she felt a body leaning against hers and then a hand against the small of her back. She knew that touch, leaned into it, and lifted her head. And then with her eyes still closed, she turned and felt Justin's lips touch hers and all of her cares rolled out to sea. They lingered in the kiss until they both needed to breathe. She leaned her head back against his chest.

"Is that what you had in mind when you said, 'need to talk'?"

"Not exactly, but it's a good bonus." He leaned in and kissed her again, and they didn't stop until they heard talking. Allie opened her eyes to see an older couple walk by, holding hands. They smiled, and Justin and Allie smiled back.

"So . . . what is it you want to talk about, or was that just a ruse to get me out here in the middle of the afternoon?"

Justin leaned back on one arm with his other arm around Allie's back.

"I want . . . we need to talk about us . . . and the future."

"Hmm . . . us, huh? Is there really an us, or is there just a you and a me? I haven't been so sure about that."

"That may depend on what we do with what I'm about to tell you."

Allie leaned away from Justin so she could look him in the eyes. He continued:

"My father called and he's made me an offer. He wants to ramp up his medical ministry, but he wants to be up-front and legal with it and needs someone to handle the logistics on a full-time basis."

"Okay, that sounds like a good thing. You'll need a job when you finish school."

"Yes I will. I haven't been clear on what I want to do, and this is a good option or at least a good start while I figure it out. But here's the twist . . . the job would be in Miami. That's the gateway to all of Latin America and that's where I need to be to ship medical supplies through mainstream, legal channels."

Allie looked down. She understood. Justin was leaving Port Aransas. And then she shook her head because she understood that he was always going to be leaving Port

Aransas. He wasn't going to get his graduate degree and hang out in Port Aransas for the rest of his life.

"I'm happy for you. It's a wonderful ministry, and you and your father will work well together."

Justin took her hands. "I don't think you understand. This isn't just about me leaving. This is about you going with me."

Allie looked at him, her forehead knotted. She was taken by surprise—not just about what Justin was saying but by the fact that she had not given any thought to leaving the island herself. She stared out at the Gulf and saw the blue-gray silhouette of a tanker on the open water. From that distance it looked like it was sitting still, but she knew it was moving at full speed northward toward the refineries of Houston. As she watched, she scooped up a handful of dry sand and clutched it, but the more tightly she tried to hold it the more the sand sifted out between her fingers until her hand was empty.

"I don't know. I just don't know. . . ."

"Allie, there's nobody I care about more than you. But I can't stay here. I was never going to stay here. I want you to go with me, but only if you want to. Miami will be a new experience for me and it could be an adventure for both of us and . . . I'd rather not be there alone."

Allie opened her hand, and the dust that remained was joined by her tears. She reached up to wipe her eyes and smeared her cheekbones with sandy mud. Justin offered his thumb and gently wiped away the brown residue.

"We don't have to figure this out today. I'm not leaving till the end of the term."

Allie spent the next week pondering and debating in her heart. She kept the news to herself. There was no girl talk with Shelly, no wisdom sought from Sam. She didn't want a group discussion about her future. She knew she was a grown-up and this was a grown-up decision. One night, as a gentle breeze blew through the Sea Garden, she looked across the crowd and saw Nancy and Sam sitting at a table talking, and Dave and Shelly leaning against a railing. And from a distance she saw a couple—a large burly, bald-headed man and a short, thin woman with long hair of brown and gray. She imagined it was Bo and Cassandra, her father and mother, even though she had never seen them together. And yet she knew that this is what they might have looked like had Bo not run away from Cassandra and had each of them in their own time not been swept away into the sea. She wanted to run to them, embrace them, and be a family, but she knew that if she got any closer and saw their faces the spell would be lost forever. So she stepped back out of sight and watched them from a distance, imagining their conversation—him being gruff and proud and she being gentle but firm.

In watching them and listening, Allie found her answer for Justin, which she gave him the next night.

"I don't want to be lonely like my mother, and I don't want to be a loner like my father. I do want there to be an us. But . . . this has become my home, and this is my family, and I can't just walk away from them. So I'm going to say yes to us, but no to going with you to Miami. At least not now. I have to continue this chapter in my life and see what happens."

Justin looked up at the stars and then his eyes met Allie's. He thought there might be more tears but there were none. He knew her decision was firm. "I'm disappointed, but I'm not surprised. I guess the timing for us is not right just now."

"No, it's not."

Justin stood up and gently raised Allie by her elbows until she was facing him. He pulled her close and kissed her, and then he held her tight. When he released her, something was taken away from her, and she knew that if she was ever an "us" it wouldn't be with Justin. Something was missing—she didn't know what—and she was okay with that.

Two weeks later, when most of the part-time college students who worked at the Sea Garden said they were leaving town and moving on, Allie knew the school term was over. She also knew she would never see Justin again.

Chapter 27

Allie leaned back in Bo's chair on the deck of the *Cassie* and looked at her watch; the beer truck was late. She didn't mind so much because there was nowhere else she needed to be—or wanted to be. She leaned back and put her feet up on the gunwales as Bo would do and looked out at the empty Sea Garden. Just a few hours earlier it was bustling with people, and in another ten hours or so it would be brimming again. The people came and went like the waves on the sea, and in between was the silence and the preparation for the next wave.

"You thinking about him?"

Allie turned to see Shelly wading through the empty tables with a tall cup of coffee in her hand. She stepped on the deck, handed it to Allie, and asked again, "Are you thinking about him?"

"Who?"

"Justin."

"No, not at all."

Shelly knew it was an honest answer because she had seen how completely Allie had poured herself into the *Cassie* and the Sea Garden. She wasn't just running the business now, or worse, letting it run her; she was putting herself into it completely, anticipating problems and making decisions that kept everything running smoothly. That included staying on top of supplies, which is why she was waiting for the beer truck at seven in the morning instead of lying in bed.

"It's ironic, you know," Shelly said.

"What's that?"

"That I used to be right over there at the Bean and your father would walk over from this boat to my shop and get his coffee. And now I'm walking from the Bean to his boat to give his daughter coffee. Just interesting how things change."

"Or how about this," Allie said. "I wouldn't be here on this boat if you hadn't given Bo attention at your shop and followed him to Freeport."

"Well it wasn't like I could ignore him. He sort of forced himself on me."

Allie laughed. "Yes, he did. You still could have ignored him, but you didn't, and instead of standing in an aisle in the middle of Walmart, earning minimum wage with no future in sight, I'm sitting here watching the sunrise and waiting for a beer truck."

"And that's an improvement?"

"Waiting for a beer truck at my own place? Yes it is."

"That's the spirit." Shelly patted Allie on the knee. "Gotta get back over and keep my own place going. Check you later."

Allie watched as Shelly walked back through the tables to the Dream Bean. She realized she hadn't given Justin any thought at all until Shelly mentioned him. She wondered if she would have been inclined to go to Florida with him if it hadn't been for the *Cassie*, but then Bo and the *Cassie* and all that happened here was the reason she was in Port Aransas in the first place, so it was really a pointless question. Justin and Florida never had a chance.

Just then she heard the rattle of a diesel engine and looked up to see the beer truck roll up and grind to a halt on the oyster shell side street. The door swung open and a young man in a uniform dropped out of the cab with a clipboard in hand and got to work unloading cases onto a hand truck. Allie watched him mindlessly for a moment as he hefted a case, checked his list, and grabbed another. And then he turned and she saw his bright blue eyes framed by his shaggy hair and red Bud cap, and the shadow of a thought crossed her mind until she stood up and pushed it away with an audible "No."

"Huh?" The driver looked up from his list. "Is this wrong?"

"Oh . . . no . . . I'm sorry. I was thinking about something else." She blushed. "When you're ready I'll show you where it goes."

He loaded another case, tilted the hand truck, and rolled toward her. She led him to the *Cassie* and to the large cooler in the pilothouse. She held the door open, enjoying the cold air as he unloaded the cases and rolled out into the sunlight and handed her the invoice to sign.

"I'm new on the route but I've heard about this place. Looks cool."

"Thanks," she said, handing the invoice back. "We're having fun."

"I saw your order sheets. Looks steady. Business must be good."

"Good enough," she said.

"Great. I'll see you next time unless they move me."

She watched him walk quickly back to the truck, hang the dolly on the back, and climb up into the cab. A grind of gears, a groan of brakes, a nod to her from the open window, and he was gone. "Cute kid," she thought, and then she shook her head. "No."

"No?"

The echo startled her and she turned to see Sam walking toward her, a cup of coffee from the Dream Bean in his hand. She blushed again. "Sorry, Sam, I was just thinking out loud."

"Better be careful. That's got me in trouble more times than I wanted."

Allie shook her head. "You're out early. Must have some business."

"I'm not sure what it is but I'm going to find out."

"Anything's fine as long as it's not another bar built around a boat next to a coffee shop," Allie said.

"Don't think you have to worry about that," Sam said

and started to walk on but paused. "Demolition Crew playing tonight?"

"Yep. We'll save you a seat." Allie smiled and now it was Sam's turn to blush. She watched him walk away and went back to the storeroom. The Demolition Crew always drew a good crowd, including Sam.

When Sam got to the Pier Association, a man in gray dress pants and a freshly starched blue shirt stood up from the steps where he had been sitting.

"Appreciate you meeting me early," he said. "I've got a lot of work to do and I wanted to get an early start. Thought I'd begin with an informal look-see here."

"No problem. Glad to help if I can." Sam dug his keys out of his pocket and aimed one for the keyhole but dropped them on the wooden deck. He heard an impatient sigh as he picked out the key again and unlocked the door. He pushed the door open and reached in to turn on the lights. The man entered and waited to follow Sam into the one small office. Sam motioned to a chair, but the man remained standing and waited as Sam rolled a large map across the top of his desk. The man dropped a legal pad and pen down in the Gulf of Mexico and leaned toward the beach as Sam spoke.

"So, this is Port Aransas. I know from your email that you're interested in the pier area, and as you can see, there's nothing available that's big enough for what you have in mind. The only undeveloped land near the piers is Nueces County Park and that'll never be available."

"Never say never," the man said.

"I think 'never' will outlast us both," Sam replied.

"Hmm . . . we really wanted to be near the heart of town." He made a note on his pad and leaned over the shoreline again. With his finger he slowly moved down the beach, reading the property labels under his breath as he went.

Sam, hands in pockets, followed with his eyes until the man paused at a couple of houses facing the beach and surrounded by grassy dunes and scrub. "That's protected public land with a few private plots that are grandfathered in. That's not going to change, either."

The man's finger traveled further south and paused again. "What about this parcel?"

"Which one?" Sam craned his head.

"Here, at the corner of Beach Road and Access Road 1-A, across from these condos."

Sam looked and swallowed. "It's private. Been there for decades."

"It's further out than what would be ideal, but then it does have direct access to the beach and that's a plus. And how far would you say it is from where we are right now?"

"Hmm . . . couple of miles . . . maybe more." Sam wished it was further.

"Not ideal, but not impossible either. We could market the idea of strolling down the beach for dinner and entertainment and then riding the free shuttle back to climb into bed. And we'd have our own bar and restaurant, of course. You know who owns it?"

"No."

"Hmm, well I can get that at the tax office. That's my next stop anyway, as soon as they open." The man stood straight and looked down at the map. "It'd sure be an improvement. That end of the beach is probably due for a cleanup. Just a bunch of old rusty trailers from what I've seen." He plucked his pad from the map, made a few notes, and shoved his pen in his shirt pocket.

"That should do it. Appreciate your help, Mr. Barnes. Now, where's that Dream Bean coffee shop?"

"Uh . . . a couple of blocks that way. Next to the boat."

"Thanks." The man rushed out the door. He didn't offer a handshake, and Sam was glad he didn't because he wasn't in the mood. He did too know the owners of the piece of land on the beach. They were Mike and Candy Hailey. They rented RV sites by the day, week, or month. Most of the renters came and went with the seasons but a few stayed year-round. The Haileys were nice folks; they left their tenants alone. They weren't sticklers for rules, and they were patient when the rent was late. Sam knew that because he'd paid late, many times.

Chapter 28

Nobody noticed that Sam wasn't at the Sea Garden that night until Nancy looked out from the stage and saw another group having fun at his regular table. Between sets she asked Shelly and Allie about him.

"Hmm, must have had some late business. He'll probably come around in a while," said Allie.

But Sam never did, and after the band finished playing and the crowd began to go home Dave was sent down the highway to check on him. Dave saw lights on in the trailer, and when he knocked on the door he heard the shuffle of feet and watched the door slowly open. Sam was dressed in shorts and an unbuttoned shirt but his hair was matted and he rubbed his eyes like he'd been sleeping.

"Sorry to wake you," Dave whispered. The other trailers were dark. "Allie thought you said you'd be there tonight, and when you didn't show we were sort of worried."

"I changed my mind. Just tired."

"Good enough. I can certainly understand that. See you later." Dave turned to leave.

"Wait a minute. Got time to talk?" Sam asked.

"Sure."

Sam stepped down from the door, letting it swing shut behind him, and walked past Dave toward the gate.

"So this is a walk and talk, huh?" Dave asked.

"Oh, sorry." Sam stopped and let Dave catch up.

They walked in silence down to the beach with the cool breeze in their faces, and when they got to the edge of the damp sand, Sam stopped and looked back toward the trailer park. "I'm losing my home."

"How so?"

Sam turned to walk south down the beach, and with Dave beside him he recounted the meeting early that morning. "I know he went to the tax office and by now everyone at city hall knows."

"So what happens next?"

"It's probably up to the Haileys, the owners."

"Do they know yet?"

"Yes, because I told them. That's where I was this evening."

"And?"

"They're in shock. They can make a lot of money selling that land."

"That's good for them, right?"

"I suppose. If they want to have a lot of money and no more worries, but . . ." Sam stopped and looked back toward the trailer park, "they don't have any worries now. They're in their seventies and their life is sort of set.

They weren't looking for a big change at this age. They're sort of like me—they like things simple."

"I guess that's a decision they'll have to make," Dave said.

"Yep . . . better them than me. Too much pressure."

And the day did come when the Haileys were asked to make that decision. But not before a lot of debate at city hall and throughout the town. Some people thought the island needed a fresh boost of energy, and others wanted to leave things alone and keep Port Aransas quaint and quirky.

"I don't want to wake up one day and find our nice little town has turned into another Rockport, or worse yet, Corpus Christi," said a longtime resident one night at a meeting. The opinion was echoed by many in the room.

The Haileys were quiet through it all and in fact stayed away from the public meetings, asking Sam to listen for them and report back any details. During one meeting, the Haileys' absence was seen by one contingent as a sign that they were against the hotel and progress, while another group speculated they were already making plans for how they would spend their money.

"None of that is true," Sam said. "They stayed home because they don't want this to be about them. They want this to be about what is best for the island. They're okay with it either way."

"And what's your stake in this?" asked a member of the planning commission. "You seem to be their proxy. I'm guessing you're going to get a percentage of whatever they get."

"No, that's not true either. I'm just one of their tenants. I'm new to the island compared to most of you so I don't think I'm due a say in the matter. I do like living down there, but I suppose I could get used to living somewhere else too."

"Especially if you have a pocket full of money," said the commissioner under his breath.

"No, I have no stake in this. We've not talked about money and we're not going to." Sam stood up and walked toward the door.

"Wait a minute. Wait a minute. Don't go storming off. I'm just trying to figure out what's what. A town like this can get hijacked and the next thing we know we've got outsiders running the show. So please, just sit back down." He motioned Sam back to his chair.

The commissioner looked at Sam. "So . . . people say you're some kind of business expert. They talk about how you saved the Dream Bean and built that Sea Garden place. They say you're some sort of branding guru. So what would you recommend for the site?"

Sam looked around and saw that all eyes were on him.

"I think a hotel is fine, but it would be nice to have something different. We've already got some high rises. I understand the desire to build tall and sell out lots of rooms, but a smart company might do just as well if they went smaller and more exclusive. Maybe just two stories, more of a garden setting. With walkways and palms and private patios."

"Like your trailer park but with more privacy and room service?" someone asked.

"Sure, that's one way of looking at it," Sam said.

In the end, the city council gave the developer the green light to negotiate with the Haileys for the property but stipulated a low-rise plan based on Sam's recommendation. The Haileys were nervous about it all and asked Sam to help them, but he told them real estate wasn't his world and he brought in a member of the Pier Association who had that background.

And then something unexpected happened: the Haileys threw a picnic one night for their year-round tenants and with everyone gathered, they handed out cashier's checks of $5,000 to each family.

"That's to help you resettle," the Haileys said. "We feel bad about throwing you out."

"What about you? What are your plans?" they were asked.

"We're gonna buy a new pickup and try dragging our home around for a while—see what else is out there while we still have our eyes and our teeth. After all these years on the beach, we might find we like the mountains better."

One by one, the trailers left the park until only Sam's remained. He rented it from the Haileys and they told him to do with it as he wished. He wanted to move it to another location, but an inspector said it would fall apart before it ever got past the gate. "It's sort of grown into the ground," he said.

"Darn, I was hoping we could park it next to the *Cassie*," Dave joked, but Shelly and Allie both shook their heads in a silent but unified "No."

"I'll find something," Sam said, and he did find a one-bedroom house to rent. It was close to the office and the Sea Garden, but that was the only thing he liked about it.

"Now I understand what Bo was feeling when he left the boat and moved in with you," Sam told Allie when she came to visit on his move-in day. "I can't see the Gulf. I can't smell it. I can't even hear it."

"That's amazing, Sam."

"What?"

"You lived most of your life three hundred miles from the Gulf and now you're a beach snob. Port Aransas has definitely changed you."

"Yes, I guess it has."

After everything had been moved to the house, Sam went to the trailer one last time. He didn't go inside again; he circled it as if it was a dead, beached whale. He patted its rusty side, and indeed, it was dead.

Chapter 29

It was going to take at least a year to build the new hotel, and while some people still grumbled about the invasion of more people that it would attract, others were excited. "This one's gonna bring more folks with money, and that's what we need," they said.

Based on Sam's recommendation, the planning commission told the developers they couldn't build higher than two floors so as not to cast long shadows on the beach or properties nearby. The developers promised their hotel would have all the latest luxuries and conveniences that a wealthier class would want, but it would feel more like a beach village than a steel and concrete building.

When earth moving finally got under way, some folks went down the beach to check the progress but Sam stayed away. If someone said, "Let's go take a look," he'd say, "I'm too busy." That was mostly true; his work was at the piers and the new hotel was two miles away. But mostly he declined because it hurt too much. While he could easily walk to the beach from his office, at that end of town it was too busy, too commercial, nothing like the unbroken expanses of sand farther south, so he stayed near the piers, the Dream Bean, and Sea Garden.

On one of his visits to the pier, Sam ran into Louie, and when Louie saw him bend down to tighten a line on a cleat, he said, "I heard you crewed once."

"A little, when I first came down. Had to eat."

"Want to go with us tomorrow?"

"Where?"

"North, up to Matagorda Bay. It'll just be overnight; we'll sleep on the boat. There's a storm that may blow up in a few days so we're not going far."

Sam was aware of the storm—a tropical depression named Harvey when it roughed up the island of Barbados some 2,600 miles away. From there it moved toward Colombia and was downgraded into a tropical wave, but it gained strength again after passing over Mexico's Yucatan Peninsula. A hurricane warning was issued for most of the Texas coast, and the mood in Port Aransas was cautious but not panicked. The natives knew that these storms were unpredictable, and this one could land hundreds of miles away.

Sam was feeling fidgety and impulsive, and it didn't take him a heartbeat to accept Louie's invitation. "Sure." And he was sitting on the deck of the boat the next morning when Louie and his two mates, Paco and Arturo, arrived. Louie looked at Sam with a small backpack sitting at his feet and smiled. "On time and travlin' light—you'll do great."

And Sam did do great. The little he had learned during his brief time on the shrimp boats came back quickly, and mostly what he had learned was to do whatever he was told to do. After sailing to the shrimp beds and getting everything set up, they dragged and pulled the nets until midafternoon then took a break for a lunch of crackers and Vienna sausages and worked until the evening. Dinner was the same as lunch with the addition of some fresh fruit packed in an ice chest.

That night, while the other men slept on the deck, Sam lay awake looking at the stars. He thought about the first time he went out on a boat and wondered if one of these men had been there too—perhaps Louie before he had a boat of his own? But he couldn't draw up a memory of what any of those men had looked like because at the time he wasn't paying attention to anyone. He was just following orders and going through the motions of living. His thoughts were no deeper than that of a crab digging a hole.

~ ~ ~ ~ ~

Sam was awakened by the sound of a splash and opened his eyes to find it was dawn and Arturo had just jumped into the water to wash off. Paco laughed loudly and shouted something in Spanish as he reached down to help Arturo back up on the deck. Louie and his mates chattered in Spanish as they ate a breakfast of bread and fruit, and then Louie said it was time to go.

Sailing back toward Port Aransas in the calm waters of the inland waterway, Sam noticed a pier up ahead on the island side.

"Where are we?" he asked Louie.

"That's Matagorda Island State Park on the port and the National Wildlife Refuge on the starboard."

"How far are we from Port A?"

"Twenty-five miles maybe."

Sam thought about it as the pier got closer. Twenty-five miles was a one-day hike when he was in Scouts.

"Could you put me off on that pier?" he asked, pointing toward the shore.

Louie craned his neck and saw the pier that he'd passed many times before in the calm of the small bay.

"This side is protected for Whooping Cranes. You'd have to stay on the outer bank. It's about a mile across."

"Yes, but can you put me off?"

"Yes . . . but are you sure? That storm may come in." He pointed toward the clouds gathering on the southern horizon.

Sam looked but he wasn't worried. "Yes."

"It's a long walk home, and when you get . . . "

"I can take care of myself."

"But when you get to the end of the island . . ."

"Please . . . just let me off."

Louie nodded to his mates and they took positions at the bow to watch for stumps as he steered toward the pier. Louie cut the motor and let the boat drift; when they got a couple of yards away, Paco jumped onto the pier with a line and pulled it tight. Arturo handed Sam some bottled water and a package of crackers. Sam dropped them into the top of his backpack.

"You be careful," Arturo said. "There's snakes in there. They may get you before the storm."

"See you back in town," Sam shouted to Louie and then jumped onto the pier.

Sam watched the boat float away, and then he slung on his backpack and walked onto the land. It was mostly scrubby grasses and brush no more than waist high. The topography was flat, and while he couldn't see the other side of the island he sensed it was there and walked toward it until he broke through to the beach. He stood still for a moment, drawn in by the silence. Not the absence of noise—the breakers and the breeze rushing at him from across the Gulf filled his ears with a noise that was almost deafening—but there was no human noise at all. No boats, no vehicles, no people playing in the surf. He looked up the coast to the left and down to the right and there was no sign of human activity. Sam dropped to his knees for a moment and rested in that thought. He recalled a time when he considered turning south from his trailer and walking all the way to Mexico. That seemed the best way at the time to get away from all that bothered him. Now, it seemed he had found just such a place without the long walk. He let his mind play with the idea that he could forage for food in the grasses behind him or even the water in front of him and find enough to be content.

The spell was broken when a gust of wind kicked up a cloud of loose sand that burned his cheeks and stung his eyes. He turned away and brushed the grit from his face. Shading his eyes with his hand, he looked back out toward the water and saw that the clouds on the horizon had grown thicker and darker. High above he saw long tentacles of clouds spiraling out toward the coastline, and in the deep blue heart of the clouds he saw a flash of lightning. Sam stood up, turned his left shoulder to the Gulf and his face toward what he knew was his only real home.

Sam walked for almost four hours with little change to the view in front of him except for the occasional small inlet that he had to wind around and the long wade across the mouth of Cedar Bayou, which separates Matagorda and San Jose islands. But he was getting warm by then and the waist-deep water felt good on his tired legs and feet. He knew he was getting closer to civilization when he came upon the end of a sandy roadway leading over the dunes to some unknown destination. On the horizon ahead, he saw the dark line marking the top of the jetty leading into Aransas Pass, and as he got closer, puffs of white he first saw along the top of the jetty became more defined until he realized it was clouds of white spray as the waves crashed against the rocks.

When Sam reached the jetty at the southern tip of San Jose Island, he climbed to the concrete top and looked across the channel at the town of Port Aransas just a thousand feet away. And that's when he realized the colossal mistake he had made, and what Louie had tried to tell him on the boat: there was no way across; he was stranded. He would have to flag down a boat going by, and while there were plenty passing through the channel, they were large and appeared to be in a hurry. He would have to get the attention of a craft that was small enough to pull up close to the jetty. So he sat on the cut rocks and waited for what felt like an hour until he finally saw a long, sleek sailboat entering the channel under motor power. Sam stood and shouted but was seemingly invisible until he pulled off his shirt and swung it above his head. He watched as the boat slowed and turned toward him. It floated up and turned parallel to the jetty. Sam slung his backpack on his shoulder knowing he had just one chance to get aboard as the boat passed by. He leapt across the divide into the arms of two men who pulled him down onto the flat, open deck.

"How'd you get stuck over there?" asked one.

"I wasn't stuck." And that's all Sam said.

A few minutes later he jumped into the shallow water on the other side of the channel and waved at the boat as it pulled away. Sunburned and windblown, Sam at first thought he'd walk back to his house on a route that would keep him from being seen by anyone he knew. But all around him he could see that people were too busy to notice him. On the streets pickup trucks rolled by in a hurry, some laden with lumber and others with furniture and boxes. Over at the piers he could see sailors and their crews working to secure everything they could. The ferry horns blew to the north and Sam could see them floating toward the mainland with their decks packed with cars and people. Sam hastened his steps as he moved toward the heart of the island town knowing that the world was about to change.

Chapter 30

The wind blew up clouds of rain mixed with grit off the pavement as Sam rushed toward the Dream Bean and climbed the front steps into the eye of a different type of storm.

"After we board up these windows we need to get off the island," said Dave, dragging a sheet of plywood in front of the plate glass window.

"No, this is my home," said Shelly. "You go if you wish, but I'm staying here."

"But the mayor issued a mandatory evacuation. You're just going to ignore that?"

"Yes. And I'm going to ignore you too, so you can go jump on the ferry with everyone else if you want, but I'm staying here."

Dave exhaled loudly. "We could die if we stay, you know."

Shelly stood firmly, hands on hips. "How do you know so much? Been through some hurricanes in Dallas, have you?"

"No . . . but have you?"

"Not directly, but . . ."

"But what? Allie's the only one of us who knows anything about this." Dave shot Allie a glance that said, "Need your help here," but Allie, who had been drawn outside by the loud talk, wasn't going to help the way Dave wanted.

"My mother was swept away by Ike because she went out in the storm," Allie said. "We'll be okay if we stay inside."

Dave struggled to hold the sheet of plywood by himself, and when he reached for the drill he lost his grip and the wood fell back against him. "A little help would be nice," he growled at the women, but Sam stepped up to help hold the plywood in place while Dave drilled the screws into the corners and across the sides.

"Where you been? We were looking for you," Dave asked after pulling a screw from his shirt pocket and pushing it flush into the wall with the drill.

"Fishing . . . so . . . what's the latest forecast?"

Dave brought Sam up to date as they finished covering the windows at the Dream Bean: Harvey's path was still uncertain but he was gaining strength, so everyone was preparing for the worst. The rain and wind were coming in waves now, and Dave and Sam went next door to the *Cassie* and covered the windows on the boat, and then moved tables and chairs from the Sea Garden into the pilothouse and inside the Dream Bean. Standing inside the *Cassie* with the rain blowing hard outside, Sam had a flashback to that night on the boat with Bo and Allie. He recalled the helpless feeling that they wouldn't survive and yet they did. With his feet on the firm ground this time, he didn't feel lost like he had, but he was still anxious knowing there were a thousand ways this could go bad.

Inside the Dream Bean, with everything stowed away, Shelly looked around while unconsciously wiping the counter with a dry cloth. Dave put his hand on Shelly's and stopped her movement.

"I think we've done all we can," he said. "And I'm sorry if I'm edgy but I just don't like taking risks when there are other options. If it were up to me, I'd have us a hundred miles north of here. But I guess if I'm going to live here with you then I better start learning how this is done."

The ferry wailed from its landing down the street and everyone looked at each other. Dave shook his head knowing they wouldn't hear that much longer.

Shelly looked around the room and changed the subject. "Thanks everyone for helping here. I know you all have work to do at your own places so better get going. I'll be fine here."

Nobody moved. Shelly made a shooing motion with her hands but nobody would shoo.

"I've done all I can do," said Allie.

"Me too," said Dave. "I got everything off the floor this morning and I've got shutters so I'm protected . . . sort of."

"What about you Sam?" Shelly asked.

"The house is okay. I've got nothing worth protecting but my vinyl records, and they're waterproof. I could use a hand at the Pier Association, but then so could a lot of folks down here. Let's spread out and see what we can do."

"I'll go with Sam," said Allie.

"And we'll check on some of the other shops," said Shelly. "We'll keep the door unlocked and meet you back here later."

When Sam and Allie got to the office, they found the windows already boarded up.

"Looks like you've taken care of everything," Allie said.

Sam shook his head. "It wasn't me."

"Well you've got people watching your back," she said.

"Yes, and we should do the same," he said, and for the rest of the afternoon and on into the evening they meandered from business to business, boat to boat, house to house, lending a hand wherever they could. Sometimes that was helping hang plywood, sometimes loading cars and trucks with furniture and boxes of belongings. But many of the locals had made the same decision as Shelly and were sheltering in place, so Allie and Sam helped tie down or move indoors anything loose that might become airborne or be washed away.

At one house they helped move a cabinet freezer from

a carport into a living room. The owner offered to pay them for their help with a couple of T-bones. "You can throw those on the grill and celebrate when this little show is over."

"Thank you, but I don't think any of us will be eating steak anytime soon," said Sam.

"I think this Harvey fellow may change his mind and decide to head on over to Louisiana," the man said.

"I wish you were right."

Walking down another street they heard shouting behind them—"Motley . . . Motley come back"—and then a cat ran between their legs and jumped up a wall and into a gaping hole in the roof of a vacant building. With the cat's owner calling loudly for Motley, Sam helped hoist Allie up into the hole and then stood in the rain with the woman as they heard cat cries and bumping around and then a crash. A side door opened and out came Allie, covered in dirt and insulation and holding Motley tightly in her arms. The woman pulled the shivering cat from Allie's clutch and raced away to safety somewhere down the street, leaving Sam and Allie standing in the rain.

As they turned back toward the Dream Bean, Allie used the blowing rain and her hands to clear the debris from her hair and clothing. She stopped walking and raised her face as if she was in the shower, and Sam turned away feeling like he was seeing something he shouldn't.

"Where do you plan to ride out the storm?" Allie asked as they continued walking.

"What are the options?"

"Well, the mayor told everyone to leave but a lot are staying, so they've opened up the civic center."

"Is that where you're going?" Sam asked.

"Shelly's staying at the Bean, so I'll be there too . . . and so should you. It's up off the ground."

As they walked back toward the Dream Bean and passed the bow of the *Cassie* resting in her earthen dock, Allie stopped and patted her bow. "She's been through a lot. I hope she's ready for this."

"Me too," Sam said, but he wasn't thinking about the boat.

Inside the Dream Bean, they found Shelly and Dave drying off and looking as drowned and beaten as themselves.

"Did you have as much fun as we did?" Shelly asked, slumped in a chair with a towel on her head at the one table they had not secured away for the storm.

"That depends. Did you chase any animals through an attic?" Allie asked.

Shelly and Dave shook their heads.

"Then we had more fun than you," said Allie.

Shelly had brought a small TV from home and had it tuned to a channel in Corpus Christi. The forecaster said Harvey was twenty-four hours from landfall and the exact location was still not certain.

"He looks sort of young. You don't want to check the Weather Channel?" asked Dave.

"That man on the Weather Channel is in Atlanta and he's watching the storm on TV. The kid in Corpus is living the storm the same as us," Shelly said.

It was close to one in the morning and the rain was coming in bands, each one stronger than the next. Allie and Dave had already moved sleeping bags, blankets, and spare clothing to the Dream Bean to ride out the storm with Shelly. Sam hadn't been home in two days so during one of the breaks in the rain he decided to go home.

"I'll be back in the morning," he said.

"Are you sure?" asked Allie. "This thing could speed up and you'll be stuck."

"I trust Shelly's boyfriend in Corpus," Sam said and winked at Shelly. He was almost out the door when the clatter of the bells on the glass startled him. He untied them and handed them to Shelly. "I don't think we'll need these to tell us Harvey has arrived."

Shelly took the bells and hugged him. "If we hear it's coming sooner we'll come get you."

Sam nodded and walked out into the dark. The rain was down to a sprinkle but even then it stung as the wind blew it sideways into his face. It was only a few blocks to his house and while usually it would be dark and quiet at this time of night, Sam encountered people still working to get their houses in order.

"You got a place to ride out the storm?" asked a neighbor.

"Yes, gonna stay at Shelly's. They're thinking it will be better a few feet off the ground. How about you?"

"We're staying here. We're staying home. Best of luck. Tell Shelly we'll be back in as soon as we can."

Sam nodded and pushed on down the street to the house that looked even less familiar and less inviting in the dark, swirling rain. Inside he took a hot shower to wash off the grit and sweat from the work around town. He fell into bed and thought he would go to sleep right away, but the roar of the wind filled his head so he reached over to the bedside table and twisted the knob on the phonograph, bringing Mozart's "Clarinet Concerto" up over the noise outside. It was an odd pairing—the mellow solace of the clarinet and the shrill whine of wood members pulling against their nails—and for a moment the rocking of the house and the rhythmic whoosh of the wind reminded Sam of a blustery night in his trailer and he longed to be home in that space. But then he heard the breaking of glass and the moan of metal bending somewhere nearby and his fantasy was shattered by the truth: even if the new hotel had not forced the trailers off the beach, the storm would have swept them away forever.

Chapter 31

The last ferry left Port Aransas for the mainland at eight on that Friday morning, and those who had stayed behind knew they would have to endure whatever Hurricane Harvey threw at them from across the Gulf. That reality was heavy on Sam's shoulders as he dodged the tumbling debris on the streets from his house to the Dream Bean. He set out for the coffee shop between the bands of rain, but while the rain had slacked the wind grew stronger by the minute, and when Sam reached the door a violent gust shoved him across the threshold. He dropped the small bag of clothing he clutched and pushed hard against the door with his body until he could turn the deadbolt.

"Good morning," Shelly said without a hint of irony. She was in her "let's get it done" zone, which for her was always a good place to be. While she filled every carafe and decanter she could find with coffee, Allie baked muffins by the dozen and Dave built what looked like an endless supply of sandwiches, all of which went into the walk-in freezer. And all along the walls on the floor in the kitchen were jugs filled with water.

"We're stocking up because the power and water could get shut off at any moment," Shelly said.

That moment came at midafternoon, darkening the Dream Bean with the only natural light coming from the glass panels on the door. They had thought about boarding that up too but realized they might need to break the glass to get out later. They were grateful to have the walk-in freezer because even with the power out it was insulated enough to hold the cold and preserve some food for a long time.

The day was as slow and tedious as the storm was loud and oppressive, with the four occupants of the Dream Bean sitting in the shadows cast by battery-powered lanterns Dave bought at the hardware store the previous day. The gaps between the bands of rain being pushed ashore by Harvey became narrower and narrower until they blended together into one continuous deluge. The power outage put an end to weather reports on the TV until Dave's phone buzzed with a text from his friend Jeff in Dallas. Dave replied and Jeff followed with hourly updates including screen shots of radar showing the center of the storm moving closer and closer to the island. With a direct hit looking more likely, they moved from the table in the dining room to the floor behind the counter. Sitting in the dim light they passed the time with magazines and naps, but real sleep was impossible with the noise of the storm stirring up their adrenaline. Occasionally one of them would venture toward the door to look out the window, but there was nothing to see through the thick gray film of rain.

Allie couldn't calm her nervous energy so she pulled out a deck of cards. "Hearts anyone?" When nobody answered she started dealing anyway and everyone picked up their hand and began playing. In between discards and pulls another game evolved—a sort of "truth or dare" where they went around the circle asking each other questions and sharing little tidbits of their lives. The questions were softballs and the answers were light until Allie asked, "Okay, Sam, worst storm till now?"

Sam sat quietly and looked blankly at the cards in his hand. The sound of the wind and rain outside stroked his memory and from out of the bottomless pit of forgotten days came a moment that caused him to close his eyes and smile.

"What is it?" Shelly asked.

Sam opened his eyes, the smile still on his lips but his eyes moist.

"I was probably about ten. I'd gone fishing with my father—not because I wanted to but because that's what he said we were going to do—and dark clouds began to roll in. I would have been scared but Dad was scared of nothing. He kept fishing, and so did I. And then from nowhere there was a crack of lightning on the water right in front of us. Dad dropped his rod and grabbed me by the arm and we started running up the hill toward the cabin. When lightning struck again right behind us, we both dove head first into a muddy puddle."

Sam shook his head and smiled again. Shelly started to speak but Dave squeezed her arm.

"Up until then I thought my father was king of the universe, afraid of nothing. But I learned then that he was just as scared as me."

Sam laughed. "I also didn't know how goofy he could be until we got in the cabin and saw each other's faces covered with red mud and only our eyes showing. I started laughing at him and that got him laughing too, and the next thing I knew he was jumping up and down and grunting like a caveman. He dubbed us the Mud Brothers, and we made up tales about fishing with our hands and eating tree bark to tell my mother when we got home. Up until then I sort of feared him, but after that it was more a feeling of respect because I knew he was flesh and blood, the same as me."

Allie sighed. "Sounds like you had a special bond. Wish I'd known Bo like that; wish I'd had more time with him."

"Our time didn't last long either," said Sam. "He was gone by the time I was in high school. He was better at taking care of others than himself. Worked too hard and wore himself out."

"Any other family?" Shelly asked.

"My mother died about ten years ago, and that's the

last time I saw my younger brother. Not sure where he is now."

Sam leaned back against the wall and stared out a window that wasn't there. Allie gathered the cards and started to deal again but realized interest had waned so she lay out a game of solitaire on the floor between her legs. She was picking and stacking when they heard the shatter of glass and looked up to see that a two-by-four had burst through the glass door and buried itself in the opposite wall. And then the ceiling began to peel back like the top of a sardine can and the room was swirling with wind and rain and debris.

"Into the freezer," Sam shouted and started pushing the other three toward the metal door of the freezer.

"What?" screamed Shelly.

"The freezer!"

They scrambled across the floor grabbing sleeping bags, blankets, and lights, and tumbled into the dark chill of the freezer. Sam pulled the door shut, which cut the noise of the storm in half but also killed the light until they got a lantern set up on the floor between them. They grabbed the blankets and sleeping bags and wrapped up, because while the power outage hours earlier had raised the temperature inside it was still chilly. Dave typed a quick text to Jeff in Dallas, and a moment later he received a radar picture and the words, "On top of you—San Jose Island actually. Max wind 130." Dave passed the message around to the others and

Sam realized San Jose was where he had been walking so foolishly just hours earlier.

"Do we have enough oxygen?" Allie asked. Nobody knew the answer exactly but Dave said they could open the door a little if anyone began to feel faint.

"How did you know to come in here?" Shelly asked Sam.

"Up north they recommend this as a makeshift tornado shelter, and the wind speeds can be double what we have here," he said.

"Anybody hungry?" Shelly asked as she pulled a bag of sandwiches off the shelf. "We may run out of air but we won't starve to death in here."

The freezer rocked and rumbled but held strong. Allie looked at Sam and he saw in her eyes the same look they both had in the cramped quarters of the *Cassie* the night of the storm on the Gulf. Her eyes got bigger when the noise outside suddenly got louder. They all knew the roof of the Dream Bean had been torn away and all that stood between them and the storm were the layers of metal and insulation around them.

In the hours that followed, they each retreated into their own minds, each pondering their own life—what they had done, what they had failed to do, what they would do with the days they had left if God allowed. Shelly and Dave held tightly to each other as lovers do when considering they might not hold each other again. Sam drew Allie under his arm for warmth in a fatherly way, and Allie accepted the gesture as she would have had it been Bo instead. And then a sort of stupor fell over them all and they slumped into a kind of hibernation with nobody moving or talking. They were in a quiet place of peace that comes from knowing you've done all you can do and it's up to God now to deliver you or take you to whatever comes next.

~ ~ ~ ~ ~

Dave was awakened by a loud thump. He checked his phone: it was seven in the morning. Then he opened a new text from Jeff from several hours earlier showing the center of the storm had moved inland over Victoria and Cuero. Dave moved his shoulder a little and that awoke Shelly, and she reached over and touched Sam, and he likewise moved a little and roused Allie. One by one their eyes fluttered open and they each took inventory with their senses. They could still hear the rain pelting the outside of the freezer, but the wind was not as loud. Most important, they were still in the shelter of the freezer and they all were alive.

Dave crawled to the door and put his hand on the cold, flat surface. He looked back at the others.

"What do you think?" Sam asked.

"I think we're okay. Ready?"

They all nodded. Shelly had tears in her eyes, her mind already picturing what she thought they would see outside. Dave pressed the round safety release and pushed on the door. It opened about an inch, letting a thin shaft of light in but not budging any further. He leaned his shoulder into the door and when he couldn't get any movement, Sam joined him and they pushed hard together against debris that had piled up on the other side. When the door finally opened wide enough, they stepped out one by one into a world they didn't recognize.

Chapter 32

The first thing they noticed when they stepped out of the freezer into the kitchen and dining room of the Dream Bean was that it was raining—it was raining inside. And of course the reason was clear: there was no roof overhead. Everything in the room looked pretty much as they recalled—the checkerboard floor tile, the light blue walls with the seascape murals that Shelly had painted—except that everything was a shade darker from the soaking of untold inches of rain. The second thing they noticed was that it was quiet. No traffic, no gulls, no wind, no boat horns or clatter of rigging. Just the sound of the falling rain.

Shelly stood in the middle of that space, turning slowly in a circle to assess what was left. She found it difficult to focus with eyes that were watery from a mixture of rain, tears, and sweat. She saw that the walls had held and the windows were intact behind their protective plywood, but the room was scattered with wreckage from the ceiling and roof—wood, drywall, ductwork, ceiling tiles, and insulation.

Allie brushed past Shelly and went to the front door,

pushed it open and walked out onto the porch. She turned to the left to see what she had come to see: the *Cassie*.

While boats at the piers had been tossed about like toys—some washed up on top of each other or up onto parking lots and on top of cars—the *Cassie* sat firmly in her berth. Her bow had faced the storm and had ridden it out with seeming aplomb. The only sign of damage was a section of gunwale that was broken by a trash dumpster that floated over from somewhere down the street. Otherwise, she was in better shape after Harvey than she had been after the collision with the tanker that ultimately had retired her from the water.

Allie walked around her and across her deck and then into the pilothouse. She sighed and hugged herself as if she was hugging her father Bo and then wiped away a tear before returning to the shell of the Dream Bean where Shelly and Dave were picking up and sorting through the remnants of their business.

"Where's Sam?" Allie asked.

"Gone to check on the others and see what needs to be done," said Dave.

And what needed to be done was everything. There wasn't a structure on the island—not a home or a business or a shed or a doghouse—that had not been changed in some way. Some got by with just a little damage thanks to some odd luck but often because they were blocked by a structure that stood between them and the brunt of the storm. But even then the rain was so fierce and so constant that even if a roof or a wall held strong, the water found its way through a crack or a seam, leaving the interior soggy and potentially ruined.

But as devastated as the town appeared, the most important immediate task was to account for its citizens. While most of the islanders had heeded the mayor's order to evacuate, a hundred or so had chosen to ride it out. That included a handful of city directors who sheltered at the Marine Institute so that they could get back to work quickly. They and volunteers went door-to-door checking on people. Sam joined the effort at the piers, walking into clusters of people asking each other: "How'd you make out? Have you seen so-and-so? What do you need?"

During one of these conversations, someone looked around and said, "Where's Calvin?" When they realized that nobody had seen him they went to his slip and found his boat, the *Lucky Strike,* missing.

"Did he sail out before the storm?" Sam asked.

"No, he was here with the rest of us yesterday morning stowing his gear," said Louie who had come from his own boat. "And glad to see you made it back." Sam nodded, knowing that Louie understood how close he had come to disaster with his walk home down the coast.

So they spread out to search for Calvin and word came back that the *Lucky Strike* had been found a few blocks away, resting upside down inside the top of a small retail building. Sam and the others approached, and when one of them called out they heard a yip from a dog.

"Calvin . . . you in there?" Sam shouted and then all stood quiet.

"Uh huh. Is the storm over?" came the muffled response.

"Yep. You just stay there and we're gonna come in and get you."

"No hurry. I got no other appointments today."

With sledgehammers and shovels they broke through the wall of the building and tunneled through the debris to the door of the pilothouse, which was upside down and bearing the weight of the boat above it. They heard a groan of steel and lumber above and Louie whispered, "We gotta get him out now. She's not gonna hold up much longer," so they pushed the door open slowly so as not to upset anything. Inside they found Calvin sitting on the ceiling, which now was the floor, one leg facing forward and one bent awkwardly beneath him; he was clutching his small dog Minnow and a cross, which was all that was left of the rosary he always wore around his neck.

"Was wondering when someone was going to check on me. We've had a pretty rough night," Calvin said.

Calvin handed Minnow over to Sam who passed her back through the hole in the wall and then Calvin tried to crawl forward himself but couldn't with a leg that obviously was broken. So one of the smaller men crawled in behind him and little by little they got his body straightened out lengthwise and then got a plank under him and slowly dragged him out into the open where Calvin sat up and looked around. "What the hell are we doing downtown? Take me back to the pier."

And so went rescues across the island, with neighbors pulling neighbors from the remains of their homes and businesses and wherever else they had gone for shelter. Along the shoreline and out on the Gulf a pair of Coast Guard helicopters plucked people from boats who had not heeded the warnings to stay off the water and seek shelter on land.

From the roofless Dream Bean, Shelly asked neighbors to spread the word that she had food and beverage for anyone who needed it as long as it lasted, and before long she had people coming for coffee, sandwiches, cookies, and whatever else could be salvaged from the freezer. With no electricity, coffee was heated over a fire pit that Dave dug out in the Sea Garden, but it was later joined by a propane grill that someone rolled up from the piers. Tables and chairs were pulled out from where they had been stored and the Sea Garden took on its familiar look, except that instead of hosting Saturday night revelers, it was a rest stop for weary islanders and aid workers slogging their way through the endless piles of rubble. The food and rest were free but as had become the custom at the Dream Bean, Shelly put a bucket on the counter. When it filled up with cash and loose change, Sam took it to the market to buy whatever might be turned into a meal from the dwindling supplies on the shelves.

The walk to the market was slow as Sam stepped around debris and over downed power lines. He saw the metal awnings of buildings rolled up into giant balls like tin foil, wooden stairways leading to the ghosts of second-floor decks, bright red vending machines on their backs in the middle of the street like defeated robots in a video game, cars with shattered windows and their seats full of mud and straw brought up from the dunes, booze bottles scattered around the remains of bars. And everywhere there was the sight and smell of shattered yellow two-by-fours that had been hidden behind sheetrock and siding for decades.

When Sam turned the corner that led to the market, he wasn't surprised to see that it too was damaged: sections of the brick walls were scattered on the pavement and the awning above the door was twisted and sprawled across the ground. At one end of the parking lot a large RV was laying on its side like a child's discarded Tonka toy. Inside the store, Sam found a cart and pushed it through puddles of water to where the canned goods had always been. He was picking from the shelves and even the floor when Maggie Gifford, the manager and his former boss, walked up.

"Someone said you'd been walking over at San Jose Island and hadn't come back before the storm. I figured you'd washed away," she said.

"Part of that story is true, and I'll let you guess which is false," Sam said. "So how you doing here? Got enough help?"

"We're doing okay but we'll be down to nothing in twelve hours and I won't need any help until we get another truck in here, and who knows when that will be. How's it looking elsewhere?" she asked.

Sam looked out the shattered window and nodded at the desolation. "It's pretty much the same everywhere. Have you heard anything from Marty?"

"Not a word," Maggie said. "I don't know if he and his parents stayed or got out. If it were up to him I bet they stayed."

"What about a count . . . any news on fatalities?" Sam asked

"Just one so far, and they're not sure about the cause. Might have been medical. It's a miracle if there's just one."

And indeed it was a miracle that there was only one life lost—mainly because most of the 3,500 residents got out of town and the hundred or so who stayed had some good luck. But that's only if you count loss of life because almost everyone had damage. For some, it was total.

Those who stayed had the benefit of assessing their situation almost right away. The people who left had to wait some days until the ferry from Aransas Pass was running again or until the highway from Corpus Christi was cleared. And nobody was in a hurry with the mayor asking for time to complete searches and then assess damage to basic city services including power and water.

With the Dream Bean secured, Shelly and her friends went to see what was left at their homes. Shelly had the most to lose, living in the home that her parents left her after the highway crash that took their lives. While she had sold or given away many of their possessions, she had kept some family heirlooms as a reminder of their too-brief time together. Dave offered to go with her but she told him she wanted to be alone. As she drove past the piles of debris being stacked up outside houses she began to wish she hadn't been so stubborn.

"I don't know if I can do this," she said as she pulled into the driveway. On first glance she was pleased to see that the walls were standing and the roof was still sitting on top—at least from the front view. But a split in the live oak tree in the front yard and a palm leaning against the side wall confirmed that the storm hadn't gone right past her. What's more, there was trash hanging a couple of feet up in the oleanders near the front door, and she knew what that meant. She pushed open the front door and saw what she expected to see: a dirty wet stain two feet up the walls and furniture that had floated to new locations.

Dave and Allie both had water damage inside from

rain coming through their roofs, with whole sections of shingles gone and others poking up like a bad haircut. Dave's carport was nowhere to be found, but his car was right where he had left it. Allie's little car was missing at first until she saw its bumper peeking out from behind a tree a couple of houses down. She followed its path through several flattened chain link fences and had to wonder if it had floated or flown to its new location because there weren't any of the scratches she expected to see.

Sam, who had the least to lose because he had the least personal possessions in his rent house, was spared any major damage. A cinderblock washateria next door had provided a tall wind and water break, with some backwash into his kitchen but in inches and not feet. It would just take a good stiff broom and some time to get it out.

"You can stay with me if you wish," Sam told the others when he got back to the Dream Bean. Allie said she was fine at her place, and Shelly and Dave said they would work something out between their two homes.

"Ha, it took Harvey to get you two under the same roof," Allie smirked.

Shelly would have sniped back, but the sight of the roofless coffee shop kept her attitude in check. "Actually, I may just stay here," she said. "I could put a tent in the corner over there and that way I could keep an eye on things until we get her closed up."

Dave took her by the hand. "Shelly, I know that would make you feel better, but it's not realistic at all."

"He's right," Sam said before Shelly could object. "It could be weeks and probably months before there're crews and materials enough to put your roof back on. And that won't happen until an adjustor looks it over—provided you or your landlord have insurance." He looked at her and the others did too. "He does, doesn't he . . . or you?"

A glaze came across Shelly's face. "To be honest, I don't know." Her shoulders slumped.

Dave put his arm behind her to hold her up. "Let's not worry about that right now. Let's look at what we can do to carry on with what we've got."

Shelly stood in the roofless shell of what once was her dream and looked up at the open sky above. "What we've got is nothing."

"Not true," said Sam. "You've got this space and the *Cassie* and the Sea Garden. The only difference right now is that where two were outdoor venues, all three are now. So you just need to change directions a little—give people a reason to come and enjoy coffee or even a meal outdoors. We'll get electricity back soon, and the freezer will be up and running again. And it's just August so we've got some mild months ahead."

Dave rubbed his chin. "And we've got a unique opportunity."

"What's that?" asked Allie.

"To have a concert—to benefit Port A. We'll get some bands in here that'll donate their time and we'll let folks pay what they want. We'll help our neighbors the best way we know how and we'll keep ourselves on the map."

Chapter 33

After shaking off the initial shock of Harvey's destruction, the people of Port Aransas began the seemingly impossible task of digging out, cleaning up, and assessing the future. Wreckage was dragged to the curbsides to be gathered up in trucks and carried down the highway to a makeshift landfill that grew in height day after day. In time it was taller than any building on the island and someone with a sense of humor named it Mount Trashmore.

When the highway reopened and the ferry resumed its crossings, the developers of the hotel at Sam's old trailer park came to see what was left. With the island in disarray, they let the mayor and council know they might scrap the project; they couldn't see any hope that Port Aransas would ever come back to life.

"Well, then you just don't know us and maybe you don't belong here after all because we WILL rebuild, and we'll find someone else for that piece of property," they were told by the city leaders. So the developers huddled, made phone calls, and came back with a promise to build as planned. What's more, they would lend their manpower and heavy equipment for the immediate need to clear rubble wherever needed.

Word began to spread that help was needed in Port Aransas, especially since Houston had received more media attention with hundreds of thousands of people stranded by flooding and power outages. Dave was awakened early one morning by a pounding on his door, and he opened it to see his friend Jeff from Dallas.

"Work's a little slow so I filled up the truck and came down to see what this is all about," he told Dave. "Looks to me like someone made a huge mess so I'm gonna see what I can do to help clean it up a little. Can I crash on your couch awhile?"

"Well, that's where I've been because Shelly, my friend, has taken my room right now."

"You always were a straight-laced gent," Jeff said with a big laugh. "Say no more. I brought my pup tent and I'll make camp out back."

"Or you know what? We might set you up at the *Cassie,*" said Dave.

"With who?"

"The *Cassie.* She's a boat. I'll show you."

"Sounds fine, but right now I'm going down to where the volunteers are lining up. I'll find you back at this *Cassie* place later." And like the whirlwind that he was, Jeff was gone. Later in the day he pulled his truck up to the side of the *Cassie* and jumped out. "Now that's a landlubber for sure," he bellowed as he patted her bow.

Dave dropped what he was doing and filled Jeff in on the details, and then he introduced him to Allie and Shelly.

"Jeff's the one who sent us the weather reports inside the freezer," Dave said.

"That's a big reason I came down. Had to see what I was texting about. So is that where you all rode it out?" he asked, pointing to the shell of the Dream Bean.

"Yes, and we appreciate you keeping us up to date during the storm. You kept us safe inside until it was over," said Shelly.

"Glad to help in some little way, and now I'm here hoping to pitch in wherever I can. And speaking of pitching . . ." Jeff pointed to his tent and other gear in the back of the truck.

"Oh sure, just set up behind the *Cassie*," said Allie.

"Great. Just add night security guard to my job description," Jeff laughed and started to unpack.

"I'm glad to have him, but how long do you think he'll stay?" Allie asked Dave from a distance as Jeff laid out his camp.

"I don't know since he didn't tell me he was coming. But I'm guessing he'll stay until he needs to get back to work at home."

"He's got a big personality, like Rosie," Allie said.

Dave sighed. "Yep, always has, and it wears me out sometimes. But he has a huge heart too."

When Dave went to check on him later, Jeff said,

"Well buddy, I don't know which of those young ladies is the one, but I'd be happy to get to know whoever you haven't claimed."

Dave glared. "Jeff . . . please."

"Okay, okay, I get it. So . . . which one of the two made you sell your house and move to ground zero?"

"Shelly."

"You chose well, my friend," said Jeff.

Dave walked back to the Dream Bean, unsure of what to do with Jeff except to keep him busy. But Jeff was no stranger to work, and nobody saw him around the coffee shop or boat between sunrise and sunset. He'd come back to his camp dirty and grimy and disappear inside his tent. Dave knew Jeff was an independent sort and so he left him alone.

But the bigger surprise than Jeff blowing into town came a few days later when Allie was on her knees, scrubbing down the deck of the *Cassie* and heard a familiar voice. She looked up to see Justin's red head gazing at her from over the gunwale. Shocked, she tried to get up quickly and kicked over the bucket, sending soapy water everywhere. Justin laughed and then scampered aboard to help pull her up off the deck.

"What are you doing here?" she asked, unable to hide the surprise in her voice.

"I saw the reports and knew I needed to come help," he said, holding her by the elbows and then letting go when he saw the look on her face.

Allie's head was spinning and her heart was pounding as she tried but failed to stop the flushing in her cheeks. She couldn't remember the last time she had even thought about Justin since he left for Florida, but now the sight of him brought feelings rushing back and especially the uncertainty of what to do.

"Where are you staying?" she asked. "A lot of us have been displaced."

"Oh, don't worry about me. I've already been to the beach and there are lots of folks camping out there right now. I brought my gear and I'll do the same. So . . . how can I help? I'm ready to do anything. Clean up, tear down, rebuild. Just don't hand me an apron and a spatula because I'm not much of a cook."

Allie pointed to the roofless Dream Bean and the grill next to it. "We're not doing a whole lot of cooking around here right now," she said, thinking a moment. "But we definitely could use some help cleaning up. And I bet Sam has some projects around the piers."

"Let's do it," Justin said with a big grin.

Over the next couple of days Shelly, Dave, Allie, and now Justin dragged out all the debris and scrubbed down the inside of the Dream Bean and all the kitchen equipment that could be salvaged. And then with some scrap lumber and all the tarps they could get their hands on Dave and Justin built a sort of temporary roof over as much of the Dream Bean as they could. It wasn't structurally sound and in fact didn't do anything to remove the red "Unsafe" sign that code inspectors put on the front door as they did on doors all over the island; their goal was to keep out the rain and the dust until the money and materials were available for a new roof. Dave confirmed with Shelly's landlord that the building was insured, but nobody could predict when reconstruction would start.

Down at the Pier Association, Sam organized work teams to help captains and crews get their boats back in working order as well as help the shop owners in the neighborhood. The shrimpers needed to get back out on the water to salvage what was left of the season, and the shops and restaurants needed to get closed in again before the fall and winter storms began to blow in as they always did. But looming larger for everyone on the island was the return of spring and tourism and especially SandFest. Everyone knew that if they weren't ready in time for SandFest, people wouldn't come and it might take years to convince them to return.

And floating out there on the horizon like a ship that couldn't find its way home was a question that nobody could answer: When Port Aransas came back to life—and there was every reason to believe it would thanks to the strong will of the people who called it home—what would it look and feel like? Would it be the quirky but loveable seaside town that generations of Texans had come to adore? Or would it be some sort of corporate reimagining—its cozy bars, shops, and rentals replaced by flashy hotels and restaurant chains rolled into town on the backs of flatbed trucks? For a town that depended on tourism, it literally was the million-dollar question.

Chapter 34

"Oh dear, it's so good to hear from you. I've called and called but couldn't get through. Is everyone okay?" Nancy asked.

"We're all safe and sound," Dave said. "Can't say the same for Port A, including the Dream Bean. And that's why I'm calling." And then he laid out the plan for the benefit concert.

Nancy had ridden out the hurricane in Victoria, which had gotten its share of wind and rain when the storm passed directly overhead and then circled back over for a second round of destruction on its way to Houston. She and the Crew had given up performing in the aftermath to tend to their own families and properties but now they were ready to get back on stage.

"You just name the date and we'll be there," she said.

Sam and Dave met with city leaders to make sure there were no objections to the plan, and indeed there were concerns. Not the least of which was that the town wasn't prepared to host a big party. Basic city services were still questionable and law enforcement was stretched thin by continued worries about looting with so many properties looking like soggy, torn-open trick-or-treat bags.

"We can't handle a spring break or SandFest crowd right now. Not sure if we'll ever be able to do that again," said the police chief.

"It's not going to be anything that big," Sam said. "It'll mostly be regional folks who know Port A and want to help get her going again. And the music will be local with no big draws." Sam looked at Dave and he nodded in agreement.

The chief and the other city leaders huddled a moment while Sam and Dave waited, and then they turned around and said it would be okay but with some stipulations: it would have to be one day only—on the first Saturday of October; there would be some beach access, but other streets in town would be blocked with attendees having access only to the venue and temporary parking on some cleared lots nearby; the show would have to be over at midnight with everyone cleared out by one in the morning. "And you'll have to rent enough porta-potties to handle the folks. We've had enough natural disasters around here," said the head of public health.

With the rules set, everyone pitched in to get the Sea Garden cleaned up for what was hoped to be a manageable crowd. Nancy and the Crew contacted other musicians they knew and the event expanded from a concert to a half-day music festival. Sam and Maggie at the market talked her suppliers into providing the fixings for burgers and hot dogs at half off wholesale. Allie was able to arrange the same deal with the beverage distributor with some nudging from her favorite truck driver. Sam got the businesses near the piers busy gathering up whatever souvenirs and trinkets had survived the storm to sell from vendor tents on the street across from the Sea Garden.

Dave worried aloud that the Demolition Crew's name might be a little insensitive considering what was happening all over town. "Maybe they could call themselves the D Crew or something like that," he said, but Sam wasn't troubled by it.

"Just let it be. The name isn't offensive; in fact it's ironic and irony sells because it sticks in the mind. But it's a festival now and not a concert so they'll just be part of the mix. By the way, do we have a name for this event?"

Dave thought about it a moment. "How about 'Port Aransas Revival'?"

"Works for me," Sam said, but the name was changed to "Port Aransas Reborn" a couple of days later after a church in Rockport called to ask who the visiting evangelist was and whether they could bring some of their flock to sing in the revival choir. Sam was surprised to learn that Jeff was a freelance writer and PR consultant, and he put Jeff to work creating flyers and posters to distribute all over South Texas.

On the day of the festival, nobody was quite sure what to expect but it became clear early that word had spread well. As the sun rose up out of the Gulf and began to light up the streets and homes as well as the lingering piles of rubble, cars began rolling off the ferry in larger numbers than typical for early October. And while some of the people headed straight to the stretches of beach that were finally open again, many followed the barricades and signs to the Sea Garden and began claiming their spots with lawn chairs and blankets.

Sam moved around with a clipboard and a borrowed cell phone, looking every bit the event planner that he had become, while answering questions and directing people and supplies to their destinations. And then he heard a crunch on the pavement and looked up to see the Crew's SUV roll up.

"Now this looks like a real party," said Chip as he slid out of the driver's seat onto the pavement. The back doors opened and Gary and Tom popped out. And then from around the front of the van came Nancy, looking sunnier than ever in Sam's view.

"So good to see you after all you've been through," she said, and while Sam juggled his clipboard in search of a free hand to shake he was greeted with a hug instead.

"Great to see you too. Glad to know you made it okay," he said.

"Can't quite say the same for you," said Chip,

pointing to the blue tarps flapping in the breeze over the top of the Dream Bean.

"Yep, Shelly's waiting in line for a new roof just like everyone else, but she's strong as you know and we're doing the best we can. Let's get you unpacked and I'll fill you in on the details."

The festival was to kick off at noon with Nancy and the Crew taking the lead. They were scheduled to close the night and fill in gaps in the lineup that Dave had arranged.

"This is Marty—he'll DJ between acts to keep the music going," said Dave as he walked Nancy and the Crew through the setup. "But he's got strict orders to keep it casual and coastal, and above all else, Texan."

Nancy stuck out her hand. "Pleased to meet you, Marty, and what's this . . . a trumpet?" she asked, pointing to the familiar shape of a trumpet case resting under his table.

"Yes ma'am. I've been afraid to leave it at home for looters to grab," he said.

"Do you play it or do you just carry it around?" Chip asked.

"I play it."

"Great, then today you can play with us."

"But . . . we haven't rehearsed," Marty said.

"Neither have we," Chip said. "Just doodle in some notes when it feels right."

Marty looked at Nancy and she winked. He tried to

hide a grin, and Dave left him with a pat on the back and a reminder: "Just don't forget why you're here. Gotta keep the music going."

Nancy and the Crew hit the stage at noon, and after a couple of songs Chip waved Marty up to join them. It didn't take too long for him to get a feel for their sound and what he could add, and by the end of their first set he was feeling loose and couldn't wait for their turn to come around again.

"You got it," said the usually quiet Gary.

"This Crew may be for you," added Tom.

The audience came and went as they pleased throughout the day because there were no tickets for the show. Keeping with the Dream Bean tradition, tips and donations were collected in buckets placed around and emptied when they filled up. Shelly, Allie, and other volunteers kept the food and drinks moving with Justin and Jeff taking turns at the grills and helping the bands get their gear on and off the stage.

After one of the changes when the Demolition Crew returned to the stage, Dave was rounding the bow of the *Cassie* and was cornered by Jeff.

"So what's her story?" Jeff asked, pointing to Nancy.

"Hands off," Dave said.

"Really?" Jeff said loudly, causing people nearby to turn and look. "You can't have 'em all . . . unless you're starting a cult or something." He laughed loudly and Dave pulled him backwards by the shoulder.

"Shush," Dave hissed, and then whispered. "Not me. I'm with Shelly. And in fact . . . we're engaged."

"Why didn't you tell me? That's great news," Jeff roared.

Dave shushed Jeff again. "Please."

"So what about her?" Jeff whispered, pointing toward Nancy again.

Dave pulled Jeff's hand down. "She has her eyes on someone else . . . or someone else is eyeing her."

"Do tell," Jeff said, but Dave was silent, and when Jeff realized he wouldn't get any more information that way he started scanning the audience, working around the perimeters until his eyes found Sam leaning on the railing of the Dream Bean, staring straight at Nancy.

"Him?" Jeff asked and pointed at Sam.

"Just leave them alone, okay?" said Dave.

Jeff laughed loudly and moved on around the perimeter of the crowd, picking up empty bottles and trash as he went.

Sam was oblivious to the attention, because as Jeff had noticed, he was focused fully on Nancy. And Nancy was oblivious to it all too because she was singing with her eyes closed. And that was part of what had Sam transfixed: she wasn't just singing the music; she was swimming in it.

And the audience—that had come from Corpus Christi to the south and had crossed the channel on the ferry from far and wide—was swimming with Nancy too.

And the food and drinks were flowing and the buckets were filling with cash and there was no doubt in the minds of anyone there that night that Port Aransas was going to survive.

It was a little after one when the last of the crowd had left the Sea Garden and even later by the time everything had been cleaned up and put away. Arrangements were made for Nancy to stay with Allie and the Crew to stay at Sam's little house. Sam opted to give them extra room and sleep on the sofa in his office but not before walking Nancy the few blocks to Allie's house. On the way they talked about the night and the future of the town, and Sam thought about taking Nancy's hand but he left her at Allie's door with nothing more than a friendly hug. Lying on the sofa in the dark of his office, Sam's inner teenager chastised him for being so timid.

The Dream Bean had always been closed on Sunday mornings and that was definitely the case after the hurricane and on the morning after the festival. Even so, Shelly was restless and crept out of the house quietly, leaving Dave asleep in the room down the hall. When she got to the Dream Bean, she was surprised to find Allie sitting in Bo's chair on the deck of the *Cassie*.

"You could've slept in. I don't think we'll have much business at noon considering we kept most of the town out late," Shelly said.

"I know, but I wasn't really sleeping anyway so I

decided to come on over and find something to do."

"Oh yeah? What's up with that?"

"Just restless I suppose. Maybe too much coffee last night."

"Not too much Justin?"

"Oh, good God no," Allie said. "He may be in town and helping us out, but I have no idea or care where he goes or what he does."

"Hmm," Shelly said.

"Hmm what?" Allie asked.

"Nothing, just hmm."

"Well good, because there's nothing for you or anyone else to be 'hmming' about," Allie said.

Shelly nodded and walked through the tables and chairs of the Sea Garden and through the front door of the Dream Bean to start some coffee.

Dave arrived at the Dream Bean a couple of hours later, but first he went around to the back of the *Cassie* to check on Jeff and was surprised to find his tent and truck gone. He rounded the corner and found Nancy and the Crew sitting at a table in the sunshine, drinking coffee and eating omelets that Allie had stirred up on the grill.

"Anybody seen Jeff this morning?" Dave asked as he pulled up a chair.

"Yes," said Allie. "He got some coffee to go, and he told me to tell you and everyone else that he appreciated the hospitality and that he'll be back for the wedding if you remember to tell him when it is."

"Wedding? Who's getting married?" Nancy asked.

"Those two," Allie said, pointing to Shelly and Dave.

"That's wonderful. Count on us for the reception," Nancy said.

"We'll see," said Shelly. "We've been pretty busy just trying to get this town back on its feet. That's the biggest priority right now."

"Well you can't always wait for the perfect moment," Nancy said. "Sometimes you just have to go ahead and do what you know you need to do."

Nancy took a long slow sip of coffee, and then she looked at the guys, who appeared to be just half awake. "And what the Crew and I probably need to do is get on back to Victoria." She stood up and stretched out her hand toward Chip. "Give me the keys. I'll drive."

By the time Sam drifted over from his office, Nancy and the Crew were gone and he was left with a verbal message from Nancy similar to what Jeff had left for Dave: "Tell Sam thank you and we'll talk again soon."

From across the island the ferry horns wailed, and Sam turned his head as if there was something to see.

Chapter 35

As the days crawled by the piles of rubble on the streets and sidewalks of Port Aransas began to shrink and Mount Trashmore grew ever taller until it could grow no more and was carried by trucks to a landfill outside of Corpus Christi. The raspy groans of demolition were replaced by the smooth buzz of saws and the rhythmic chucks of nail guns, and the shrieks of gulls were joined by the beeps of trucks backing onto lots with their loads of lumber and shingles.

The transition from cleanup to reconstruction brought handshakes and hugs as volunteers who had put their own lives on hold to help Port Aransas dig out boarded the ferry and floated back to their homes. Meanwhile, men and women still needing part-time work huddled around contractors' trucks on Monday mornings to sign up for any jobs available.

"Packed up and moving out?" Allie asked Justin one morning as he arrived at the Dream Bean with his car full of his belongings.

"No, just moving. I was on the beach and then in a room and now I've rented an apartment that just got cleaned up and was available for cheap," he said.

"When were you going to tell me this?" Allie snipped.

"When were you going to ask?" Justin countered, and then seeing the irritation on her face he took her by the hands and tried a softer tone. "I know . . . I know . . . things have been in flux and I just wanted to make sure I knew what I was doing before I said anything."

"And so . . . you know what you're doing now?"

"Yes, I do," he said and explained that he had done all he could for his father's medical ministry in Florida and he was ready to find his own calling. "There are plenty of people in Texas who need help, especially here on the coast, so I'm working part-time at the food bank while I look for something more permanent."

Allie was skeptical because she knew Justin had the means to go anywhere and do anything he wanted, and yet he was talking about doing social work.

"And what will you do when Port A has been rebuilt and all the people have been helped?" she asked.

"People needed help long before Harvey hit," he said.

It took all the will power Allie could muster to not openly scoff at Justin's high-minded words. She wanted to believe him, and yet she wasn't sure if she should. He had led her on and then let her down when he left town the last time. And even if he was being completely honest, Allie didn't trust the way he was laying all this personal news at her feet as if it would sway her back into his arms. It's not like she had been waiting for him to come back to her, and she definitely wasn't going to pick up right where they left off.

"You may be right about the need," Allie said. "I mean . . . Shelly and me and most of the shops on the island are just one bad season away from having to ask for help ourselves."

There—she'd thrown Justin a conciliatory bone, but if he was playing a game, she was too. She looked deep into his eyes and thought she saw a hint of disappointment even though his face carried his usual sunny smile. She knew she had cut him with her questioning but she wasn't going to fall back into his arms if that was his angle. In fact, he had frayed their tenuous emotional bond with his sudden departure to the point that all that might be left between them was raw physical attraction, and even that wasn't as strong for her as when they first met. The novelty of his red hair had worn off. And if she was looking for a hunk, the beer truck driver would do fine, but "hunk" had never been her type or ever in her vocabulary.

"Okay, well . . . I'm glad you've found a new direction," Allie said finally. "And now I need to find my keys and go pick up some stuff for Shelly." She pulled off her apron and reached under the counter, jingled her keys, and walked to the back door, leaving Justin standing alone in the Dream Bean's empty dining room.

Before Allie could pull out from behind the Dream Bean, she had to wait for a man driving a front-end loader to push a pile of wreckage away from a house that had been knocked down earlier that morning. And then once she cleared that, she had to stop again while a flatbed truck backed into a lot with a load of fresh lumber. If there was anything Justin said that rang true, it was the fact that people still needed help, and help didn't come equally to everyone or at the same time. Tenants had to wait on landlords, and landlords had to wait on adjusters and lenders. Property owners who were under-insured or not at all had to make do until they found enough cash to make whatever fixes they could— or make the hard decision to board the ferry and start over somewhere else.

Shelly practically jumped over the wall of the Dream Bean on the early November day when her landlord came and announced he had received his settlement check and he'd have a crew on site in a week to begin rebuilding her roof.

"You'll still have to stay out of here while they're working," he said.

"No problem. We can do all we need to do at the Sea Garden and the *Cassie*," Shelly said. She swung around and drew Dave up in a big hug. "Finally . . . we're gonna get back to where we belong."

Dave closed his eyes and snuggled into Shelly's hug. She had been so distracted and driven since the storm that he wondered if they had lost their spark completely. He had come to know that Shelly's emotions were wound up like a tangled ball of seaweed and as long as the Dream Bean remained unsettled, so would the rest of her world. He knew that while he couldn't control everything, he at least could make sure he wasn't the one tying her in knots. So while the roof was being rebuilt, he jumped into overdrive to take inventory of equipment and dry goods and order whatever they would need to get up and running quickly. They looked at the calendar and mid-December looked like a reasonable target to reopen for full business.

"This may be the best Christmas ever," Shelly crowed from the middle of the Dream Bean.

"You know you have the opportunity to do some things differently if you wish," Dave said.

"I liked things just the way they were—serving people what they want and keeping them coming back," Shelly said.

"Uh . . . I was really talking about the way the room is arranged," Dave said.

"Oh . . . that . . . well, whatever you think is best. Just make sure there are enough electrical outlets inside and out," she said and walked back into the kitchen.

Slowly, day by day, the Dream Bean began to look like itself again but with a clean, level roofline, fresh paint outside, and touch-ups on the inside. Shelly took the opportunity to clean up her murals, and in a surge of boldness she added a new scene: the dark clouds of a hurricane boiling on the horizon with a man and woman standing on the beach, leaning toward the storm with their hands raised and ready to push it back out into the Gulf.

"Hey, great picture of you and Dave," Louie said one morning when he came to get his cup filled before going out on the *Rainbow*.

"That's not us," Shelly said, but Allie snickered from across the room. "Ah, yes it is."

Shelly shook her head as she counted out Louie's change, and then she walked to the middle of the room and stared at the mural. Just then Sam came in the door.

"What's up? Something wrong with the new picture of you and Dave?" he asked.

Shelly whirled around. "Really . . . you too? Is it that obvious?"

"Well . . . yes," he said.

"It was unintentional."

Sam stood beside her with an arm around her shoulders. "Intentional or not, there's nothing to be embarrassed about. You've built a business from nothing and when it got torn up by the worst storm in a century you rebuilt it. There's no quit in you or anyone else in Port A. It's rubbed off on us newcomers and we're going to have a great Christmas at the Dream Bean."

Shelly reached up and patted Sam's hand. "You always know just what to say."

"I'm only saying what's true."

Shelly turned to look out at the porch. "But the

holidays won't be complete unless you string lights outside like you did that first Christmas here. I'll get you the money to do that."

"Keep your money," said Sam. "You've not only rebuilt the Dream Bean but you've rebuilt me. I can pay for the lights."

Sam did, but he went on a spree and bought lights not only for the Dream Bean but the Pier Association office and for other shops that were willing to pay for the electricity. Then, with help from Marty and Justin, he strung lights down the pier itself and over to as many of the boat masts as they could reach. And then he asked all the shops to open their doors or set up tents on a Thursday night for what he dubbed "Get-and-Give" with sales going to help their neighbors.

All the lights were switched on and people roamed the shops and tents until almost midnight. Shelly and Allie and their helpers served hot chocolate and cookies from the Sea Garden, and local musicians added some Christmas tunes to the mix.

Sam wandered around through the crowds and was surprised to find Nancy among the shoppers instead of the musicians.

"You left the Crew at home?" he asked.

"I heard about this and decided to come down by myself and do some shopping. So am I right in guessing you had something to do with putting this all together?" she asked.

"Yes, but it's no big deal because it's actually part of my job description to organize events," he said.

"Well it's fabulous of course and I know it's a wonderful help to the community," she said.

"Maybe so."

Nancy locked her elbow in Sam's and they walked on down the sidewalk together.

Far out on the Gulf a couple of workers on a drilling platform stood at a railing and looked out across the open water toward the shoreline.

"What's all that light over there?" one of them asked.

"I don't know," said the other. "I've been out here three months and that's the first time I've seen that much glow. Looks like they're having a Christmas party in Port Aransas."

Yes, they were, but it was more than that. Sam made sure the lights stayed on through Christmas and on past New Year's. It was his way of telling anyone who was looking: "We're still here and we're not going away."

Chapter 36

Despite the lights and party of Christmas near the piers, the new year stumbled into Port Aransas like a groggy drunk that woke up on the beach and was trying to find its way home. Business was slow at the Dream Bean as it was for everyone else in town as the locals got back to rebuilding their lives and the out-of-towners stayed home to work on their New Year's resolutions. Even with her roof back on and ready for full service, Shelly didn't have enough business to need more than one of the Florez sisters in addition to Allie and Dave.

Shelly was discouraged and fearful too, so one midmorning, when it was clear that nobody else was coming in, she locked the doors and took a walk through the neighborhood to check on some of the other shops. She walked into Jenny's Memories and meandered through the antiques and thrift shop junk until she rounded a corner and found Jenny sleeping on a cot.

"Oh," Shelly said, which startled Jenny awake. She sat up and rubbed her face and combed her shoulder-length hair with her fingers.

"Everything okay?" Shelly asked.

Jenny stretched and yawned and then stood up and looked at Shelly. "I guess I forgot to lock the door again. What can I help you with?"

"Nothing, I was just visiting around. Are you . . . are you living here?" Shelly asked.

"I was doing just fine at home, but the city came and told me I had to leave," said Jenny. "Imagine that— getting tossed out of my own house. I really don't think it's any of their business," and then she leaned toward Shelly and whispered loudly, "and they probably won't like me sleeping here but that's not their business either."

Later that day when Shelly saw Sam, she told him about Jenny. He rounded up some volunteers and they went to Jenny's house to see what was needed and what they could do. As it turned out, it was no minor situation: the wall facing the brunt of Harvey's wind had been pushed inward a couple of feet at the top and the roof was sagging above it. Jenny had hung tarps in the gap to keep out the rain, but nothing had been done that would prevent a collapse of the roof or the wall.

"Jenny, why didn't you say something?" Sam scolded her softly.

"Everyone else was patching up their own places and I didn't want to be a bother. My son gets back from his Marine deployment in six weeks and he can fix just about anything," she said.

"Well, this isn't right and we're going to get you fixed now," Sam said, and within a week they had Jenny's house repaired enough to satisfy the city code office.

"I can't pay you, but come to the shop and I'll sell you anything you want at half price," she told the volunteers. "And Sam—I've got some new records to show you, and I've still got that old trombone you were looking at."

Sam laughed as he recalled the first time he went into Jenny's Memories and she misunderstood him when he asked if she had anything to play music on. He was looking for a phonograph but she led him through the junk to a tarnished brass trombone.

"I'll come by the shop and look at the records but I still don't need the trombone," he said.

"Just be warned: Someday you're gonna want it and it'll be gone," she said and hugged his neck.

And it was that way up and down the island five months after the hurricane as the people of Port Aransas worked and often struggled to get their lives and livelihoods back on track. Jenny's story was just one of countless examples of the resilience and determination that comes from living on that beautiful but dangerous line where land and water meet.

While the Dream Bean struggled through the weekdays, the Sea Garden focused on Friday and Saturday nights when the locals got off work and others rode over on the ferry from the mainland, but it wasn't as busy as before the storm because the folks in Rockport and other towns up and down the coast were still working to clean up and rebuild. Nancy and the Crew became the regular Saturday night band with Marty sitting in with them until the day when he announced he had his own band and asked for an audition.

"What do you play?" Dave asked, looking at Marty with his trumpet and three other high schoolers who had set up with keyboard, bass, and drums.

"Jazz standards and some improv."

"What do you call yourselves?"

"Port A Pirates."

"With names like the 'Demolition Crew' and the 'Pirates' we're gonna start drawing a rowdy crowd," Allie said under her breath.

"Go ahead . . . let's see what you've got," Dave said.

Marty counted off a very slow four and the Pirates settled into a clumsy rendition of Miles Davis' "My Ship." But the longer they played the more their nerves subsided and they began to sound like something. Dave and Allie looked at each other in disbelief, but Sam nodded with approval.

"I knew he was a natural when he showed me his record collection. You better sign 'em up and lock 'em in right away or they'll be unavailable soon," Sam advised.

With the Pirates and the Demo Crew bringing listeners back to the Sea Garden on Friday and Saturday nights and with other restaurants and clubs slowly reopening and reclaiming their own fans, it was starting to feel like Port Aransas was ready for guests again. But the big test would come in April with SandFest.

Chapter 37

Sam was up and getting himself ready for the day when he heard a knock on the door and opened it to find Nancy standing there.

"What are you doing . . . I thought you guys were playing tonight?" he said.

"We are but I came down early. I want to see what SandFest is all about, and I thought maybe you could show me around. I got your address from Shelly," she said.

"Well . . . I was just . . . I guess you could . . . " and he glanced back over his shoulder.

"Don't worry, I've been around the Crew enough not to care about male messiness," Nancy said.

Sam moved aside to let Nancy in, and she was shocked at what she saw: not only was there not a mess but there was very little in the apartment at all.

"Oh my, did you lose everything in the storm?" Nancy asked.

"No, I didn't have anything to lose. This is just . . . me. I'll finish getting ready. Make yourself at home. There's coffee in the pot if you want it."

Sam slipped down the hallway, entered a room, and closed the door. Nancy stood for a moment and then sat down in a chair at the end of the coffee table. Her purse slipped off her shoulder and brushed across a stack of papers, receipts, and magazines, causing a few items to slide onto the floor. She bent down to pick them up and her eyes caught the headline on a yellowing newspaper clip: "Ad Exec No-Billed in Accidental Death." She was almost finished reading the article when Sam came back into the room. He stopped and looked at her with the clip in her hand.

"What are you doing?" he asked.

She touched the pile on the table. "I bumped it. I'm sorry. But . . . why do you keep this?" And she held up the clip.

"To remind me."

"Of what?"

"Of what I did . . . to her, to her family, to my family, to my career, to my colleagues."

"That's a heavy load. How long do you intend to keep carrying it?"

"As long as it takes."

"I think that's too long. The article says it was an accident. That ought to be the end of it. Accidents happen."

"Yes, but they don't always end a life."

Nancy handed the paper back to Sam and watched as he cut the stack like a deck of cards and put the clip back in. She looked around the apartment and noted again how empty it was. There was nothing that really said that someone lived there except for a phonograph and a few records sitting on a shelf, and that stack of papers. It sat on the table like a sedimentary boulder with each layer representing a slice of Sam's life and that clip buried in the middle. She had accidentally excavated it and brought it back into the light. She had no idea how many days or weeks or months it had been safely buried. Or if he dug it out from time to time to keep himself in his place. She looked around the apartment again.

"The trailer and now this empty apartment—is this your penance for accidentally ending that girl's life?"

Sam sat on the edge of the couch, looking down at the floor.

"The trailer was all I could afford when I got here and I can't afford much more now. Maybe it became a penance, I don't know. It certainly has kept me grounded. The whole island has done that. It's hard to stray when you're surrounded by water."

Nancy stood in front of Sam. "You know . . . it's okay to have more . . . to want more. You don't have to feel guilty or be afraid of being happy, of enjoying yourself. I sort of think that's why God put us here."

She walked toward the door.

"Where are you going?" Sam asked.

"Outside. That's where the world is. My world, anyway. Out there. Yours might be out there too. Come on, let's go see." She held out her hand and Sam took it.

Nancy and Sam walked without talking through the streets of Port Aransas that were still ringing with the sound of saws and hammers and then down onto the beach that was teeming with its own music. Thousands had come to SandFest even though there weren't half of the rooms available on the island as there were before the storm. But the sand carvers had come—pros with their tools and families with plastic buckets and shovels— and so the party was on and as big as ever.

As they walked and stopped to watch the carvers turn mounds of dark wet sand into angels, dragons, and magnificent castles, Sam's muscles began to relax and with them his reticence. The questions back in his house were unexpected and at another time they might have pushed him back into the shadows, but Nancy's gentle persuasion had loosened a knot that still was binding him when he hadn't even realized it.

As they walked they said nothing of what happened earlier and instead talked about what was in front of them. They had just stopped to watch the progress on a carving that was one-half man, one-half woman, when Nancy looked out a distance and saw Allie and Justin, kneeling in the sand, making a small castle with a plastic cup. They were smiling, laughing even, and appeared to be having fun.

"What about those two?" she asked and nudged Sam.

"What about them?"

"Will those two halves ever make a whole?"

"Don't know for sure, but they're at a good age. They don't have to be in a rush. They can just enjoy playing."

When Sam and Nancy got down toward the end of the beach where the crowd was thinning out, Sam wheeled back around toward the sand carvings and the thick of the crowd.

"Sorry, but that's as far as I can go," he said.

"You'll have to see the hotel some day," Nancy said.

"Yes, maybe when it's finished and there's nothing left of what was."

Nancy had heard the story from Dave and knew the painful irony in Sam's statement—that he had played a key role in the sale of the trailer park to the developers. But even if that hadn't happened, it would have been destroyed by the hurricane.

As they walked back toward the crowds, Nancy looked over her shoulder and caught a glimpse of some new wooden steps leading over the tops of the dunes toward the hotel. "That's interesting," she said, but Sam didn't turn to look.

That evening the Sea Garden overflowed with people, and Allie and Shelly had everyone working that they could find. The crowd was noisy but not unruly.

"Not what I expected for spring break," said Chip.

"SandFest is different," explained Dave. "More of a family event, and you can bet those two will make sure it stays that way." Dave nodded toward the deck of the

Cassie where Allie and Shelly were standing with feet spread and hands on hips, looking out at the crowd.

Chip whistled softy through his teeth. "Glad to know we're not competing with wet T-shirts tonight."

"Never," Dave assured.

And as docile as the crowd was, it became tamer still when Marty and his Port A Pirates played a set, followed by Nancy and the Crew.

As Nancy sang, Sam noticed how the day's sunshine had brought highlights to her hair and a tan to her face in a natural and pleasing way. He looked around and knew without question that she was the loveliest person on the island.

When Sam returned alone to his apartment that night, he pulled the newspaper clip from the stack of papers, carried it outside, laid it in an empty clay flower pot, and struck a match. He watched as the gray smoke rose in the air and disappeared into the ink black sky.

Chapter 38

Before the grand opening, the hotel invited city leaders and business owners to a preview tour. As they walked the property, everyone marveled at the garden feeling as they wound between what looked like individual bungalows with private patios and gardens. Sam was finally coaxed into taking a look at the transformation of his old stomping ground, and he remarked at how well it had turned out. But then he stole away and Dave found him standing on the deck beside the terraced pool, staring across the top of the dunes at the beach and the Gulf beyond.

"You miss it, don't you?" Dave asked.

"Yep."

"Change is hard. It'll never be like it was that first day when we met on the beach—not for you and not for me. I was grieving my loss and you were still dealing with your own tragedy."

Sam stood silently, squinting at the glitter on the water, the sea breeze tousling his hair. Dave continued:

"We can't undo anything that's happened. You weren't planning to get involved with Shelly, Bo, Allie, me, and the Pier Association, and I wasn't expecting to come down here and get tangled up with all of you and especially not Shelly."

"So what about that?" Sam asked. "When's that wedding going to happen that you've been talking about for so long?"

"We got busy with the Sea Garden, and Bo died, and then the hurricane blew everything off track. And then we decided we wanted to wait till after the hotel is finished because we want to have the ceremony on the beach right about there," Dave said, pointing out to the left a little ways. "You'll be there of course, but you won't have far to travel."

Dave turned to walk away.

"Huh?" Sam asked in a daze.

"Come . . . I want to show you something."

Dave turned Sam's shoulder to get his attention and led him around a corner to a wooden fence, through a gate and onto another deck. In the corner was a metal table and chairs. To the right was a boardwalk that stretched over the dunes to a stair that led down to the beach. To the left was a large window and a home-style door framed by terra-cotta flower pots planted with bright red geraniums.

Sam stood and looked around.

"What do you think?" Dave asked.

"I think the hotel will charge a premium rate for this cozy hideaway."

"More like a cozy home if you ask me," said Dave.

Sam turned his back to the door and looked back out toward the beach, drawn by the familiar sound of the waves and the wind. Dave leaned into his field of vision.

"What?" Sam asked.

"Sam . . . this is *your* home."

Sam looked at Dave with the same lost look he had given him on the first day they met on the beach.

"Sam . . . the hotel, the Haileys, everyone made this happen for you. Nobody believed for a minute you'd be happy in town, most of all the Haileys. So when you weren't looking, they made this apartment a requirement before they would sell the property."

Sam shook his head. "This is outrageous. I can't possibly accept that. This should remain available for the Haileys. They made this happen."

"Oh, don't worry about them. Turns out old Hailey is a shrewd negotiator. He also worked out a permanent trailer pad and hook-up for whenever they're back in town. Rent free. And by the way, so is yours."

"What?"

"Your rent—it's free, as long as you live here."

Sam rubbed his forehead with both hands.

"Like I said, shrewd negotiators. The Haileys were just tenants at the trailer park until they hadn't heard from the out-of-state owners and discovered they were way behind on taxes. Hailey bought the property at auction for a song. He could afford to be generous when he sold it because he hadn't put much into it. And with your help, they got much more than they ever expected."

Sam didn't know what to say. Dave handed him a key and motioned him to go inside and look around. "I'm going back to the party. Take your time."

Sam explored every corner of the apartment, which was furnished more like a lived-in home than a sterile hotel suite. Going into the bedroom, he realized he was on a corner because the windows in that room looked northeastward up the beach toward town.

On the kitchen counter he found an envelope with his name on it, and inside was a store-bought thank you card with messages from folks including the Haileys. Sam read the words and felt like it was meant for someone else.

When Sam had seen enough, he walked back out on the deck and down the boardwalk to the steps descending onto the beach. He sat down on the top step, just in front of a little metal sign that said, "Private."

He sat there alone for a while until he heard footsteps on the planks behind him. A moment later, Dave sat down beside him and asked, "So, will this work for you?"

"I think I can make it work," Sam said dryly.

Dave put his hand on Sam's shoulder. "That's good, but if you can't, Shelly and I were thinking we'd give it a try ourselves."

Sam shook his head again and let out a deep sigh that mingled with a chuckle and floated out across the beach before tumbling into the breakers.

Chapter 39

When Dave and Shelly finally set their wedding date—
the one-year anniversary of Hurricane Harvey—some
thought it was a bad joke.

"Are you kidding? Of all the days on the calendar you
picked that one? There's still so many folks trying to get
themselves right," someone said.

"Well for starters, it's a Saturday in the summer and
that's like 'Wedding Planning for Dummies,'" Shelly
said. "But . . . we can't keep waiting for the world to get
right around us. We've gotta get ourselves right and so
that's the day we've chosen. And besides, it'll be a
happier reason for us to remember the day."

With that decided, they stuck to their original plans.
Allie would be Shelly's maid of honor and Sam would be
Dave's best man. The loss of Bo left Shelly with nobody
to walk her down the aisle. Other names popped up—
including Louie and a few other loyal customers at the
Dream Bean—but Shelly rejected them all. "I want
Sam," she insisted, and it was decided that Sam would
escort her and then fall in next to Dave.

When Nancy and the Demolition Crew offered to

play at the reception, Shelly was quick to say no. "I don't want any of my family working at my wedding; we'll get Marty to DJ."

But Shelly's iron will was challenged one morning at the Dream Bean when the Florez triplets cornered her in the kitchen with spatulas raised high and demanded that they sing her wedding march.

"Okay, okay . . . but what will you sing?" Shelly huffed.

"Trust us," said Angelita. "It will be perfect," piped in Bernita. "You will love it," added Carmelita.

"Okay, okay . . . but please, no mariachis," said Shelly.

The sisters backed away, giggling, while Shelly leaned against the wall, a little shaken and uncertain about what she had agreed to. The girls were great in the kitchen, but she'd never heard them sing. And just when she thought she had everything else under control, Nancy came to her and insisted—in her gentle manner and with no kitchen utensils in hand—that she sing one song too, but at the reception.

"I just really don't want any of you to have to work," Shelly pleaded.

Nancy watched bewildered as Shelly scrubbed the dry, clean counter with all her might until Dave stepped alongside her, stopped her hand, and whispered in her ear, "Nancy just wants to give you a wedding gift in the form of a song."

Shelly looked at Nancy, sighed, and let her shoulders fall in surrender.

"It'll be special. I promise," Nancy said.

Dave shot a look at Nancy that said, "You better get it right," and Nancy answered back with a wink.

But Shelly put her foot down on one critical detail, and nobody objected: "We've all been through so much. Just wear something that makes you feel at home—that makes you smile." For Shelly, it was a white cotton dress with a lapis necklace that her father gave to her mother. Dave would wear his khakis and a blue shirt.

And so on the evening of August 25—exactly a year after Shelly, Dave, Allie, and Sam huddled in the freezer at the Dream Bean—with the sun still high above the dunes and throwing its diamonds across the top of the water, family and friends watched as Sam escorted Shelly down the sandy aisle to the perfect harmony of the Florez triplets singing "Llegaste Tu," and then Shelly took her place beside Dave. Following cues from the preacher at the Community Fellowship Chapel, they recited their vows, promised their love, and exchanged their rings. It was all very straightforward and sensible the way Shelly had wanted it until the couple kissed and a small flotilla of boats bobbing in the shallow water sounded their horns, followed by an "amen" from the ferry on the other side of the island.

And then the chairs were rearranged and tables were set up with food and drink and Tiki torches were lit.

There was no dance floor, so the guests pulled off their shoes and rolled up their pants and just moved around in the soft sand. But not before Marty called Shelly and Dave up for the first dance. As Nancy softly strummed the guitar and began to sing, Shelly gasped a little and buried her face in Dave's shoulder.

"What's that?" he asked.

"It's 'The Sweetheart Tree,'" Shelly whispered. "From 'The Great Race,' my favorite movie. Pop and I watched it together just about every year. Once he laughed so hard he fell off the couch."

"Interesting choice . . . but I like it," Dave said as he pulled her close and turned her on the sand.

Shelly sniffed and rubbed her eye and put her head back on Dave's shoulder, and then just as quickly she popped up again. "How did Nancy know?"

"Don't look at me. I've never seen it. You'll have to share it with me . . . maybe tonight," he said.

"Oh no . . . not tonight," she said.

"Good choice," Nancy said later as she sat down beside Sam on the steps leading over the dunes to his apartment.

"I bet she forgot she told me about that when her parents died," Sam said. "She told me a lot when that happened, and I just sat and listened."

"And that's what you do, isn't it Sam? You listen," Nancy said.

"Maybe so."

"Well, it's a gift that not too many people are willing to share. Everyone wants to be in the spotlight, although that is less so in Port A. People here . . . they just want to live."

Sam didn't answer, but his thoughts rolled back to fuzzy memories of a man he once knew in Dallas who lived for the spotlight. For a moment it was as if he was recalling a life he had read about in a book or seen in a movie, and then he hung his head when he realized that he was that man. He was brought back to the present when he heard a shout from the beach and looked up to see Dave's friend Jeff waving at them and motioning to "come on down."

Sam and Nancy both waved back and smiled.

"Speaking of spotlights, I heard he's had his sights on you," Sam said.

"Well, it takes two to tango so he'll have to find another dance partner. But I appreciate the warning," she said.

And with those words Sam realized how little he knew about Nancy—like why she had never married. Some men would be hungry to know, but Sam was, as Nancy had observed, a listener, and he would wait to let her tell him if she wanted to someday. This was not that day, so they sat quietly and watched the party from a distance. They stood briefly to make way for the Haileys as they walked back up to their RV parked in its private berth. As they sat down again, Nancy noticed Allie and Justin standing ankle deep in the water, apart from the crowd, fingers interlocked loosely at their sides.

"Will they be next?" Nancy asked.

"That depends a lot on Justin. He sort of burned Allie once already," said Sam.

"From what I've learned, Bo would have had an opinion about that. I wish I could have met him."

"In some ways you have," said Sam. "Allie's not as brusque or stubborn, but she has his strength. She won't let Justin hurt her again. He'll have to earn her trust."

"I guess that's what it always comes down to—trust," said Nancy. "So . . . Sam . . . are you thinking what I'm thinking?"

Sam didn't reply. He'd been to enough weddings when he was younger to know there is a sort of matrimonial mist that can float in the air and get people caught up in the magic. He didn't know Nancy well enough to know if she was caught up in that too, although he sensed she was better grounded than that.

Sam turned his body and leaned against the railing to face Nancy. She read his eyes like a book and smiled softly before answering all of his questions.

"I'm thinking that as happy as I am for Shelly and Dave, and as hopeful as I am for Allie and Justin, I love my life as it is," she said. "In fact, I can't imagine it being any better. I mean . . . I'm having a great time with the Crew, I still enjoy teaching, I have some wonderful new friends here in Port A . . . and especially you."

Sam turned forward and looked out beyond the beach to the horizon, his go-to place when he was searching his own feelings. He recalled how when he first arrived on the island he would sit on the beach at night and stare at the lights out on the Gulf. They all looked the same to him at first, but then he began to notice that some moved and some stood still. In time he learned that the moving lights were ships, while the stationary lights were drilling platforms.

Nancy locked her elbow in Sam's and leaned against him. "Remember what you said about Allie and Justin at SandFest, something about, 'They're at a good age. They don't have to be in a rush. They can just enjoy playing.' Well even though I'm twice their age, that's how I feel. I hope you're not disappointed."

"Not at all."

"Really?"

"Really." He took her hand and held it gently.

Sam knew it was an honest answer. He had come to Port Aransas to escape, not to find new love. In time it had come to him but not in a way that most people want. It was a comfortable, familial love unlike anything he had ever known. He was at home. He was content. He no longer was one of those ships on the horizon, churning the waters toward some unknown port. He was one of those platforms anchored to the floor of the ocean—like an island, like Port Aransas.

About the Author

Jeff Hampton has based his life and career in Texas writing for newspapers, magazines, businesses, and institutions. His interest in observing the people around him has led him to write essays, short stories, and novels that explore relationships and communities in their many forms.

Aransas Evening is his sixth book, following *Aransas Morning, Grandpa Jack, When the Light Returned to Main Street, Jonah Prophet,* and *The Snowman Uprising on Hickory Lane.*

Watch for a collection of devotional essays on the importance of community in 2019.

www.jeffhamptonwriter.com

www.ingramcontent.com/pod-product-compliance
Lightning Source LLC
Chambersburg PA
CBHW032234010726
47494CB00002B/494